SECOND
CHANCE
GOLD

JOHN H. CUNNINGHAM

Other books in the BUCK REILLY ADVENTURE series
by John H. Cunningham

Red Right Return
Green to Go
Crystal Blue

SECOND CHANCE GOLD

A BUCK REILLY ADVENTURE

JOHN H. CUNNINGHAM

SECOND CHANCE GOLD

Copyright © 2014 John H. Cunningham.

Published by Greene Street, LLC

Book design by Morgana Gallaway

This edition was prepared for printing by
The Editorial Department
7650 E. Broadway Blvd.
Suite 308
Tucson, Arizona 85743

Print ISBN: 978-0-9854422-7-9
Electronic ISBN: 978-0-9854422-6-2

www.jhcunningham.com

This book is for Marius Stakelborough

"A sailor can't just go to bed at seven o'clock in the evening, so we decided to open a bar. There wasn't one on the island. There we could get together, play dominoes and cards, just shoot the breeze for awhile." Le Select opened in 1949.

Merci, Marius.

Île Fourchue

Île Pelé

Île le Boulanger

Île Frégate

Île Toc Vers

Île Chevreau

St. Barthélemy

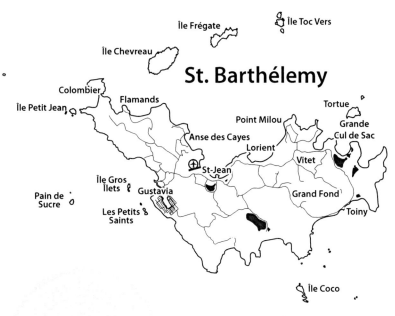

Colombier

Flamands

Point Milou

Tortue

Île Petit Jean

Anse des Cayes

Grande
Cul de Sac

Lorient

Vitet

St-Jean

Île Gros
Îlets

Grand Fond

Pain de
Sucre

Gustavia

Les Petits
Saints

Toiny

Île Coco

CONTENTS

Familiar Names, Different Faces   1

This is Not My Beautiful Beach Trip   63

My Reputation Exceeds Me   123

The Gold, The Guy or The Girl?   195

Familiar Names, Different Faces

1

THE MUDDY TRAIL OF THE HUDSON LED ME PAST MANHATTAN, A CIVILIZA-tion now foreign to me, as the voice of Air Traffic Control whispered vectors into my headset. I followed instructions and banked east over Central Park. Just south of the Queensboro Bridge, I was given clearance to land. The brown channel was free of boats, ferries, and trash barges, so I added flaps and held my breath as the Beast splashed down into the East River. I'd salvaged her a year ago, a forgotten relic from a CIA operation gone awry. The G-21 Goose had been designed and built in the late 1930's to accommodate businessmen coming from Long Island to New York City at the same seaplane base where we were now headed. Hell, she'd probably landed here in her eighty-year existence.

I decreased power, still a thousand feet from my destination. I hadn't been in New York City since the crash of e-Antiquity, my former treasure-hunting company. Losing e-Antiquity had only been the first domino in a cascade of failures that included divorce, bankruptcy, the death of my parents, and a still open FBI investigation into insider trading. Returning here now made me cringe. I'd gone from the cover of the *Wall Street Journal* to living one tank of gas at a time, chartering tourists, and salvaging the occasional lost soul just to pay my bills.

I had no regrets.

I kicked my heel against the safe beneath the seat that held the old treasure maps I'd spirited away before the creditors descended upon e-Antiquity. I had yet to give them my full attention, but today's return to the Big Apple was in response to an old friend and investor who'd summoned me. The entire flight up the coast had me wondering if he was interested in getting back into the treasure game.

The seaplane base was hidden behind a huge residential complex, the only building on the east side of the FDR highway. I taxied past it and hoped there'd be room for me to—

What the hell?

A Grumman Widgeon was already tied up at the dock.

By last count, there were fewer than a hundred Widgeons worldwide, but that's not what caused my white-knuckle grip on the wheel. My first flying boat was a Widgeon I'd named Betty, after my mother. I'd lost the boat a year ago. The odds of seeing her twin here, now, seemed astronomical.

I aimed the Beast toward the pier and rushed through the checklist to shut her down. With repeated glances out the starboard side window, I could tell the Widgeon's paint was fresh, a nice porpoise-gray with blue floats. She was equipped with factory standard radial Ranger engines, just like Betty had been. And I could tell from various details, that this plane had been built in 1946—just like Betty. Aside from the color, she was the spitting image of my old flying boat.

I glanced back at her N number: CU-N-1313. CU was the registration code for airplanes from Cuba—which was where I'd lost Betty and salvaged the Beast.

There was a knock on the hatch.

I swung around to find the heavily clothed ramp agent waiting outside. He'd already secured lines to my bow cleat and to the ring below the tail.

My fingers tingled as I turned off batteries, closed off fuel lines, and took a deep breath. The restoration of the Beast's interior was nearly complete, and if not appointed for luxury, she was now presentable enough so passengers didn't balk at riding in her.

Cold air hit me in the face when I climbed out. I hiked up the zipper on my old leather jacket.

"Great old plane," the man said. He thrust a clipboard in my face with a contract flapping in the breeze. "Can't believe we have two old Grummans here at the same time. Bet that hasn't happened for fifty years."

"I can't believe it, either."

I handed him back the clipboard. He nodded toward the Beast.

"Love your silver and black color scheme," he said.

"Thanks, just finished it."

I stepped up to the Widgeon, peered inside the left side window and found an orderly cockpit. The fuselage windows revealed a few duffel bags and a metal storage locker on the starboard side, with seats on the port. I started to reach toward the hatch, then balled my fist and turned away.

Every detail of her fuselage stirred memories.

I glanced back at the tail. CU-N-1313. Two eighty-year-old flying boats from Cuba. Here at the same time.

"How long you going to be here?" the ramp agent said.

I checked my old Rolex Submariner—I'd be late if I didn't get moving.

"Only a few hours."

"Need a yellow?"

"Supposed to be a car here to get me."

"Let me guess, the Rolls?" He laughed. "It's out front. Follow me."

The man had the logo of the New York Skyports on the back of his insulated coveralls. The wood planking groaned under our weight, and the wind cut through me with a whistle. I didn't miss the cold or the concrete jungle of big city living. New York's a great town, but I now preferred flip flops to Ferragamo loafers, cargo shorts to custom tailored suits, and filing flight plans between islands instead of business plans to investment bankers.

The ramp agent nodded toward the burgundy Rolls Royce outside the fence.

"That ain't no rental."

I smiled. It sure wasn't

The driver who sprang from the vehicle had on an immaculate cashmere full-length overcoat and a black cap. He walked around the rear of the car, met my eyes, and pulled the back door open.

"Nice to see you, Percy," I said.

"Mr. Reilly." Was that a smile?

"Where're we headed?"

"Mr. Greenbaum is expecting you at Riverpark, just up on 29th."

I sank into the cream-colored leather, and the door closed with a quiet thud.

Here we go.

2

WE TURNED ONTO 29TH STREET AND DROVE UNTIL WE REACHED A LAND-
scaped cul-de-sac where taut flags snapped in the swirling wind. A
broad open plaza stretched out toward the FDR and beyond to the East
River, with Long Island City visible across the white-capped water.

"Riverpark Restaurant is through the lobby," Percy said as he jumped
out to open my door. "Mr. Greenbaum's waiting for you there."

"Thanks, Percy. Great to see you."

He nodded, his hand on top of his cap.

I stepped out into cold my bomber jacket was no match for and wind off
the river that nearly knocked me over. I dashed across the brick sidewalk
to enter a massive glass and steel building. I rubbed my palms together and
shook off the chill, then continued through the cavernous lobby toward
a broad, luxurious spiral staircase that ascended into a marble and glass
atrium.

A man came around the corner of the elevator bank. I stopped in my
tracks. As he approached, he stopped in *his* tracks.

"Jack, is that you?" I said. Jack Dodson, my former partner at e-Antiquity,
but he looked leaner and meaner. When did he get out—

"Long time no see, Buck. Thanks for all those visits while I was in Sing
Sing. Really let me know how much I meant to you."

He'd spent five years in prison for insider trading—a fate I very narrowly avoided. "And for the bullshit pittance you and your brother sent my wife?" He shook his head.

"Hold on, Jack!" I wasn't about to let that pass. "I'm fucking bankrupt, my brother got all the—"

He laughed, but his eyes showed no mirth.

"We were best friends, Buck. Partners. You were like family to me. We created e-Antiquity together." His voice was a whisper, but the fire in his eyes made me look down at the floor. "And we had a deal—I take the fall, and you take care of my family—"

"My brother sent checks every month. Son of a bitch cut me off, but kept sending money to her—what the fuck was I supposed to take care of your family *with?* I've got nothing left to give."

This perfectly reasonable—and truthful—explanation got me a dry laugh as Jack glared at me, slowly circling past. I turned, still facing him, adrenaline keeping me on high alert.

"That was the one thing that kept me going," he said, "knowing that when I got out I had my money stashed and you had shit."

A thought lit up my brain.

"Were you here to see Harry?"

His smile twitched and his eyes narrowed.

"Keep clear of me, Buck. Run your little charter service and chase tail in the Keys. I've got a lot of lost time to make up for."

"But—"

"Nice bumping into you, *ex-partner.*"

He turned sharply and continued through the lobby at a brisk pace. The women watched him pass, maybe because he was dressed all in black, tight pants, boots, a black turtleneck, and a designer leather jacket.

I watched him walk outside—and froze when Percy appeared and opened the rear door to the Rolls. Jack slid in without looking back. A moment later the car continued around the cul-de-sac and up 29th Street.

I exhaled a deep breath.

Jack Dodson was out of jail, he hated my guts, and he'd met Harry Greenbaum before me.

The Widgeon? Jack was a pilot too, but it had a Cuban registration.

What the hell was going on here?

It took a few moments for me to collect myself. My heart rate had shot up and the cold I'd felt on entering the building had been replaced with a light sweat. I pulled off my jacket and swiped my fist across my damp forehead.

"One for lunch?" The pretty brunette hostess asked.

"I'm looking for Harry Greenbaum."

She smiled, nodded for me to follow, and led me toward the back of the restaurant.

I replayed the surprise encounter with Jack in my head as I walked through the crowded restaurant and bar.

What the hell's going on here?

3

HARRY WAS SITUATED PAST THE BAR, IN A PRIVATE ROOM WITH TWO UNIFORMED waiters, a long table, and a river view I barely noticed. Jack had persuaded Harry to invest in e-Antiquity back in the day, having met him through our bankers at Goldman Sachs. It had been Jack's job to raise money while I scoured the globe for antiquities, and Harry had been his coup.

"Buck Reilly." Harry stayed in his seat. "It's been far too long." I shook Harry's doughy hand. The lines around his blue eyes had been etched deeper in the five years since I'd last seen him, and there were a few pounds more of him to like. His gray flannel suit sported a red handkerchief in the breast pocket, perfectly accentuating his blood-red tie.

I swallowed. "It certainly has, Harry. But I've sure appreciated you being there for me these past few years."

He held a hand out to the chair across from him and one of the waiters rushed over to pull it out for me. Was this where Jack had been seated?

He laughed. "You've always been attracted to adventure, haven't you? That's what persuaded me to invest in your company in the first place."

"Yes, well, your sixty-four companies—"

"Down to fifty-five now." He must have seen my brow lift. "Just completed an IPO of several I'd bundled into a conglomerate, dear boy. Sorry for not offering you friends and family shares, but I know your means are limited these days."

"Congratulations." I paused. "You never slow down, do you?"

"At my age, slowing down means death." Harry's British accent added authority to whatever he said, often tinged with just a touch of sarcasm. It was one of the things I always enjoyed about speaking with him. "And that wouldn't be much fun, would it?"

The waiters delivered salads, and for the first time I noticed there was both white and red wine poured for each of us. Harry sipped the red, no doubt a rare French vintage. Among his many interests, he was a oenophile. He supposedly had a twenty-thousand-bottle cellar in his country estate outside London. As much as I wanted to guzzle both glasses, my plan was still to fly south right after lunch.

"Could I get an iced tea, please?"

One of the waiters jumped at my request.

"I bumped into Jack out in the lobby," I said. "Did you invite me here for the same reason you met with him?"

Harry's eyes narrowed, but only for a moment.

"No, dear boy. He contacted me a week ago and asked to meet, so I fit him in to my schedule today. I summoned you for a completely different purpose."

Harry must have rented the private dining room for the entire day. That was his style—have people come see him away from his office or residence or at a location under his control.

He sat back in his chair and gripped his armrests.

"When you and Jack were partners, I'd always felt you were the more cunning, someone who'd stop at nothing to attain your goal." He paused. "But while incarceration has sharpened Jack's focus, the island life has muted your ambition."

"That's not true—"

"I don't mean that as a slight, dear boy. I know you've been through a lot."

"I just don't care about money like I once did. It drove my every decision, determined my every relationship—and what did it get me?" I sat back and took a deep breath. What's the point of arguing the pitfalls of wealth with a billionaire?

"You're a better man now. You've matured. You were what—twenty-five or six when e-Antiquity struck gold?"

"So what did Jack want?"

The waiter delivered my iced tea and Harry used the interruption to consume his salad in four bites. My appetite was gone.

"The reason I asked to see you today, Buck, is extremely important to me." Harry's eyes locked on mine. "And it's for a personal reason, not business."

I waited.

"A dear friend's nephew has been missing for several weeks now," he said. "When I spoke to him two days ago, he had all but given up hope that the boy would be found."

"How old is the boy?"

"Forty, I believe."

I tried not to roll my eyes. To Harry, every guy under fifty was a boy.

"I assume the police have been doing everything possible to find him?" I said.

"Perhaps not," Harry said. "He lives in the Caribbean, and as you know, the levels of investigative expertise there aren't exactly up to par." He sighed. "And to be perfectly frank, the young man is not well liked on the island where he resides."

"So you want me to go look for him? What do you expect I might find that the police haven't?"

"Perhaps nothing, dear boy, but if there *is* anything to be found, my bet is on you to find it."

I ran through my obligations back in Key West. There wasn't much—a couple of charters that could wait, no salvage, and not much income potential on the horizon.

"What island?"

"St. Barthélemy," Harry said. My jaw tightened. When e-Antiquity was at its pinnacle, just before the financial fantasy collapsed, Jack and I had rented a 140-foot yacht with a crew of 22 and parked it in Gustavia harbor at St. Barths the week before Christmas through New Year's. We'd flown in our top investors, Harry Greenbaum being the biggest, and lavished them with every comfort. Caviar, champagne, foie gras, no expense spared. The million-dollar tab was one of the catalysts for our company's quick demise. I looked at Harry—was that a smirk on his face? It was.

The French island was the epitome of the fast lane lifestyle, the sophisticated playground to the world's rich and famous. Russian magnates, Hollywood movie stars, top fashion designers and celebrities. It remains one of the most beautiful places I'd ever been.

"Who's your friend?"

"Lou Atlas. His missing nephew is Jerry Atlas."

"*The* Lou Atlas? Former presidential candidate and software billionaire?"

"I'd not say he's sentimental, but his nephew is one of his few heirs. I suggested I might have someone who could pursue a private investigation."

My turn to smirk.

"Harry, you know I'm not a PI."

"You've said it yourself. Salvaging lost treasure or lost souls, it's all the same."

Good grief. The Atlas fortune was huge, multiple billions. But so was Harry's. Normally, there wouldn't be much for me to wrestle with—I loved that island. And I'd make a decent payday. But there was something else I wanted from Harry.

"Can you tell me what Jack's up to?"

Harry frowned. "Picking up where you boys left off, I'm afraid. But no more public company, no more newspaper coverage, and limited investors."

"Is that what he wanted from you? Money?"

"Of course. And, dare I say, respectability. As I mentioned, Jack's like a sharpened razor now and his focus is precise. He claimed not to need much money, but a select investor with contacts like mine would be advantageous. He also claims to have copies of all the old research materials that e-Antiquity had yet to pursue."

The air whooshed out of my lungs. If Jack had the same maps and information I did—and if Harry was funding him . . .

Harry handed me a piece of stationary with Atlas's address and phone number printed on it. He lived in Palm Beach.

"He's expecting you tomorrow morning at nine. And I'm sorry, dear boy, but my next appointment will arrive at any moment. Please give Lou my regards—and of course keep me apprised."

Had I said yes?

"Just tell me what Jack's going after, Harry. Please."

He dabbed at the corners of his mouth with the cloth napkin.

"The wreck of the *Concepción*."

I felt my eyes bug open. "Hispaniola or Saipan?" There were two famous Spanish galleons named *Concepción* that had sunk three years and nearly 10,000 miles apart.

Harry frowned. "Hispaniola, dear boy." A vision of my future suddenly crystallized. Using copies of the same maps I had, Jack would pick off the treasures one by one, dooming me to eternal poverty. My hesitation to pursue those treasures had been based on fear of failure—or maybe of success—but either way, the luxury of hesitance had just vanished.

"Back me, Harry."

He squinted. "What's that, Buck?"

"Forget Jack. Back me to pursue the treasures—I have the same maps, the originals, and I—"

Harry held up both his palms, and I pressed my lips together. My heart raced. What was I saying?

"I need you to help Lou Atlas get answers about his nephew."

"But I—"

"If that goes well, we can discuss your proposition." Harry checked his watch.

I headed back into the lobby, dazed by the events of the past hour. The *Nuestra Senora de la Concepción*, which had sunk off the coast of Hispaniola, was one of the wrecks I'd gathered information on while e-Antiquity was still on a roll. While I still carried the details with me in the Beast, what use were they to me now that Jack was out, had money, and was hell bent on succeeding?

Unless I could get Harry to back me. Again.

New York had not been kind to me today and I couldn't wait to get out of the city. The tree limbs and bushes whipped wildly outside and the sky had turned gunmetal gray. I had to get to the Beast and head south or I'd be stuck here for the night and never make the meeting with Lou Atlas.

Harry's Rolls Royce was back in the cul-de-sac. Approaching the car felt like the walk of shame, and I remained pissed off about Jack Dodson's ruining my day until Percy pulled into the seaplane base.

The Widgeon was gone.

I ran past the heavily clothed ramp agent to check the Beast. Her lock was secure, and once inside, I bent down to check the safe under my seat. Still locked. I entered the combination anyway, just to make sure.

I felt the fat folder inside and my breathing finally began to slow.

4

AWOKE TO THE SOUND OF SOMETHING SLAPPING AGAINST THE SIDE OF THE Beast.

I lurched up in a sweat—had I fallen asleep while flying?

A small jet roared by. Now I remembered—I'd arrived at North Palm Beach County Airport at 1:45 a.m., triggered the landing lights from my microphone, and landed on runway 26. After refueling and a brief conversation with my brother at the Leesburg, Virginia, airport, instructing him to stop sending money to Jack's wife, and start sending it to me, I flew another 746 nautical miles and landed at this little field, running on fumes. The operating hours here ran between sunrise and sunset, so my presence this morning would have been a surprise to management—which, a quick glance out the side window confirmed, was the guy currently beating on my hatch.

I glanced at my watch: 7:18 a.m. Sleeping in your plane here was a no-no too.

Apologies, cash for the tie-down fee, and the news that I'd be departing in a few hours placated the line guy, who pointed me toward the pay phone and the pilot's lounge where I could take a shower. But first I called the number Harry had given me for Lou Atlas. I told his assistant where I was and asked if someone could pick me up.

A shower and change of clothes restored my humanity, while scrambled eggs, bacon, and a double-espresso got me ready to face the day. When I walked outside at 8:30, a black Mercedes limo awaited, which didn't so much as raise an eyebrow from the line guy who'd waked me up.

"Can you have her fueled up in an hour?" I yelled to him. "I won't be long."

"I wouldn't have charged you the tie-down fee if I'd known you were gassing up," he said.

I didn't actually have the cash for a refuel—I was counting on coming back with an Atlas expense account.

AFTER A TWENTY-MINUTE RIDE IN SILENCE, THE LIMO TURNED DOWN South Ocean Boulevard and a mile later entered a gated driveway that included two uniformed guards, a pair of Dobermans, and several cameras. The palm-lined stretch of crushed oyster shells led to an incredible 1920's era red-tile roofed mansion that resembled the Breakers Hotel nearby. Lou Atlas was one of the richest men in the country—hell, the world—and he wasn't shy about it. He was a self-made man who'd come damn close to being president, voodoo economics and all.

I was greeted by a doorman with a Texas accent and delivered to a special assistant in her late-twenties, dressed in a tight pencil skirt, silk blouse, and stiletto heels. Her long brunette hair was so glossy she could have stepped right out of a shampoo commercial, but it was her silky French accent that had me following her as if in a trance. Well, that and the view from behind.

Money did have its perks.

She left me in Mr. Atlas's private office, which was as big as the lobby at the La Concha hotel, where I lived in Key West. Every surface was covered with rich marbled wood, probably from rare trees of the Amazon. Lou Atlas wasn't known for being concerned with the environment, which had been one of the knocks against him in the election he lost some dozen years ago. I sat in a leather chair that faced the massive gold-washed desk, which looked like it belonged in Versailles.

A different set of French doors than the ones I'd entered burst open, and Lou Atlas stormed into the room. He might only be 5' 9" but he had the frenetic presence of LeBron James. He crossed the room so fast I just got to my feet in time for him to thrust out his hand and take hold of mine.

"Lou Atlas, pleased to meet you."

"Buck Reilly. Harry Greenbaum sends his regards."

"Ha! That Limey bastard's beat me out of a few deals over the years, but I just love his suave demeanor, know what I mean?" His Texas accent was still strong, even though he hadn't lived there in twenty years. "I tell you, their days as an empire may be long past, but those Brits still have some classy sons of bitches over there, and Harry's one of 'em." Lou dashed around the end of his desk. Pretty spry for eighty-three.

"I'm sorry to hear about your nephew," I said.

Lou dropped down into the chair and his face went from jovial to squint-eyed in a blink.

"Don't feel too bad—he's a sorry piece of shit." Lou grunted. "My only sister's only child and nothing but a bum, but hey—" His lips bent into a smile his eyes didn't share. "He's family!"

The blunt description pushed me back into my chair.

"And you're what—one of Harry's investments that didn't pan out? Former treasure hunter, something like that?"

I swallowed. "Feels like a lifetime ago."

"Bet it don't for your former stockholders." His smile faded. "But Harry says you're still good at finding things, and while I think this is a damned goose chase, I owe it to my sister to check the box."

I rubbed my palms across my jeans. "What can you tell me about your nephew and his disappearance?"

"I already told you he's a piece of shit, but that's as much my fault as anything. You give a young man a few million a year for life, you're gonna get one of two things—someone who wants to prove he deserves it or a slacker who sits on his ass and does shit. Well, that's Jerry, the latter of the two."

I found myself nodding. I'd known plenty of people with trust funds, and sadly, most of them fit Jerry's category. A steady flow of money for nothing is not a recipe for hard-won success.

"And Jerry lives on St. Barths?"

Lou cackled. "That's right. Not a shabby little rock, is it?" He nodded toward the doors where I'd entered the room. "That's where Annette's from, the little beauty who brought you in here. Father owns half the waterfront in Gustavia, the main harbor in town. Doing him a favor bringing her up here. Hell, doing me one too." He pumped his eyebrows.

"I know it well—St. Barths, that is."

"So Harry told me. That's another reason you're sitting there."

I wondered if he actually knew his nephew. Or was all his information second-hand?

"What else can you tell me about Jerry that might help me learn what happened to him?"

"Aside from being a drunk who spent his days at a circuit of beach bars, he went and got married to a local girl and had a few kids he hardly ever sees. Hasn't worked since he was in the Air Force in his late teens—he's forty now, and aside from a brief failed attempt at trying to buy and build a business, he ain't got shit to show for the millions he's pissed away." He paused. "Sound good so far?"

"And he's been missing—"

"About a month now. Plumb disappeared—wife don't know shit—and given their pre-nup, he's worth more to her alive than dead, drinking buddies ain't seen him, police don't much give a damn since Jerry's caused more problems than probably any other resident on the island—wrecking cars, starting fights, that kind of thing."

"Any chance of foul play?"

"Wouldn't surprise me none, but more likely he drove one-a his cars off one-a them steep-ass cliffs and vanished into some desolate scrub."

Jeez, no love lost here. Guess he did know Jerry.

"What about his mother—your sister?"

"Dead seven years now. Like I said, feel I owe it to her to find out what happened, otherwise when I see her next she won't be too happy with me." Lou slapped his palms down on the top of his paper-free desk.

I licked my lips. "Pretty cold trail, sir."

"Yep, I don't expect much out of your efforts but I'll give you a week, cover your expenses, pay you twenty grand, and if by some miracle you find him alive I'll garnish his trust and pay you a quarter million. It's high season down there, so it'll be expensive, but I don't give a damn."

He leaned toward me and thrust his jaw out. I felt like he was waiting for me to counter, so I did.

"I'll need a cell phone and credit card."

He pulled a drawer open, took out a Visa Black card and a cell phone, and slapped them down on the desk.

"They don't like American Express down there. Hell, they don't much like Americans, but what else is new?" He snickered. "Even though the damn Russians make us look genteel by comparison. So." He slapped the desk again. "We got a deal, or what?"

Going to St. Barths with what I assumed to be an unlimited expense account and getting paid while being there?

"You have a deal, Mr. Atlas."

"Call me Lou, I'm retired now. Got enough people kissing my ass, so I need straight shit out of you, Treasure Hunter."

Once we nailed down the terms, he pushed the credit card forward—fast— and I caught it as it was about to fly off the desk. He pulled a piece of stationary from another drawer, took out a fat Mont Blanc pen, and scribbled down some names and numbers of contacts he thought might be helpful. He also wrote out a note on a separate piece of monogrammed paper that stated I was looking into matters on his behalf. He must have pressed a button somewhere, because Annette reappeared and stood next to me.

Lou said something loud and indecipherable that made Annette giggle. I realized he must have spoken in French, the one language I spoke enough of to get by, but his nasally Texas accent made it incomprehensible to me. Annette, however, seemed to understand.

Lou turned back to me.

"I hear you got your own plane," he said. "When you gonna leave?"

"Soon as I get back to Key West and pack some things." He sneered when I mentioned Key West but didn't say anything. "I like to have help when I work on salvage projects. You mind if I bring an associate?"

"Long as it ain't some girlfriend." He paused and rubbed his chin. "Or *significant other*, as they say down there. This ain't no paid vacation, Reilly. Harry damn-Greenbaum or not, I want a daily report."

And there I had it—my dream job.

And while I was searching for trust-fund trash on St. Barths, Jack Dodson would be searching for the treasure of the *Concepcion*.

5

THE FLIGHT DOWN THE KEYS USUALLY PUT ME IN A RELAXED MINDSET, BUT Jack had left a reality hangover even Lou's Visa Black card couldn't erase. I thought of my binder with each potential treasure file stored in archival sleeves. I couldn't wait to review what I had on the wreck of the *Concepcion* to assess whether Jack had a shot to find it.

To get my mind straight, I repeated my down-island process of naming the different islands as I flew over them. Tavernier blended into Islamorada and then the Matecumbes were followed by Fiesta, Rattlesnake, Grassy, and Marathon. I flew over the old bridge at Bahia Honda, past No Name, Big Pine, and down through the Saddlebunch Keys. I vectored west to stay clear of the naval air traffic at Boca Chica, got into line behind a commercial Dash-8, and followed the air traffic controller's cue to cross over A1A and set down on runway 27.

With my binder of maps tucked into my flight bag, I checked the private terminal for Ray Floyd, then remembered he was at a video game convention at the Hard Rock Hotel in Fort Lauderdale. Good grief. He'd counted down the days to that gathering like a kid before Christmas. I pictured the beaches in St. Barths, most of which were dotted with nude sunbathers, and wondered whether Ray would have chosen that over the digital warriors he was gaming against now. Then I remembered one of his 'Floydisms.' He called it the Wealth / Narcissism factor: the more money someone has, the more self-obsessed they are. St. Barths was not his kind of place.

My old Rover Series II took several tries to start and I exhaled hard when she finally caught. The old girl needed a tune-up and several parts replaced, but the restoration of the Beast had exhausted my funds. As soon as I collected the $20,000 from Lou Atlas, the Rover was next in line for some TLC from Jonesy, my Australian mechanic.

The La Concha was crowded, augmented by the new lobby bar and change in circulation that came with the renovation, and the holiday season was now in full swing since the annual snowbird migration had commenced. Once the massive spa was finished where they had torn down The Top on the roof, the traffic here would be insane. I held my breath as I passed by reception, hoping to avoid Bruce, the day manager—

"Buck!" A female voice sounded.

Emma, one of the reception staff, held a FedEx envelope out to me. Why would someone be sending me an overnight package? I took the lumpy parcel, thanked her, and hastily bumped and jostled my way to the elevator. I squeezed in between cocktail-carrying tourists with glassy eyes and fixed smiles. They had that comfortably numb-and-on-the-crawl look.

Once in my room, I dropped my gear and tore open the envelope. Inside was a DVD and a number of photographs. There was a handwritten note clipped to the pictures.

> Buck,
>
> Not so nice to see you yesterday. Better be the last time. If we cross paths hunting for artifacts, then a package just like this will be sent to the FBI. I took the fall, you take a hike.

It wasn't signed.

I pulled the photographs apart and—shit! They were all from a folder inside our former office safe—the same folder I still kept inside the Beast. My sheaf of maps and more damning stuff in the folder, laid out page by page. Which, dammit, we'd documented for insurance purposes. The photos were dated before e-Antiquity went bankrupt.

My fingertips were numb as I removed the DVD from the jewel case. #5 was written in black magic marker on the disc. I hurried to my machine, turned it on, and watched what I instantly recognized as security footage from what had been our conference room. My father was standing there.

My heart lurched—I hadn't seen him in video since he'd died four years ago, and what was worse, I recognized the moment even before I saw myself rush into the room, the same sheaf of documents now in my hands. Younger, hair slicked back, Hugo Boss suit, face pale and wild-eyed. I heard my voice fill the room.

"Dad, thanks for coming—"

"What's so urgent, son?"

"It's over—this crazy run's over."

"What are you talking about?"

"The market—our company—the auditors—everything. We're toast."

"e-Antiquity?"

"What else would I be talking about?"

My father sat down. I remembered this scene as if it were yesterday. Jack and I had destroyed all the security tapes before the Feds stormed our offices—at least, I thought the tapes had been destroyed.

My father shook his head, a pained, terrified look on his pale face. Hot tears streamed down my cheeks as I watched, just as they did on the screen.

"Your mother and I have everything invested in—"

"Sell it now," I said, "before news hits the press. You have a couple of weeks, I hope. And take this for safe-keeping." I pushed the sheaf across the table toward him. He just stared at it. "It's the best maps and information we have on other missing treasures—it's worth a fortune!"

"But what are we supposed to do—"

"Take it, put it somewhere safe, sell the damned stock, and go away. Take Mom and go."

The screen went black.

A sudden nausea built inside me. I leapt from the couch and just made it to the bathroom, where I threw up in the toilet. Perspiration seeped from every pore as I grabbed the sink, the small room spinning slowly, my equilibrium blown off its axis.

Fucking Jack.

He'd taken the fall all right, but he'd hidden his money. He obviously knew I'd taken the maps—hell, he'd made copies for himself first—had probably been planning this the whole time he'd been in prison.

Where I never once went to see him.

6

I RIFLED THROUGH MY RESEARCH MATERIAL ON THE *CONCEPCÍON*. OVER TWO hundred men had died when she sank on a reef, some seventy miles off the coast of Hispaniola. The ship had foolishly left Havana on November 2nd, 1641, as a hurricane approached. When the storm ripped the ship's mast off, the captain tried to steer her to Puerto Rico, but the violent seas smashed her into the reef. Even though 190 men lived to tell their story, it took until 1687 for the wreck to be salvaged by New Englander William Phips, who recovered over 68,000 pounds of silver and a modicum of gold. Although certainly a fortune, records of the *Concepcion's* manifest indicated that was at best only a third of her hundred-ton cargo. Numerous efforts to find the balance failed until 1978 when a private salvor named Bert Webber recovered six thousand silver coins and valuable artifacts. Yet an immense amount of the treasure—thousands of pounds of silver and gold—remained missing.

While at e-Antiquity, I'd assembled significant GPS data, detailed information from Webber's records, and little known accounts from the original survivors that I'd hoped could lead a well-financed effort to the area where it was likely buried by coral in what was now called Silver Shoals.

Information Jack and I both possessed.

If I went after it, he'd throw me to the wolves. But as far as I knew, he was focused on the *Concepcion*. There were still other treasures I could pursue—with Harry's help—once I returned from St. Barths. I wouldn't just sit back and let Jack banish me to poverty, but I *would* steer a wide path around him.

I checked the weather, flight time, and logical course to St. Barths, which was 1,120 nautical miles away. I decided to stop in Punta Cana in the Dominican Republic for fuel, then plotted the course. Like most islands in the Caribbean, neither the DR nor St. Barths allowed water landings, so the Beast would stay dry on this trip—fine with me, since saltwater was so difficult to clean out of the plane's many nooks and crannies. Corrosion was one of the biggest problems for salt water based flying boats.

With Ray Floyd out of town, I still hoped to get one of my other friends to join me on the trip. Plus, I needed information. With that in mind I flipped through the tattered pages of my address book. An automatic grimace twisted my lips, but I dialed the number from the hotel phone anyway.

"Special Agent Booth's office. Can I help you?"

Booth qualified for an assistant now?

"This is Buck Reilly. Is he available?"

After less than a minute the familiar voice came on the line.

"Charles Reilly, III? Are you calling to confess your crimes and turn yourself in?"

I swallowed back acid reflux.

Booth was the Special Agent in Charge of Florida and the Caribbean basin, and he'd dogged me since I moved to Key West. He'd made it clear the FBI believed I was guilty of insider trading—specifically of having warned my parents before e-Antiquity's stock crashed—and Interpol still suspected me of plotting their deaths in Switzerland as if I had them killed to get the inheritance. Booth had forced me into being an under the radar operative a few times, to go places he couldn't, all under the guise of keeping the heat off my case. He was a royal prick, and if he got his hands on the information Jack now held over my head, he'd happily arrest me. So, like any gambler, I wanted to keep an eye—or in this case an ear—on the opposition.

"Very funny, Booth."

"Then to what do I owe this honor?"

"I've been hired by Lou Atlas to—"

"*The* Lou Atlas?" He paused. "Your client list is improving, but you're wasting your time."

"I'm looking for Lou's—"

"Deadbeat nephew. That is what you were going to say, right? Jerry Atlas?"

I bit my lip. "Why is it a waste?"

"He's just a missing person—no foul play, no interest to me. Just another drunk gazillionaire who pissed his life away."

Pretty much the same summary Lou Atlas had offered.

"So the FBI doesn't have any intel?"

"What makes you think you can call me looking for information, Reilly? You're *my* gopher, not the other way around. And if I—"

"Okay, Booth. I thought you might benefit if I can find him, figured you'd be willing to give me some insight. Sorry I called—"

"Hold on, hotshot. I'll tell you this. Since the guy's related to Lou Atlas, of course we looked into his disappearance and called the local police—or *gendarmes* as the French call them. They had nothing but a lengthy rap sheet of drunk and disorderly, fighting in public, disturbing the peace, and a case of domestic violence."

"Jerry's a wife-beater?"

Booth snickered. "No, apparently his old lady kicked his ass at some beach bar once when she found him hanging all over a bathing suit model. Anyway, bottom line is, the local police assume he drowned because he hadn't gone through Customs, which he always did when going island-hopping, and his body hadn't been found, alive or dead. They claim to have conducted an exhaustive search, but who knows what that means. So from their perspective, case closed."

I checked the list of names Lou Atlas had provided and saw one labeled *gendarmes.*

"That's what I figured, but thanks for confirming my gut. I told his uncle it was a pretty cold trail, but he didn't seem particularly concerned one way or the other."

"Keep me posted, kid. If you learn anything to the contrary, I can help."

We hung up. I knew if I teased Booth with Lou Atlas he'd drop his drawers. He didn't have much to offer, but at least it corroborated what I'd expected, and I now knew the FBI had made an inquiry, missing person's case or not. The best news, though, was that Booth was his usual charming self, which meant Jack hadn't sent any evidence to the FBI.

Yet.

And I wouldn't call Booth for help unless the Caribbean froze over.

7

With that I set out toward Blue Heaven. Once outside the La Concha I decided to walk rather than take the Rover or my bike. In the back of my mind, I knew it was to avoid Bruce. Management at the La Concha had been busting my chops lately, and I wasn't in the mood to face that right now.

The walk down Duval was as eventful as usual. Drew, the doorman at Margaritaville, gave me a wave; Susie Pizzuti, formerly of the Conch Flyer and now at Willie-T's, shouted my name from across the road, and when I got to Petronia Street one of the drag queens in front of the 801 Bourbon Street Bar gave me a wolf whistle.

I stopped and smiled. "How you doing, Edward?"

"Be better if you came over and hung out with us, Buck!" His deep voice belied the curvaceous physique, accentuated by a mini-skirt and tank top.

"I'm headed over to see Lenny, but next time."

"That's what you always say," he said.

I waved and made my way up to Bahama Village and into the open air bar and restaurant known as Blue Heaven. Shaniqua, Pastor Willy Peebles's daughter, had replaced her cousin behind the bar. She gave me a big smile. While she lacked Lenny's gift of gab, she more than made up for it with her almond-eyed and mocha-skinned beauty. I'd rather look at her than listen to Conch Man—Lenny's nickname.

She glanced at her watch, then me. I nodded, and within a moment a glass of Papa's Pilar dark rum on the rocks was in front of me.

"Why you look like someone ran over your dog, Buck?"

I took a sip of the rum. "You ever have your past sneak up and bite you?"

"Don't be *sneaking* in here to make a move on my cousin, man."

I smiled as Lenny Jackson slid onto the stool next to me. Shaniqua blushed. She and I had a long history of flirting with each other, partly to tease Lenny, but also because there was real attraction, at least on my part. But I'd reluctantly concluded that Shaniqua was just too close to home. If it didn't go well, the fallout would be costly.

"You available to accompany me on a boondoggle for the next week?" I said.

"The hell you up to now, man?"

"I've been hired by one of the richest men in the world to go to—"

"Stop right there, Buck. I got a City Council meeting three days from now—only my second one—so no way I can miss that."

"Not even to go to St. Barths with me?" I pulled the Visa Black card out of my pocket. "And this?"

He shook his head.

"Nah, man. Much as I'd like to, I can't miss that meeting. I got shit to propose that's gonna blow those people's minds. I'm taking this gig serious, cuz."

Some locals arrived, and soon Conch Man was on a roll. Next thing I knew there was a crowd around the bar. I asked Shaniqua to place a call for me to another potential partner.

Pretty soon the sun was down and the restaurant was packed. I nursed my drink and checked my watch.

I felt a heavy weight on my shoulder.

Bruiser Lewis and his brother Truck stood next to me. I slid off the stool and Bruiser threw a few short punches at me, which I blocked before he grabbed my arms and gave me a quick bear hug.

"The hell you up to, Reilly?" Bruiser said.

We caught up. Bruiser told me he had a heavyweight bout in two months, which if he won, would put him in line for a title shot. He was headed to Tallahassee tomorrow to train with famous corner man, Caspar Johnson.

"And to think I almost knocked you out that time we fought," I said.

"Yeah, almost." He grinned at me.

"What about you, Truck?"

"Busy season's coming quick and I'll be up to my ass in tourists on the *Sea Lion*." As long as I'd known him, I still had difficulty imagining Truck as the captain of the largest, circa late 1800's schooner and sunset cruiser in Key West. He'd be lucky to get a day off once the tourist season really kicked in.

"How'd you like to join me on a salvage trip to the French West Indies?"

His face showed no expression. He turned toward Bruiser who was also impassive.

"Don't speak no French, man," Truck said.

I told him I did, along with the details of who'd hired me, and a little about St. Barths. His eyes widened with each additional fact. He started to nod, then stopped.

"I get paid anything?"

"All expenses, plus five grand. Should be a cakewalk, and St. Barths is amazing."

He looked at Bruiser, who was drinking sparkling water.

"You two together are usually like matches and gasoline," Bruiser said.

Truck smiled. I pumped my eyebrows and we slapped a high-five.

We spent another few minutes on logistics, set a pre-lunch departure time for tomorrow, then I paid Shaniqua and made my way back toward the La Concha. I was ready to get this trip done, get paid, and get back on Harry Greenbaum's calendar.

Jack could have the *Concepción*, but the fire was building inside me to beat him to the next target.

8

THE SOUND OF ENDLESS RINGING FINALLY PENETRATED MY TRAIN OF THOUGHT from inside the hot shower. I slid across the floor to grab the phone, worried it would be Truck calling to cancel.

"Reilly, that you?"

"What do you want, Booth?" I stood with water puddling below me on the floor. I thought of Jack's package and held my breath.

"Listen, after you called yesterday, I double-checked the news on Jerry Atlas."

I wrapped myself in a towel.

"And?"

"All his money's still on deposit at the *Banque Nationale de Paris* branch in Gustavia—freaking eight figures, I might add, so nobody's cleaned him out—"

"Wouldn't his wife have access?" I did remember Lou Atlas mentioning that Jerry was worth more to his wife alive.

"She's not on the account. Typical for the super-rich—but hey, you ought to remember that, right?" He laughed.

My ex-wife, former super model Heather Drake, had been on all my accounts—and she'd cleaned them out before the IRS could do it.

"The French authorities have totally abandoned their search efforts, but the money will stay in the account until the body's found or the equivalent of a petition of probate is made by his family to release the funds. I'm not really up on French estate laws."

I glanced at my alarm clock. Is that why Lou Atlas wanted me to find him? To free up the frozen money? A dull ache began to throb in my right temple.

"Not much help . . ."

"You're welcome, hotshot. The money being there tells a story, so figure it out." He paused. "And if you learn anything, let me know. The French don't much like non-licensed investigators poking around."

"Thanks for the call," I said. "I'll let Lou Atlas know you were helpful."

"That would be—"

I dropped the phone on the cradle. Booth pandering in the hopes of getting an audience with Lou Atlas was predictable, and one of the reasons I called him yesterday. And it kept me semi in the loop if Jack dropped my dime.

I'd taken more care in packing my bag last night than I usually did. St. Barths at high season required me to dig out what few decent clothes I had left from back in the day. After a quick check-in with Flight Services, I grabbed my bags and took the elevator to the lobby. The door opened—

"Buck Reilly, there you are!"

Damn. It was Bruce, the day manager.

"I'm kind of in a hurry, Bruce—"

"All I need's an answer, Buck. Are you going to renew your lease here, or are you moving out on the tenth?"

"That's in, what, three days? I'm leaving town—"

"I need an answer."

"Is it even legal to triple my rent?"

A smile turned the corners of Bruce's pinched lips.

"Not my call. After spending millions on the renovation, management out of Dallas isn't happy with this month-to-month deal, and it's way below market, you know that."

I took in a deep breath. "I can't afford—"

"They want a year commitment *and* security deposit if you're going to stay." He held his palms out. "So what's it going to be?"

Dammit!

"I don't have the money right now."

"They're up my ass, Buck. They want an answer before the tenth. So if you can't tell me now, and I don't hear from you by then, we'll put your stuff in storage, okay?"

The headache that had quietly begun to throb when Booth called now pounded like a jealous boyfriend on his girl's door.

"I'll call you, Bruce. And thank those sons of bitches in Dallas for me, will you?"

I pushed past him into the blinding sunshine behind the La Concha.

"Fuck!"

Heads turned toward me as I hurried through the parking lot. My throat burned with rage, or from throwing up after viewing Jack's video. What could be worse than having the chance to be rich again but knowing that if I pursued it I'd end up in jail? Thanks to my ex-best friend and partner, Jack Dodson. But once I finish this wild goose chase to find information about Jerry, then at least I could pay my rent and not get evicted.

9

"I'D TELL YOU BOYS NOT TO DO ANYTHING STUPID, BUT I'D BE WASTING MY breath," Bruiser said.

"You just worry about training for Petro Kamikov, little brother," Truck said. "Buck and I'll be just fine." He brushed his hands down the nicest shirt I'd ever seen him wear. "You get past Petro and you got a title fight, man. Don't fuck it up."

"And don't you fuck up the clothes you borrowed," Bruiser said. "That shit's Ferragamo."

Truck snickered. "I read up on this place, man. Movie stars and billionaires be hanging out there. Gonna find me a French model, maybe a Swedish princess. Or even better, both."

I opened the front door to their Patterson Street duplex.

"We'll be back in a week, maybe less. Good luck with your training."

Bruiser groaned but I didn't wait to hear him complain. Training for a fight like that would be a 24/7 effort, and all forms of recreation, including booze and women, would be off limits the minute he arrived at camp.

I'd picked up a double buche and Cuban sandwiches from the Cuban Coffee Queen on the way to get Truck. Once we arrived at Key West International Airport I packed the plane, did the pre-fight check, measured the fuel level, and glanced around the tarmac.

Wasn't the same without Ray here.

We climbed aboard and slammed the hatch shut.

"This old bird looking pretty good since you got it painted," Truck said. He was pressed into the right seat, built for a man half his size. I heard a hissing sound as he breathed in. "Smells good too, all leathery like a new Escalade."

His face turned serious.

"Hope it runs like one."

As we flew, I filled him in on what I knew about Jerry Atlas, but Truck was more interested in his uncle, the former presidential candidate. I reiterated what Lou and Booth had both inferred—that this was a perfunctory investigation to ease Lou's conscience, and the French police in St. Barths considered the matter closed. That bothered Truck about as much as it bothered me, since we were getting paid to go to one of the swankiest places on earth.

"By the way, if by some miracle we do find Jerry alive, Lou's paying me $250,000."

Truck's brow furrowed. "You didn't say nothing about that."

"Because nobody expects it to happen. It's a bullshit incentive, kind of like giving me a lottery ticket."

Truck worked his jaw back and forth, puckered and unpuckered his lips.

"Just the same, what's my cut if we find him?"

"$20,000 make you happy?"

His smile lit up the cockpit. "Damn straight."

We flew southeast along the Cuban coast and continued on that course until Haiti appeared ahead. Truck stared out the window.

"Dear Lord," he said. "Keep us away from that voodoo hell hole."

The fear of voodoo from a big man like Truck Lewis made me smile. The barbed wire tattoo around his left bicep made him look like much more of a hard-ass than he really was.

Rather than fly across Hispaniola, I vectored north and watched my GPS until I was over the point where my records indicated the *Concepcion* had sunk. There was no boat in sight on the rolling deep blue seas. I couldn't imagine Jack mounting an expedition that quickly, but I had to see for myself. I exhaled a long breath. These were now forbidden waters.

I turned toward Punta Cana and after another thirty minutes got permission to land at the eastern tip of the island. I circled around, added flaps, reduced power, and put the Beast down smoothly on runway twelve. While primarily dominated by major resorts, many of which had walls like fortresses to keep the natives out, the Dominican Republic had several commercial airports.

To pass the time, I explained to Truck that the DR had the second largest populace and economy in the Caribbean and Latin America. The island had come a long way since Christopher Columbus first set foot here in 1492 and proclaimed it *Le Espanola*, or Hispaniola.

"Back in those days the island was occupied by Taino Indians that had emigrated from South America. Unfortunately the Europeans brought disease that led to epidemics of smallpox and measles—killed off most of the native inhabitants, cleared the path toward a plantation economy and a slave population that—"

"Gotta take a wicked leak," Truck said.

I swallowed back any further history lesson.

Air Traffic Control directed us across a series of taxiways toward the Fixed Base Operation where we'd fill the twin 110-gallon fuel tanks—we were close to empty after the nearly thousand miles we'd flown.

Something caught my eye amidst the few dozen private planes tied down in rows beside private hangers—a gray Grumman Widgeon, CU-N-1313.

Jack Dodson *was* here. Crap!

Guilt stabbed my heart at the recollection of my former plane—destroyed and abandoned in Cuba—more a family member than an airplane, and this one looked just like her. I aimed the Beast toward an open spot away from the Widgeon and went through the checklist to shut her down.

Truck left fast in search of the restroom. I radioed the FBO and asked for the fuel truck to come as quickly as possible. Given the time of year we only had a couple hours of sunlight left and I didn't want to try to land on St. Barths in the dark. Plus, the last thing I could afford was to bump into Jack.

Once outside, I checked in all directions. Seeing nobody, I double-timed it toward the Widgeon.

"Buck Reilly?"

I swung around fast to find the fuel truck had pulled up behind the Beast.

"Permission to fill her up?" His Spanish accent made it sound like he wanted to "*feel* her up."

"Ah, yeah, sure."

He hesitated, and I scurried over to where he stood and handed him the Black Visa card. He nodded once, spoke Spanish into a radio, and waited. After a moment, a voice crackled a response, and he stepped into the hatch to climb atop the port wing to reach the first fuel tank.

Back to the Widgeon, I studied the fuselage. Little dents here and there stirred memories, but was I imagining them? The port wing on this Widgeon's assembly looked secure and the rivets matched those on the starboard side. I'd removed Betty's port wing and used it on the Beast, only to exchange it with an Alaskan charter service once Ray and I commenced restoration of the Goose.

Betty had been burnt down to bare metal. Could someone really have restored her so expertly? Without parts? In Cuba?

I ran my hand down her fuselage and a sense of warmth ran through me.

"Mr. Reilly!"

My heart jumped. The attendant waved his clipboard. Truck was climbing back onto the Beast and I checked the sun—well into its downward arc. Time to go.

I signed the credit card receipt without even checking the amount. The fuel jockey nodded, peeled me off a copy, and spun on his heel to climb back aboard his truck.

We took off without seeing Jack.

A shiver curled my toes.

Anticipation before a salvage trip always did that—even if it was for a human being.

10

THE RECTANGULAR PORT OF GUSTAVIA WAS ENCIRCLED IN RED ROOF TOPS and filled with yachts. Hills rose up on three sides, their tops washed in an orange glow from the sun on the horizon behind us. White beaches and hilly green contours were sparsely dotted with luxurious villas, which set St. Barths apart from most islands. Scant light illuminated the two peaks ahead, with the path between them deep in shadows that led to the drop into St. Barths' airport.

Literally.

The nose of the Beast was pointed to the crotch of two hills that rose steeply up in opposite directions but left a narrow gap to fly through.

"What the hell you doing?" Truck leaned forward. "Those hills—"

The plane jerked from an updraft. I edged forward on my seat—hands bouncing on the wheel, teeth pressed tight—focused on the short runway just ahead that began on the hill itself.

"What's the cross on the side of that peak for?" Truck's voice was an octave higher than normal.

The wing tips bobbed from side to side—full flaps—power down to stall speed, and we swooped low just over the road—

A Mini Moke honked its horn ten feet below us.

We glided across the long grass hill that led to the scant runway. It wasn't much over 2,000 feet—2,100 if memory served—so stopping the Beast was going to be quite a challenge. Focused on the beach ahead, which was getting closer by the second, I did everything possible to slow her down. Finally, we skid to a stop—the smell of burnt rubber flashing through the cabin—just before the tarmac blended into the windswept sand on St. Jean beach.

Palm trees that fringed the beach swayed languidly. A pair of topless beauties strolling along the waterline, smiled and waved to us.

I smiled back. I never thought I'd be here again.

Thank you, Lou Atlas.

An approaching Winair Commuter broke my reverie. I added power, taxied back up to the head of the runway, waited for him to land, then crossed over to the private aviation ramp area. We powered down, killed the batteries, and battened down the hatches. When Truck popped the hatch, a Customs officer took us and our bags back to the terminal, where we got our passports stamped, paid for a week of tie-down, rented a Jeep, and set off toward St. Jean.

"Where we staying?" Truck said.

"It's high season. Lou Atlas had to pull some strings to get us into a little hotel in Lorient."

"This place has a China town?"

"Lorient's named after a French town in Brittany where the French East India Company was based. It was the embarkation point for trade with China and India. When the company fell apart in the late 1760's, people scattered and some came here to trade with buccaneers and pirates."

"Figures."

The narrow yet well-maintained two-way road was clogged with cars. Motorcycles sped past idle traffic on the wrong side of the road and dodged between slow-moving cars. No sense of island time here. The population, largely French transplants, maintained a Côte d'Azur pace and treated the island like a living painting by Gauguin, with each space carefully planned and nearly every home or building colorfully and thoughtfully trimmed, just like their inhabitants. We followed the road through St. Jean, which had occasional discrete entrances to secluded boutique resorts, and scattered gourmet wine and food stores—just as I remembered it.

We drove up the hill along the asphalt strip that clung to the coast, where the view of St. Jean and the airport was breathtaking below. The road cut down through carved stone bluffs and descended into the postcard-perfect village of Lorient. Mature landscaping blended with chic restaurants amidst a small, tasteful shopping center.

A quick left turn onto a quiet narrow road took us past a small shopping center and on to the hotel La Banane. Just past the hotel was a high chain link fence.

"See that down there?" I said.

Truck looked over and shrugged.

"Jimmy Buffett's hotel, l'Autour du Rocher, used to be up on that hill."

THE OWNER OF LA BANANE, A YOUNG PARISIAN TRANSPLANT, DELICATELY steered my rusty French to his fluent English. His eyebrows arched when I produced Lou Atlas's Black Visa card.

"Ah, *oui*, Monsieur Atlas phoned me. I am Jean and I will help you arrange anything you need. I have a suite ready for you."

Truck smiled and raised his eyebrows as he glanced around the small but well-appointed open-air lobby, restaurant bar, patio and pool area that comprised La Banane. No sunbathers around the pool at this hour, but jazz, cigarette smoke, and laughter wafted from the bar.

Jean led us to a comfortable suite at the end of the serpentine path. Once settled, I pulled out the list of names Lou Atlas had given me and tried to decide where to start. All we had to do was check each box and Lou should be satisfied.

Back in St. Jean, we parked the Jeep and hoofed it toward the water down a sandy alley covered by palm trees and bougainvillea between luxurious resorts that led to the flour-soft beach. Purple lights shone from the bar at La Plage and more colored lights twinkled from homes and hotels along the bay. I suddenly felt the miles of the day pressing down on me. But a warm breeze blew my hair back, and the sound of the surf and smell of salt air massaged my senses. Truck spun in a slow circle, soaking up the view, the well-dressed early diners and willowy waitresses.

The bartender smiled at us from the small beach bar. I sat on one of the white plastic stools and ordered a Rhum JM on the rocks. Truck asked for a Carib beer. While the bartender produced our drinks, we simply absorbed the beauty of the surroundings. As he put the drinks on the painted wood counter I leaned forward.

"Pardon me," I said. "Last time I was here I met another American. His name's Jerry Atlas." The bartender dropped his eyes. "Any idea where I can find him?"

"Again? Jerry's been gone, maybe a month."

Again? How many people had asked about Jerry?

"Gone from the island?"

"Gone from the world." He took a drag from the cigarette that sat smoldering in an ashtray in the corner of the bar.

"He died?"

"That's what I'm saying."

I sighed and took a drink of rum.

"Too bad. Last time he offered to take me Scuba diving. Said he'd pay for the whole thing."

The bartender smiled. "That was Jerry. Always buying drinks for strangers, and taking them boating, diving, to dinner—"

"Nice guy, huh?"

"Nah, a lonely drunk." He paused. "And sales have really dropped since he vanished."

"Damn," I said, "guess I blew that. Never went out diving with him. What kind of boat did he have?"

The bartender laughed. "Jerry rented everything."

Truck and I ordered sandwiches.

"My buddy and I want to do some diving tomorrow. You know where Jerry chartered his boats?"

"Master Ski Pilou on Gustavia Harbor. Ask for Bernard. Tell him you were a friend of Jerry's."

I held up my rum to toast the information. The food came and Truck wolfed most of it down.

"Must have been a popular guy if other people have come asking about him," I said.

The bartender shrugged. "Aside from his wife and the *gendarmes*, just a couple of big guys, not so friendly."

"Big guys from St. Barths?"

"Maybe Puerto Rico. Spanish speakers with bad English and no French."

Truck let out a long belch that turned heads three tables away in the open-air dining area.

"I'm toast, Reilly," he said.

I handed the bartender a fistful of Euros I got from an ATM by La Banane.

The bartender stared at me for a moment, no smile in his eyes.

"Jerry was popular with tourists, not so much with locals." He leaned on the bar. "Him being rich was nothing special here."

I followed Truck back up the dark sandy path toward the road.

"Pretty slick back there," he said. Then in a lower voice: "Not sure why you need my ass, but I'm damn happy to be here."

I swatted a mosquito on my neck and saw blood on my palm. The bartender had confirmed exactly what Lou told me, but I was curious about the unfriendly Puerto Ricans. Lou never said there'd be others looking for his nephew. So who were they—and what did they want with Jerry Atlas?

11

SLIPPED OUT OF THE ROOM AT DAWN AND WALKED TO WHERE THE ROAD DEAD-
ended at the chain link fence. The ruins of l'Autour du Rocher poked out
above overgrown foliage on the abandoned hill. I paused to imagine the
debauchery that occurred there in its heyday.

The drainage ditch that followed along the fence through the woods led
me out to the water. I jogged along the narrow beach at Lorient, my feet
sinking deep into the soft white sand. Wet sea glass glistened in the pink
light of dawn, and lines of mild wake slowly broke on the shallow coral
near the shore. The smell of low tide was carried in with the morning mist,
and the air was thick with salt.

Halfway up the beach was the old red, yellow, and green surf shack. It
had been elevated and placed on a concrete foundation since the last time
I was here. I sat on its stairs, watched the waves, and thought about Jerry
Atlas. A week's worth of the same stories is what I expected, but here, now,
in the peace of this place, I was glad to be here. Lou Atlas's daily report
would only confirm what he already knew until I was as sure as I could be
Jerry had shuffled off the coil.

Back at the hotel I found Truck seated at one of the tables next to the
pool, drinking coffee and looking more relaxed than I'd ever seen him.

"We getting paid for this shit? Seriously?" he said. "I didn't vote for Lou
Atlas when he ran, but he's got my vote now."

Soon after I sat down, a petite blond waitress delivered a basket of fresh croissants, followed by two plates of eggs, sausage, and French bread. We devoured the meal, killed the pot of coffee, and I shared my plan for the day with Truck.

I drove us back down the coastal road to St. Jean, past the airport. Truck said he could the see the Beast tied down where we'd left her. We continued around the traffic circle, over the hill and down into Gustavia. Traffic was heavy in the capital as workers, shopkeepers, and tourists circulated like hemoglobin through the clogged arteries. Truck asked about the harbor, which was long and rectangular and packed with some of the largest yachts in the world.

"High season brings in the richest of rich," I said. "And they all want to outdo each other."

Truck was speechless. We followed the road along the harbor, but not before I pointed out my all-time favorite hamburger dive, Le Select. At the end of the harbor we dodged a motorcycle and took two quick lefts, doubling back, now overlooking the town and yacht basin. Halfway down the block I pulled up next to a silver Land Rover Defender with police lights mounted on its roof.

"Mind if I stay outside?" Truck said. "Not a fan of police stations."

I found myself in a small but clean reception area within the small stone building. A nondescript bespectacled woman in her late fifties gazed up at me from her desk.

"*Bonjour*—" I paused and tried to formulate my question in French.

"Yes, Monsieur?"

Screw it.

"My name's Buck Reilly and I'm here on behalf of Lou Atlas. I'd like to see Commander Grivet, if he's available."

Her eyes narrowed and she pursed her lips.

"*Oui*, he is here. And this is about Jerry?" Her voice had the sound of walking through gravel. There was a full ashtray on her desk.

I nodded. She reached for her phone, hesitated, and stood up instead.

"*Excusez-moi.*"

She walked down the corridor and disappeared around the corner. I glanced around the tidy station, quiet compared to most police stations I'd visited, voluntarily or otherwise. Late model computers, nice modular furniture, photographs on the walls from locations around the island.

The woman reappeared, followed by a tall, thin man in uniform, whose eyes met mine the moment he came into view and never looked away.

"Monsieur Reilly, is it?"

I pulled out the handwritten letter from Lou. Commander Grivet read it and handed it back with a flourish.

"As I told Monsieur Atlas on the phone, there is not much to say. His nephew vanished. According to his wife, it has been nearly a month now. We searched all of his, ah, usual places, spoke to the people who knew him best—bartenders and the like—and everyone said the same thing. One day he was here, the next he was gone."

"So that's—"

"When his Jet Ski washed up on the shore at Anse de Cayes, we concluded he had fallen off and drowned."

"What?" Lou hadn't told me this. "When did this happen?"

He shrugged. "A few days after Monsieur Atlas disappeared."

"Did you share this with his uncle? Or the FBI when they called?"

His eyebrows arched at the mention of the FBI and he crossed his arms.

"His family here, his wife, was informed of the discovery." He uncrossed his arms and put his hands on his hips. "What *she* tells Monsieur Atlas is her business, and as for the FBI, we responded to their inquiry and stated that Jerry had disappeared. They asked to be contacted if there appeared to be foul play. Falling off a Jet Ski and drowning is not considered foul play here on St. Barthélemy."

A hint of the renowned French haughtiness flashed in his voice as he relayed this information. A flash of adrenalin hit me in anticipation of the response I expected after my first report to Lou Atlas.

Job done, come home.

I exhaled a long breath and remembered what the bartender at La Plage had said about Jerry renting equipment.

"Had he rented the Jet Ski from Master Ski Pilou?"

He looked up, a new light in his eyes.

"Yes, that is correct."

"Did they say where he'd been going, or if he was alone?"

Commander Grivet pursed his lips. "He was alone, except for the bottle of rum he had taken with him, and no, he did not tell Bernard where he was going. Jerry used their Jet Skis frequently and went any number of places, mostly beach bars, but occasionally further, and often around the entire island."

"Was there anything on the Jet Ski—or any sign of trouble?"

He shook his head. "A half-full bottle of rum and his wallet full of Euros and credit cards."

"Was Jerry a regular customer of yours, Commander?"

He nodded slowly. "He was no stranger to us here." His eyes were cold as he glanced at his watch. "Will there be anything else, Monsieur Reilly?"

Hell, I could file my report before lunch and be on my way this afternoon. Almost too fast, dammit. Would I still get paid?

"One other question, Commander. How are Jerry's wife and kids?"

He slowly rubbed his chin between his index finger and thumb.

"Financially in trouble—Jerry left them with nothing, all his wealth serving no purpose other than making interest for bankers." He curled his lip. "There is an agreement she signed before they were married."

His tone made it clear what he thought of such agreements.

Protect the money was rule number one amongst the rich. Family, wives and children were replaceable. Money was not.

"They'd been staying with her family in Toiny after Jerry disappeared, but now . . ."

I waited.

"But now *what?*" I said finally.

"Gisele—Jerry's wife—is in the hospital."

"Why?"

"She was attacked. Beaten brutally, last week."

"Because of Jerry?" I said. "Do you know who—"

"We don't know who or why. Gisele is from St. Barthélemy, her family has been here for generations. They are well-liked members of the community. Jerry's death was . . . unfortunate, but we have found no connection to this incident."

"What'd Gisele say about her attackers?"

"She has no memory of it. Her young daughter found her in their driveway, behind their car." The muscles in his jaw rippled as he pursed his lips. "These things do not happen here. We have a population of six thousand, which comes with all varieties of domestic issues, but this incident was different."

"And she remembers nothing?" I said.

He shook his head. "Not that she will tell us."

I left the station and mentally ticked the second box on Lou Atlas's list of people to speak with. What would he say about these revelations? Would he care? Or would he only give a shit about the money sitting in *Banque Nationale de Paris* down the street?

"Yo, Reilly, you all right?" Truck was standing in the shade of the large tree out front of the police station.

I looked past him.

"We need to go to the hospital."

12

TRUCK ARGUED AGAINST GOING TO SEE GISELE AS WE CROSSED TO THE OTHER side of the harbor and drove up the steep hill to l'Hopital de Bruyn, which overlooked the Caribbean from the peak of the western side of Gustavia harbor. The way he saw it, we'd earned our fee and the right to take the rest of the week to chill. I disagreed with his logic. Lou Atlas wasn't known for being that generous—I wanted to make sure we pursued every lead.

Pursuing this one involved a lot of convincing, from reception to the nurse on the ward and finally Gisele's doctor, who read the note from Lou Atlas and threw it down like it was an audit notice from the French equivalent of the IRS.

"Fifteen minutes," he said.

GISELE ATLAS WAS INDEED BEAUTIFUL, THAT MUCH WAS OBVIOUS, THOUGH not entirely at the moment. The left side of her face was swollen, her left eye still closed, her left cheek yellowed and purple from bruises. There was an IV tube attached to her wrist. She was asleep under a taut sheet, face up and arms at her sides.

I debated whether to wake her. Finally I leaned in close, the antiseptic scent strong around her.

"Gisele?" She didn't stir. "Gisele?"

Still nothing. I glanced back at Truck, who shrugged his shoulders.

"Gisele?" I touched her shoulder.

Her good eye blinked open and her whole body went rigid. She struggled to raise her arms but they were pinned beneath the sheet.

"It's okay! *Ça va!*" I held up my hands. "I'm here on behalf of Jerry's father, Lou." The statement was sour on my tongue. Lou had barely mentioned his daughter-in-law and grandchildren. "My name's Buck Reilly, and this is Truck." I pointed my thumb behind me. "We're here to help you."

She frowned. "Has Monsieur Atlas come?" Her voice was scratchy.

I glanced around, saw a pitcher of water, filled an empty glass, and held it up to her lips.

"No, he sent us." I glanced at Truck. "What happened to you? Who did this?"

She turned away, her swollen eye fluttering. She murmured something in French—I picked up the words love and children, but that was it.

"I miss my Jerry." Her body shuddered. "I love—loved him. And the children . . ."

I sat carefully on the edge of her bed, my hand hovering in the air for a moment before I laid it gently on her shoulder, which made her flinch.

"Gisele, the person—or people—who hurt you . . . did it have anything to do with Jerry?"

She trembled under my hand. Was it sadness? Fear?

Finally, she turned her gaze back toward me.

"I do not remember. Anything."

"It was in front of your house. Were you going somewhere and got mugged—um, surprised by the attacker?"

She turned her head away again and bit the side of her mouth. Something between fear and anger twisted her lips. I sensed she remembered something. Was the attacker someone she knew, someone she feared—or wanted revenge against?

"I remember walking through the gate, then everything is black. Next thing I remember, I woke up here."

She studied Truck, looked him up and down, then did the same with me.

"Americans, yes?"

"Right." I pulled Lou Atlas's letter out, cleared my throat, and read it aloud.

"To whom it may concern, Buck Reilly is in St. Barths on my behalf to determine what happened to my nephew, Jerry Robert Atlas. Please accord him the same courtesy you would to me, cooperate with him, and help him to understand what happened. If you have any questions about his authenticity, please call my assistant, Annette. *Merci.*"

"He says nothing about us—nothing about his grandchildren." Tears rolled down her cheeks.

Truck shook his head, presumably because he thought the same thing I did: that Lou Atlas was a heartless prick. Another curse of wealth—you question the sincerity of everyone close to you, especially those who marry into your family.

"That's why Truck and I are here now," I said. "We're here to check on you and to find out why someone might do this."

The door swung open. Truck and I turned to find the doctor, his eyes ablaze the moment he saw his patient's tears. He launched into a torrent of French, way too fast for me to understand, then rushed to Gisele's side, placed his hand on her forehead, and spoke in a soothing tone. I understood him saying it was okay.

He turned back toward us.

"You've upset her, you must leave." He herded us toward the door. Once in the hall, his eyes and tongue sharpened. "What is wrong with you? Can you not see what this poor woman has been through?"

"Why do you think she was attacked?" I said.

He shook his head, grumbling to himself.

"Did it have something to do with her husband?" I said.

"Of course it did! Opportunists looking for money—but she has none!" His voice rose with each sentence. "Penniless, that's how he left her—good that she is a Rigaud, her family can support her—but that pig left her nothing!" Then in a low voice: "And now she is alone and terrified. It is time for you to leave. Take your letter and large friend and go home. St. Barths will take care of its own."

"But I—"

"Go, now!" He shooed us out.

Outside, Truck and I took a moment to collect ourselves. I stared out into the deep abyss of blue water and wondered where Jerry had capsized. A large sailboat tacked toward the harbor, its crew scurrying about like ants.

"Damn, Reilly," Truck said. "That was some heavy shit."

"Heavy bullshit, I'd say. "

"What you mean?"

"Someone attacked her for money she doesn't have and certainly wouldn't have on her? I don't think so."

13

"You've got a mess down here, Lou," I said into the cell phone he'd provided. "Your nephew apparently drowned, and someone beat the shit out of his widow. She's in the hospital and needs money." I bit my lip. "I thought I'd be finished early, but after seeing Gisele I feel obliged to figure out what the hell else is going on." I paused. "Consider this your first report. Bye." I hit End, then took a long gulp of cold Carib beer.

We were seated on the outdoor patio of Le Select, awaiting cheeseburgers and the arrival of my old friend Marius Stakelborough, the nonagenarian proprietor. The patio was full of locals, boatmen, and designer-clad tourists. Le Select was the melting pot on St. Barths, just a block away from the harbor, where all demographics blended harmoniously to drink, dine, smoke, and see friends. It had been there for over sixty years.

"Was starting to think I was the only black man on the island," Truck said.

The several generations of Stakelboroughs who ran the restaurant were various shades of brown, a calaloo of interracial offspring that bespoke the progressive community on the island.

"St. Barths was never agricultural," I said. "No sugar plantations, no crops of any kind—"

"So no slaves is what you're saying?"

"Basically," I said. "It wasn't considered really valuable back in the colonial days, so the island was slow to develop. The French sold it to Sweden, then bought it back in the 1800's—"

"Buck Reilly!"

Marius walked through the door from the inside bar, leaning on a cane as he went. He'd aged a lot since I'd last seen him. I slid the plastic chair back, stood up, and gave him a hug. His bones pressed against me.

He said it was good to see me and asked how I'd been, in French. He knew my history, even though the last time I'd seen him was when I was here on the mega-yacht.

"*Comme si, comme* ça," I said.

He nodded, the smile never leaving his face. Marius was a living legend, gentlemen and entrepreneur, and was considered royalty in Sweden. The wealthy from around the world had courted him. St. Barths was part of France, but if it were its own country, he'd have been the foreign minister.

We sat back down and I introduced him to Truck.

"Which yacht you on this time?"

"My flying boat—an old Grumman Goose."

"Don't be landing her in these waters." He laughed. "Not like it used to be around here."

A young man brought him an Orangina. I knew Marius wouldn't ask, so I cleared my throat.

"We're here on behalf of Lou Atlas."

"Ahh, Jerry. No prodigal nephew, that one."

"How well did you know him?"

"He came by often."

"Drinking?"

"Now and then, but usually on his way to the bank around the corner." He nodded toward the harbor. "Jerry went there a couple of times a week to meet with the manager."

"The manager?" That surprised me. Would he be checking on his money?

"We just went and saw his wife all beat up in the hospital," Truck said.

Marius winced. "Bad, bad, bad. Not right, you know?"

"Any word of who or why?"

He leaned forward. "There've been some men here, hunting for treasure."

I felt as if all my blood had rushed to my feet and left me cold.

"*What?*"

"A sunken Spanish galleon called the *Concepcion*."

Couldn't be. I glanced around to see if anyone was listening. The mention of sunken treasure always garnered attention from eavesdroppers. Even Truck was leaning in close, his attention fixed on Marius.

"I'm familiar with the *Concepcion*, but the Dominican Republic's five hundred miles away," I said. "Why would they be here?"

"Easy, because of Remy de Haenan."

The silence that followed seemed long. And unnecessary.

"I'll bite," I said. "Who's Remy de Haenen?"

Marius sighed. "One of the greatest men ever to live in St. Barths. In fact, you're much alike, Buck. He was an aviator as far back as the forties and the first to land a plane here in the fifties."

I watched as Marius's eyes grew distant.

"Remy was fearless. Went from smuggler to airline owner to mayor of St. Barths for fifteen years—even president Chirac came here from Paris to see him!" Marius glowed. "Ah, Remy de Haenen. How I miss him."

"What does any of that have to do with the *Concepcion* —or more important, Jerry Atlas?" I said.

Marius took a sip of his Orangina. "Back in either the late sixties or early seventies, Jacques Cousteau came to St. Barths—"

"*The* Jacques Cousteau? From the TV show?" I said.

"*Oui*, he came aboard his ship, the *Calypso,* to get Remy. They searched the waters off the Dominican Republic for *la Concepcion*."

"But why Remy?" I said.

Marius blew out a long, slow breath.

"Remy had covered the islands like no one before him—his airline, the first in the Caribbean—he knew everybody and everything. Cousteau needed him."

I didn't remember any mention of Jacques Cousteau from my research.

Based on the date, it would have been before Webber found his artifacts in 1978. My fingers tingled in the same way they used to when I found an undocumented detail about a treasure I was hunting for.

Would Jack know about this?

"What'd they find?" Truck's voice was a whisper.

Now Marius shrugged and looked away.

"Nobody knows. Rumors say they found gold—and if they did, well, it wouldn't surprise me that Remy kept it a secret. The Dominican government would want their share . . ." Marius waved his hand away as if to dismiss the idea as nonsense.

We sat in silence. The hustle-bustle of the bar faded into the background as I processed the information. If Remy and Jacques Cousteau did find some of the *Concepción* treasure, what became of it?

I shook off the thoughts of treasure.

"And what does any of this have to do with Jerry Atlas?"

Marius smiled. "Remy sold the Eden Rock hotel to Jerry back in the nineties."

"What? Jerry *owned* the Eden Rock?" It was probably the most exclusive boutique hotel on the island.

"Not for long," Marius said. "I've been hearing rumors about men in town looking into the *Concepción*, so I'm only guessing, but that could be the connection."

"How is that a connection?" I said.

The tinny outdoor speaker cracked and the female chef's voice said: "*Nombre sept.*"

"That's us," I said.

Truck sauntered over to the outdoor kitchen window to gather our plates, and a local man stopped by to talk with Marius. The possibility of a connection to the *Concepción* here on St. Barths had my mind spinning. The wreck was 500 miles away! What could Cousteau have known—and why would Remy de Haenen be of help all the way from here? Just because he owned the Eden Rock—and later sold it to Jerry Atlas—so what? Lou certainly hadn't mentioned that detail, and it didn't seem to fit

Jerry's drunken trust-fund brat image. The mention of the *Concepcíon* and treasure hunters here from the DR had my head spinning.

Marius put his palms down on the table.

"I have to go. Doctor's appointment. My eyes—one's dead and I just had surgery on the other."

"You look great—"

He laughed. "You've always been full of shit, Buck. I'm old and tired. I've been blessed, but my days are drawing down."

We stood. I gave him another hug and he kissed me on both cheeks.

"You've piqued my interest, Marius. We'll be back."

Marius's smile drifted away, and through his dark glasses I could see his eyes were narrowed.

"Just watch yourself, Buck. Plenty tricky currents here now. It's not the same any more."

When Truck returned with our plates, Marius was gone, though not before sending two fresh beers over to our table. We inhaled the double cheeseburgers and salty fries in near silence, still rocked by the news of the *Concepcíon*.

Truck kept glancing past my shoulder while he ate, so I assumed there must be an attractive woman behind me. When he swallowed his last bite, he leaned closer.

"Couple of dudes in the bar been watching us."

I washed down the remaining fries with the last of my beer, took a deep breath, and sat back. "Is one of 'em a skinny but muscular white guy?"

"No, man. Look kind of Latino to me."

"You ready?" I said.

We walked out and headed up the street. At the second set of open doors into Le Select, I glanced back inside. Two big men—Latino, like Truck said—stood watching us. They turned away when they saw me look their way.

At least neither of them was Jack.

We continued at a casual pace up the street to where our Jeep was parked across from the Rhum St. Barth store. We hadn't looked back, but when we pulled out I saw the same men getting into a white Land Rover 110.

"Our friends from the bar are following us," I said.

"Plot thickens," Truck said.

14

THE MYSTERY MEN FOLLOWED US ALL THE WAY BACK TO LORIENT, BUT KEPT going through the village when I turned left toward La Banane. I pulled into the shopping center across from the hotel and watched over my shoulder as they accelerated past.

"The hell's that all about, cuz?" Truck said.

"Good question. The bartender at La Plage did mention a couple big Puerto Rican guys were looking for Jerry, and Marius told us about two men from the Dominican Republic. Could be one and the same."

Truck and I went into the grocery store. If the two men in the Land Rover came back, they'd see our Jeep here and wouldn't be searching down the street for our hotel. We bought some cheese and crackers, a few liters of water, and Truck wanted candy.

We walked outside and kept looking up and down the small strip center until the men drove slowly back past. They must have spotted us—they picked up speed and kept going.

We hopped in the Jeep and drove down the narrow lane into the walled parking area of the hotel.

"If they come back, maybe they'll think they lost us," I said.

"What the hell, man? Who are those guys?"

"Could be the treasure hunters, and if they think Jerry Atlas knew something about the *Concepcíon,* they might have beat Gisele Atlas looking for answers."

"Maybe they staked out her hospital room and followed us from there," Truck said.

I pulled my long hair back and tried to tie it into a ponytail—not quite long enough.

"I need to think."

Female laughter drifted from the open bar and we both glanced over to see a pair of women seated on one of the plush couches with a bottle of champagne in front of them.

"I'll be over there," he said.

Restless, I made my way back down to the drainage ditch that led to the beach, but rather than walking along the shore I climbed the rocks up to a break in the fence, squeezed through, and continued up the loose gravel driveway toward the mass of green trees and overgrown shrubs at the top. Cactus and a variety of wildflowers grew the length of a stone wall that bordered the washed-out road that circled up the hill to the ruins of the l'Autour du Rocher. The building had been abandoned since a fire destroyed most of it one New Year's Eve some twenty years ago.

The hotel had been built on the peak of a bluff, and a huge rock formation dominated the center of what had once been a courtyard encircled by rooms, a bar, and a dance floor. The view out over the sea and back across the length of the beach some three hundred feet below was breathtaking in all directions.

Inside I saw evidence of a fresh demolition effort. I was amazed it had taken this long for someone to rebuild the one-time magnet to the likes of Joni Mitchell and Mick Jagger.

The sun was on its way down, and long shadows stretched out like giant roots overtaking their surroundings. A cool breeze gave me a chill as I sat on the edge of the small building in the back, past where the hot tub had been. I stared out over the bay that led to St. Jean and considered the findings of the day.

I checked the phone—there was a message.

"Got your update, Treasure Hunter," Lou Atlas said. "Not surprised about Jerry. Better a Jet Ski than crashing his car into a sidewalk full-a people." He paused. "Didn't know about Gisele, so thanks for telling me. And I agree, keep at it. In fact, I'll still pay you the $250,000 bonus if you can produce the body. *Habeas corpus*, as they say. I'll keep the Visa card loaded and I'll be waiting on your next update toot sweet."

Click.

Habeas corpus? How the hell can I produce the body if he drowned out there? Why does it feel like Lou Atlas knows more than he told me? Nothing but the vast silver sea spread out before me, accentuating the absurdity of Lou's statement.

A distant vibration caused me to sit up. I turned my attention to the sky—the sound—it was unmistakable.

Radial engines.

I jumped to my feet and rushed to the wobbly railing that was the only barrier between me and a steep drop into the water. I scanned the sky as the sound grew louder.

There!

A plane appeared from behind me—floats hanging from the wings, that unmistakable fuselage—a Grumman flying boat.

My stomach clenched. Had someone stolen the Beast?

I peered at it in the fading light. No, too small.

That left only a Widgeon. I swallowed, hard.

It was just a silhouette, so I couldn't make out the color scheme. Based on its gradual descent and course, I could tell it was headed for the airport here. The sound faded into an echo across the bay, like the cry of a T-Rex across the span of time.

The pit I'd felt in my stomach twisted more tightly. People were already here in search of the Cousteau-de Haenen connection to the *Concepcíon*, and if they were connected to Jack I'd be in trouble.

I rushed back toward the hotel through the darkness that enveloped the hillside, my mind churning. Harry and Lou had sent me down here under the premise of easing Lou's conscience. I'd been lured by the destination, the money, and the hope of getting Harry to back me going forward, but things weren't adding up.

Maybe because I had no idea what the equation was.

This is Not My Beautiful Beach Trip

15

CONFUSION AND CONCERN KEPT TRUCK AND ME WITHIN THE CONFINES OF the hotel for the night—that and him being half in the bag from spending the evening chatting up the pair of British divorcees at the bar. They were here to celebrate their new freedom and financial independence after catching their husbands with their mistresses on a supposed business trip to Majorca. Apparently Truck had been hard-pitching a double date for the next night. Distracted by the plane, I'd walked right past the bar and entirely missed the three of them calling my name.

Morning brought a renewed sense of purpose. After rousing Truck from his lair, I promised him breakfast on the road. I wanted to get to where we were headed early, so if the people we were going to see had jobs, we'd catch them before they headed out.

The road to the left took us out past the graveyard filled with white-washed above-ground tombs at the end of Lorient, up the meandering hill past Marigot, and down to Grand Cul-de-Sac. I told Truck that Lou Atlas wanted to keep us on the job, and we could still earn our reward if we found Jerry's corpse—good news to Truck, albeit an upside with infinitesimal odds. The idea of treasure had grabbed his attention, but I'd downplayed it for fear of running into Jack Dodson. As a result, Truck wasn't taking much of this seriously. It didn't bother me, yet, but it would if I needed him to focus.

We reached the end of the easterly road, the Hotel Le Toiny up on the left. Marius had told us Gisele's parents lived out here but not exactly where, so I drove up to the five-star restaurant and asked where I could find the Rigaud family farm.

The waiter's eyebrow rose. I realized Rigaud must be a common name on the island, so I mentioned Gisele.

"Ah, Gisele." He continued in French, slowly, and directed me a kilometer south toward the Grand Fond. Their farm was on the right side of the road, and there was a sign with their name by the driveway.

I told Truck to keep an eye out as we drove south. There weren't many houses on this end of the island, which was where the local agricultural and dairy farming industry was centered. The bulk of gourmet food was imported directly from France, but the demand for milk, cheese, and other dairy products must provide the Rigaud family a steady business.

"There it is." Truck pointed toward a gravel drive that wound up and around a hill and disappeared. "Man, this side of the island don't look nothing like St. Jean or Gustavia." He was right. Long, wind-swept, open hills covered with golden grasses led sharply up from the road, and the area was nearly devoid of the sleek villas found elsewhere around St. Barths.

No house was visible up the driveway. I turned and the tires spun gravel as we ascended the long road, fenced on both sides, where sun-beaten cows and goats watched us impassively from beyond the wire. A modest two-story farmhouse was at the top of the hill under the shade of large gaiac trees. A few old pick-up trucks were parked out front, a dusty tractor in a small barn next door.

Before we made it to the house, an elderly man opened the front door. He was holding a pitchfork. A woman peered out from behind his shoulder.

"What do you want?" he said in French.

Startled, I replied in English. "We're friends of Lou Atlas, Jerry's uncle."

The man's furrowed brow lifted, and he spat on the ground.

I waited, but he said nothing else. Truck and I glanced at each other.

"We're here to help," I said.

He spit on the ground again, and his wife said something and waved her palm at us as if to shoo us away.

"No more Atlas," he said. "Go."

"This is fucked up, dude," Truck whispered.

"We went to see Gisele at the hospital yesterday. We want to help protect her from whoever attacked her."

"You!" The man shouted. "You beat her!"

"*What?*" My jaw dropped. "We just got here yesterday!"

"No, she said two men, foreign men." He shoved the pitchfork toward us.

"Let's get outta here," Truck said. "This dude's nuts."

An idea struck me. I held up both my hands.

"I can prove it to you—I'll be right back." I jogged back toward the Jeep.

"Reilly! Don't leave me alone, dammit!"

I reached inside my flight bag and grabbed my passport. I ran back to them. The old man had crouched lower and aimed the pitchfork toward my chest, his wife hissing unintelligible French in his ear.

"Let me show you—I'm American!" I held up the passport. "We just arrived yesterday."

They let me approach, slowly, my passport opened to the page with yesterday's stamp from Customs. Monsieur Rigaud whispered something to his wife and she grunted, then stepped toward me and ripped the passport out of my hand. They studied it together, flipping through the pages. It was heavily stamped from locations all over the world, still active from my days at e-Antiquity. They whispered to each other, and I heard a loud exhale. He handed the pitchfork to his wife and the passport back to me.

They led us to an outdoor seating area and after a few questions finally opened up about their daughter's relationship with Jerry Atlas.

"He was always trouble," Madame Rigaud said. "Rich, yes, but trouble more. The drinking, always gone, never there for Gisele or *les petits enfants*."

"And Gisele, why would someone attack her?" I said.

The old man shook his head. "The money. Jerry's money."

"The men from the Dominican Republic said they wanted to help too," Madame Rigaud said. "But they lie." Her eyes were thin as razor blades, her voice as sharp.

"Dominican Republic?" I said.

"The other two men who come here asking about Gisele, and Jerry too, always Jerry," the old man said. "Then they threaten to get nasty." He reached down and put his hand on the pitchfork.

"Did they mention Eden Rock?"

The Rigaud's shared a knowing glance and nodded.

"Were they the ones who hurt your daughter?" I said.

"All Gisele told us was two men. Not from St. Barths, so could be them."

"Gisele will get even," Madame said.

"How, if she doesn't know who attacked her?" I said.

She shook her head. "With Jerry, not them."

I heard a child scream from inside the house. Madame stood, her wrinkled, knobby hands grabbing hold of her husband's shoulder for balance before she turned and shuffled inside.

What had she meant by getting even with Jerry?

"My grandchildren," the old man said. He looked into my eyes. "Why are you here?"

I pulled the letter out of my pocket, unfolded it and held it out to him.

"From Lou Atlas." He read it, nodded once, then folded it up and handed it back.

"My daughter and grandchildren will be safe. We will make sure of that."

TRUCK AND I WERE QUIET FOR MUCH OF THE DRIVE SOUTH. I WANTED TO drive through the rural part of the island to think, up over the highest point on Mount Vitet and into Gustavia from the back side of town. Neither Marius nor the Rigauds had been on Lou's list, and both had provided unexpected information.

The memory of the Grumman last night made me flinch. Was Jack

Dodson on-island now, following some obscure connection to the *Concepcíon*?

"Hey, Reilly," Truck said. "When we gonna eat?"

At least there was one question I could answer. I jerked the wheel to the right and parked the Jeep across from Santa Fe, a sports bar high above Gouverneur Beach.

"Right now."

16

ONCE BACK IN GUSTAVIA, WE LEFT THE JEEP BY THE MASSIVE ANCHOR AT THE head of the harbor and continued down the walkway. Truck was amazed by the many yachts. Dinghies buzzed around like water bugs and an air horn pierced the air. The sky was a brilliant cerulean blue, unencumbered with clouds, and St. Martin was a gray silhouette on the horizon. The sounds of boats, motorcycles, laughter, seagulls, and bells clanging provided a steady white noise. Trendy shops faced the water from the other side of the road, where smartly dressed people relaxed in cafés or strolled along the sidewalk.

Le Select was crowded, and Marius was holding court in the front corner. We hurried along the narrow street.

"Buck, *ça va?*" Marius waved to us.

I pointed to an empty table inside the bar.

He nodded and by the time Truck and I entered he was already there, calling to the bartender for drinks.

"Back so soon?"

"We went to see Gisele's parents in Toiny this morning," I said.

Marius sat back in the plastic chair. "Salt of the earth."

"They greeted us with a pitchfork."

He laughed.

"They said two men from the Dominican Republic had come asking questions about Jerry and Gisele," I said. "Monsieur Rigaud chased them off."

"That reminds me of another story from Remy's days," Marius said. "When the French government tried to impose a tax on the island and sent a tax collector, Remy, me, and a hundred others greeted him at the airport with pitchforks and machetes. He never even got off the plane! It turned around and left to loud cheers." Marius shook his head. "After he resigned as mayor, Remy moved to the Dominican Republic. He considered St. Barths his home, but he needed peace that a small island like this could not provide. Everyone knew him here, looked up to him."

"You think he told people in the Dominican Republic about his adventure with Jacques Cousteau?"

"He was an old man by then." Marius smiled. "And old men like to tell stories, so yes, good chance."

A well-dressed elderly couple came in and the man put his hand on Marius's shoulder. He turned with a ready smile as the woman bent down to kiss his cheek. They spoke together in the local French patois.

"Okay, Buck, I catch you later—"

"One last question?"

He hesitated, his face serious.

"Does Remy have any family left on the island that might know more?"

He nodded slowly and I could tell he was trying to remember names and faces, who was alive and who had passed.

"Yes, I'm sure . . . his daughter—no, granddaughter—Nicole. I think she's still here."

I stood. "By the way, you said Jerry met with the BNP manager a lot. What's the manager's name?"

"Philippe Piccard."

We shook hands and I again pulled his bony frame in for a hug. Back out on the street, Truck turned to me.

"I thought you said this *Concepción* was a wild goose chase?"

I thought of the package Jack Dodson sent me, and his demand that I stay out of his way.

"Maybe it is, maybe it isn't."

17

INSIDE, THE GUSTAVIA BRANCH OF THE *BANQUE NATIONALE DE PARIS* LOOKED like any other bank, albeit with a higher finish to the décor. But with a stellar view out onto the harbor, it was prime real estate and obviously catered to the wealthier residents and visitors on the island. I could only imagine the magnitude of funds wired through here on a daily basis.

A young man with slicked-back hair and a well-tailored gray suit approached us as soon as we entered.

"*Bonjour.*" He glanced at our shorts and polo shirts. "Can I help you?"

"We're looking for Philippe Piccard," I said.

"Your names, please?"

"Buck Reilly and my associate Clarence Lewis."

The young man nodded once, spun on a heel, and walked directly toward an internal corridor, no questions asked. Since we'd asked for the manager by name, he probably figured we had good reason to be here. Truck wasn't so sure.

"Why we seeing this guy?"

"Something Marius said yesterday made me curious."

"He on that list from Lou Atlas?"

"Nope."

The young man reappeared and waved us back. He delivered us down a short hall to an office where a bald man in an even nicer suit sat behind a paperless desk.

Monsieur Piccard stood and offered his hand.

"How can I help you, Mr. Reilly?"

I passed over Lou's letter. After a moment, he sighed and handed it back.

"I'm afraid I'm not at liberty to discuss the details of Mr. Atlas's—Jerry's—accounts, with you or the other Mr. Atlas."

"Of course," I said. "We're not here to ask about his accounts—we're already apprised of the balances and status—but given Jerry's disappearance, we'd like to get your non-confidential thoughts on him as a person."

"I cannot share—"

"Monsieur Piccard, I said non-confidential. We know Jerry came to see you several times a week, and while the *gendarmes* don't suspect foul play, we've been speaking to Jerry's associates to help advise Mr. Atlas on how to proceed. He is not looking to remove Jerry's deposits from BNP, but that could change if he feels the bank isn't doing its best to help us determine what happened to his nephew."

Piccard straightened his back and the corners of his mouth turned down.

"Naturally we would like to assist Mr. Atlas. Jerry was not only a customer, but as you say, he was here frequently, and though he could be . . . demanding, I considered him more than just an acquaintance."

Demanding?

"Thank you. And we appreciate your candor." I smiled and considered how to play this. "Jerry had many different sides, didn't he?"

Monsieur Piccard shrugged. "Here at the bank he was constantly shifting funds into different investment accounts, based on the markets or currency fluctuations. As one of our more sophisticated clients, he kept us on our toes." His smile was strained.

Sophisticated? "Not exactly his public persona, though, was it?" I held my breath.

He laughed.

"No, not at all. Jerry liked to have fun, and while he was generous, I often wondered if his reputation as a playboy was a façade—that can be excellent camouflage, you know. From what I saw, he never let anyone get close enough to know the real Jerry."

"Even Madame Atlas, his wife?"

Monsieur Piccard pressed his fingertips together.

"She is not on any of his main accounts, only a checking account for household supplies and groceries. I do not know whether she knows the extent of his estate or not, but she *is* fighting for access now."

"Jerry's estate is complicated," I said.

"Ha! An understatement."

I didn't want to press too hard. Right now, Philippe Piccard believed we were far more informed than we actually were, so I struggled with how to ask the next question.

"And Jerry's estate attorney, is he also of a high caliber?"

"Ah oui, Pierre Jardin is the best on the island. Have you spoken to him yet?"

"He's our next stop."

Monsieur Piccard provided directions to Jardin's offices, which were only a couple of blocks away. I said we might return if anything else arose.

"Thank you for coming in person. Please let Mr. Atlas know that we—I—am very saddened by Jerry's demise. Complicated, yes, but he was also caring, in his own way."

Once outside, we turned left and walked slowly in the direction of Pierre Jardin's office.

"Don't sound like the same Jerry Atlas we been hearing about," Truck said.

I shook my head. "No, it doesn't."

I pulled out Lou Atlas's list of names. Odd that neither Jerry's banker nor attorney were included.

Why?

18

Though not large by the standard of big city attorneys, Pierre Jardin's plush second-story suite had a beautiful view down Rue General de Gaulle. A lovely young pixie-haired paralegal/administrative assistant greeted us warmly in French, then switched to English upon hearing our response. She stood in front of a rosewood desk neatly covered with stacked files and papers.

"Is Monsieur Jardin expecting you?"

"Philippe Piccard from BNP suggested we come see him." I produced the letter from Lou Atlas.

She read the letter and sighed.

"Unfortunately, Monsieur Jardin has not returned from his lunch meeting." She glanced at the digital clock on the desk. "But he should be back in ten minutes or so, if you would like to wait."

There were two chairs and a couch, all pale blue leather, in the waiting area near her desk.

"That's fine, we'll wait."

As she walked down the hall I noted bright red high heels and tan legs wrapped in a thigh-high tight blue skirt. Back in a flash, she gave us two cold glasses of water, then sat at her desk.

"So sad about Jerry," she said.

"Yes, hard to believe he drowned doing something he loved so much."

She squinted slightly and nodded her head.

"You must have known him well," I said.

She nodded again. "He was very—"

The door suddenly swung open and a rotund man with gray shaggy hair, dressed in tan linen pants and a white linen shirt, walked in. He stopped when he saw us.

"Messieurs Reilly and Lewis here on behalf of Jerry Atlas's uncle," the paralegal said.

"*Oui*? How can I help you, gentlemen?"

I repeated the ritual handing over of Lou's letter. Monsieur Jardin scanned it.

"Come to my office." Without waiting he hurried down the hall to a corner room with a wonderful view of the western side of the harbor, BAZ Bar visible beyond the boats. He shifted stacks of files from his pale green leather couch to make room for us, then sat at his desk and lit a cigarette. He leaned back in his chair, which squeaked, and exhaled a long cloud of smoke.

"Jerry was not fond of his Uncle Lou," he said.

"Neither are we. However, he hired us to look into Jerry's affairs, search for anything that may have hinted at foul play." I paused, debating whether to use the banker's revelation to appear more informed. "With Gisele seeking to invalidate the prenuptial agreement, Mr. Atlas thought we should speak with anyone who knew him well, which has led us to you."

He leaned forward. "I was not aware that Mr. Atlas knew about me. In fact, Jerry specifically stated that he did not."

Crap. Strike one, and ever closer to the attorney-client-privilege brick wall.

"He didn't," I said. "The list of names he asked us to check with—" I pulled the list from my pocket and handed it over "—is comprised only of people who knew him socially. His banker, Philippe Piccard, gave us your name and suggested we come see you."

A long drag on the cigarette caused the ember to glow red for several seconds.

"That is unlike Philippe."

"We're not seeking confidential information, Monsieur Jardin—"

"Pierre."

"We're only trying to find out what happened to Jerry. We understand he lived something of a dual life."

Pierre gave me a penetrating look, then leaned back in his chair.

"With his estate in limbo—under attack, actually—and given that he is dead, I am willing to discuss certain details with you. Particularly those associated with his wife, Gisele."

I leaned forward. "What's the likelihood that she can overturn the prenuptial agreement?"

He shrugged. "Quite good, actually. They were married in the United States, and French law follows the matrimonial regime passed at the Hague in 1978—which, in essence, provides loopholes for a surviving spouse unless the agreement was updated and reaffirmed by the court in their place of residence, in this case a French court. Jerry had never chosen to do that."

I bit my tongue—another detail we'd been unaware of.

"Being a small island," Pierre said, "we found this out six months ago, when Gisele began to quietly investigate her rights to have the regime overturned. And, while Jerry chose to act as if he was unaware, we followed her progress through discrete discussions with colleagues at the firm she had retained."

Wow.

"He must have been upset."

"Yes, well, they had been married for many years, Gisele provided him with three lovely children, and he fully intended to waive his rights anyway, but he was curious as to how she would raise it with him." Another blast of smoke billowed our way. "Jerry's social life—the bars, the philandering—had festered into a sense of guilt that was eating away at him."

"You can't change your past," I said.

"But you can change your future. And Jerry was letting that play out a little before he did so."

"How did you feel about Gisele's efforts?"

He laughed. "The wives of French men, or men who have acquired French tendencies, is often a complicated affair. Given Jerry's great wealth and her lack of access or protection—his will had not been updated either—who could blame her? Now that he is dead, I am simply doing as Jerry instructed me to do before. Wait and see."

Good grief. The more I learned about Jerry, the clearer it became that he wasn't the person I'd been led to believe.

Nor was Gisele.

I glanced at Truck, who had his arms crossed and was staring at me. Time to switch gears.

"Were you Jerry's attorney when he acquired the Eden Rock from Remy de Haenen?"

Pierre laughed. "No, but that is how we met. I represented Remy in the transaction. Jerry hired me to help him sell it later."

The phone rang. We waited while Pierre had a quick conversation in French. I could hear his assistant's voice out in the reception area.

Pierre stood.

"My next appointment will be here soon, gentlemen. If you speak with Monsieur Lou Atlas, you can let him know that I was helpful. If he needs assistance here on St. Barths, we no longer have a conflict."

"One last thing, if you don't mind. Given your understanding of Gisele's situation, I'm guessing you know she was beaten and hospitalized."

His face darkened. He reached down to stub out the cigarette but did not respond.

"There are men on St. Barths looking for treasure from the wreck of the *Concepción*," I said. "Did Jerry ever mention this to you?"

Pierre's brow furrowed. "Treasure? Jerry? No, why should he have?"

"How about Remy de Haenen, did he ever mention the subject?"

He held both hands out to his sides. "Treasure? No, neither man mentioned anything of the kind. Is it purportedly connected to the Eden Rock? That was their only tie."

I studied his face, which had acquired deep contours and wrinkles.

"That's the word on the street," I said.

He shook his head. "I don't believe it. If it is true, neither man ever uttered a word to me, and I knew them both very well. Now that you mention it, I do remember Remy going off with Jacques Cousteau on some treasure hunt decades ago. He came back with nothing but stories of wine and seasickness."

My gut said he was telling the truth.

"And while Jerry Atlas liked to play dumb, he was dumb like a fox. He told me everything—at least, I believed he did."

19

GIVEN EVERYTHING THAT HAD HAPPENED, I WANTED TO CHECK THE BEAST. Since she was tied down on the private aviation tarmac, we didn't need to go to the main terminal—the access road was on the other side of the runway.

I waited for a gap in traffic and darted forward in the Jeep. A roar caused Truck and me to flinch—a St. Barth Commuter plane dropped in over the twin peaks, just twenty feet above the open Jeep.

"Damn!" Truck said.

We slowed to watch the plane float down until its wheels skidded on the scarred tarmac, which sent up plumes of smoke. A horn shrieked behind us and we jumped again. I popped the clutch and turned right toward the private aviation lot. A concrete wall with an iron fence above it, along with a private aviation hangar, blocked our view until we turned the corner.

My heart sank.

I jammed on the brakes. Truck followed my gaze.

"Hey, looky there, your plane went and had a baby," he said.

Parked next to my Grumman Goose was the Grumman Widgeon I'd seen in New York and Punta Cana. It was Jack Dodson who'd flown in last night at dusk.

A sudden numbness passed through me. Jack would assume I'd ignored his warning and was also on the trail of the *Concepción*.

Son of a bitch.

We walked to the Beast, me in a fog. The Widgeon was tied down adjacent to my plane. Jack must know about Remy de Haenen—why else would he be here?

"Why you so pale?" Truck said.

I realized I was holding my breath.

I could either let Jack know why I was here and promise to stay out of his way, or wait until our paths crossed and decide what to do then. I'd damn sure love to beat him to the *Concepción* treasure, if it was really here.

"They look so cute together," Truck said.

The Beast was still locked—no notes or obvious messages from Jack. I slowly circled the plane.

"The hell you doing?" Truck said.

"You see the tail numbers on that baby plane?"

Truck glanced back. "CU-N-1313. What about it?"

"CU stands for Cuba—"

Truck jumped back. I wasn't surprised given that he'd once had a near deadly altercation on that island.

"Damn, boy! They got chickens and boiling pots in that thing or what?"

"It belongs to my former partner, Jack Dodson, who I know for a fact is on the hunt for the *Concepción*." I glanced around in all directions and saw nobody, so I stepped toward the small Grumman. I peered inside the pilot's side window and was simultaneously impressed by the tidy cockpit and choked up—this Widgeon was the same year as Betty, had the same lines. There the resemblance ended. Jack's wasn't stock and certainly not *brand* new, but the equipment was new in the setting of a Grumman cockpit.

"Former partner? From your old treasure hunting business?" Truck said. "Why would he have a Cuban plane?"

"Exactly what I'm wondering." I glanced around again, then spied inside the window under the wing. Nothing on the two seats in the back, and the chrome metal locker on the starboard side was closed tight.

A drop of cold sweat slid down my back. My old green kayak used to hang from the top of the cabin inside Betty. I could have sworn I saw patched holes where the hooks that suspended my kayak had once been.

I stared at the dimples and told myself they were just that, dimples left from the restoration. These planes were never perfect. Was it just because this was a Widgeon?

As I stood next to the plane, I put my hand on her fuselage and a shock of warmth spread through me.

Betty?

I thought back and tried to remember who Jack might have known from Cuba, but couldn't think of anyone.

I walked back to the Beast, unlocked it, and popped the hatch open. A wave of hot air rolled over me from the inside. I sat in the left seat, bent down, and tried the handle of the small hotel safe I'd welded to the frame under my seat. When the La Concha upgraded their suites a few months ago they'd replaced the old safes with newer, larger ones. I'd asked Bruce if I could have—damn!

How many days had I been gone? Would they really have packed up my possessions and moved me out?

Truck crawled in behind me.

"The hell you doing, Reilly? Freaking hot in here."

I shook off thoughts of my room at the La Concha—nothing I could do about it right now. I bent down, spun in the combination that popped open the safe, and pulled out a sheaf of papers.

I felt Truck watching over my shoulder. He'd no doubt guess what the old maps and documents were, but Truck and I had been through a lot together and I knew I could trust him.

I removed the yellowed pages.

"This is information on the *Concepcion*."

"No shit? Damn boy. I feel like Indiana Jones's accomplice or something."

"I hope not," I said.

"Why's that?"

"His accomplices usually got killed by Nazis." I scanned each page, skipped the maps, then dropped the papers back into my lap.

"What'd you find?"

I slid the material back into its folder, placed it back inside the sheaf of other folders, stretched the rubber bands over them, and lowered it all into the safe.

"Nothing that would corroborate a connection to Remy de Haenen."

I glanced past Truck, out the starboard side window to where the Widgeon sat pretty in the afternoon sun. My stomach flopped and I brushed cold sweat off my brow.

"You look like you going to puke, Reilly."

"I might. After seeing the banker and attorney I feel like we're maybe being set up."

"So should we get the fuck off this rock and go home?" Truck said.

"We seem to have stumbled into a lot of people on the prowl for a fortune in missing gold," I said.

"What kind of fortune you think, cuz?"

I glanced back at Truck.

"Estimates were that fifty tons of gold and silver was never recovered from the *Concepcíon*." I watched his eyes pop. "Still want to go home?"

He shook his head.

"Didn't think so."

20

No way was Jack Dodson's being here in St. Barths a coincidence. No way was appeasing his conscience the only thing Lou Atlas had on his mind—Jerry had been dead for a month, for one thing, and there were others. Could Lou be after the *Concepcíon*? If Harry was backing Jack's search, was I Lou's unwitting scout on the same trail?

In any case the opportunity to dig up details on the *Concepcíon* was too good to pass up. I could use the cover of searching for Jerry Atlas to my benefit.

I swallowed. Buckle up, Jack—I'm back in the game.

Could the evidence he had against me be in the lockers aboard his plane? My former plane, if my gut intuition was accurate.

Inside the *Marché U* grocery store, across from the airport terminal, I ran my finger down through the "H's" in the skinny St. Barths phone book.

Ah-ha. Nicole de Haenen.

I dialed the number on my cell phone.

"*Allô?*" a female voice said.

"*Bonjour, je m'appelle* Buck Reilly." I continued in French and asked if she was the granddaughter of Remy de Haenen.

Silence.

"Hello?" I said.

"Your weak attempt at speaking French doesn't help. I told you people to leave me alone."

The buzz of a dial tone followed.

I looked down at the phone.

"What'd she say?" Truck said.

"That she'd told us to leave her alone." Had Jack Dodson already reached her?

"Funny, I don't remember that."

There was an address in the phone book. She lived in St. Jean.

Back in the Jeep, I had Truck use Google maps on his cell phone to find the location. The digital world made it hard for anyone to stay off the grid. If you had a name or phone number, it could lead to an address. Hell, I didn't use a cell phone or email and people still found me.

Anonymity is *so* last-century.

Truck guided me through the rocky green hills above St. Jean, around a large saltwater pond, through a hodgepodge of residential neighborhoods, and to a steep road that turned from poorly maintained asphalt to gravel. Our tires spun as the hill steepened. I had to put the Jeep into four-wheel drive.

"We're way up here now." Truck was glancing back over his shoulder toward the water.

At the top, the driveway turned right into a copse of mature papaya trees, followed by groves of sugar apples, sapodilla, and mango.

"You could live on fruit up here," I said.

The house was a simple island-style home, old but well maintained. The roof tiles were burnt orange and the exterior walls a faded white, almost yellow. The property was huge, possibly the entire top of the mountain— no other homes, signs, or fencing in sight. I pulled up next to an old sun-bleached Suzuki Samurai.

"Now that's a hell of a view," Truck said.

As the highest home on the ridge overlooking the water, it provided an incredible panorama over St. Jean that included an unobstructed view of the airport. I could see the Beast, just a small dot, with Jack's Widgeon, a slightly smaller dot, next to it.

"Let's go," I said.

More mature landscaping lined the stone path to the front door, where a sign hung on two crooked posts of native wood. Although faded, the name was legible enough: "de Haenen."

"Think she'll talk to us?" Truck said.

I smiled, confident that my persuasive powers could crack even the most reclusive of women.

The door flew open—a shotgun was the first thing I saw.

"Was I not clear—wait. You are not . . ." She paused, her brow furrowed. "Who are you and what is it that you want?"

I glanced up from the end of the double-barreled shotgun to bright blue eyes. She lowered the gun from chest to waist height.

"*Je regret . . .*"

"Damn, woman, 'bout made me pee my pants!" Truck said.

She raised the gun again. "You're the man who called earlier? With the bad grammar?"

I cleared my throat, searching for my voice.

"Yeah, that was me—I'm Buck Reilly, and this is my associate, Truck Lewis."

Her eyes widened for a second, then narrowed to slits.

"What do you want? Why did you ask about Remy de Haenen?"

I took a deep breath and held my hands up.

"Nicole, right? My friend Marius suggested we come see you—"

"Marius who?"

"Dude from Le Select—" Truck said.

"Stakelborough," I said. "We've known each other for years. We're here on behalf of Lou Atlas—I didn't know your grandfather—"

"What are you trying to say?" She said.

Truck looked at me and shook his head. "Just show her the letter, Reilly."

So much for my power of persuasion.

I started to reach into my pocket. She stabbed the shotgun toward me. "Slowly!"

I removed Lou Atlas's now crumpled letter from my pocket and held it out for her, but she asked me to read it aloud, which I did.

"Hold it up so I can see it," she said.

I pointed to Lou's name engraved on the top of the page.

She finally lowered the weapon.

"My brother was right, man." Truck said. "Trouble finds you no matter where you go."

21

THE VIEW FROM NICOLE'S SIMPLE HOUSE WAS STUNNING. THE BACK WALL WAS almost all glass, and there was a terraced patio down one level to a pool that provided an unimpeded view of the beach and water. Other red rooftops dotted the hillside below, but from this elevation it felt as if you were on the top of the island.

Nicole having apologized for the shotgun greeting, was now seated with us at an old wood dining table next to open French doors that overlooked the patio. I hadn't expected her to be so young, probably early thirties, or so beautiful. Her hair was sun-streaked, a wheat-colored blond, and her long muscular limbs were tanned the shade of coconut husk. She wore shorts and a loose fitting blue linen tank top that matched her eyes.

She'd served us cold water and now looked at us expectantly.

"Lou Atlas asked me to come down and try to figure out what happened to his nephew, Jerry." Her expression didn't change. "Did you know him?"

"Not personally." She shook her head. "Not the kind of person I choose to call friend, which was too bad, because Gisele used to be." Her response was matter of fact, not haughty or judgmental. "Why did Marius tell you to come see me?"

"About the treasure," Truck said.

Her eyes widened.

"Hold on," I said. "Let's back up." I glanced at Truck. Based on the way Gisele greeted us, I was betting she'd already been approached by someone less than friendly, and I didn't want to push her too hard. "When we learned that Gisele had been attacked, we wanted to find out why. Sure, Jerry was a drunk and nobody liked him, but everyone seemed to love Gisele—like you said—she's a nice woman from a local family. When we visited her parents, they said they'd been approached by some men from the Dominican Republic—"

She nodded her head slowly.

"So when we saw Marius, I asked his opinion. He told us the Dominicans were here searching for clues about a Spanish galleon that sank off what is now the Dominican Republic back in the 1600's." I paused, but her expression didn't change.

"You nodded when I mentioned the Dominicans—"

"They came to see me, along with two Americans this morning. That's who I thought you were when you called."

I shifted forward in my chair. Americans? Jack?

"Marius mentioned your grandfather had sought to salvage the *Concepción*—that's the galleon's name—along with Jacques Cousteau, back in the early 1970's."

"And what does that have to do with me?"

"First of all, we didn't come here for treasure." Truck shot a glance towards me. "But we *are* concerned for Gisele, and we're trying to determine why she would've been attacked a month after her husband fell off his Jet Ski and drowned."

She stood, walked to the open doors, and stared out toward the sea. Long muscular legs, regal neck, hair loose over her shoulders—

Truck elbowed me.

Nicole turned back toward us.

"And why should I trust you any more than the others who have come asking about my *grandpere*?"

"I know, I'm sorry. If you know Marius, you could speak with him—in fact, he said I reminded him of Remy. I'm a pilot, you can probably see my plane from here."

"What do you fly?" she said.

"A Grumman Goose."

Her eyes lit briefly. "Another old flying boat? That must be what all treasure hunters fly."

"We're not treasure hunters," I said. "We're here to find out what happened to Jerry Atlas."

"Mmhmm." She sipped her water, but her eyes never left mine. "I have my pilot's license but not a seaplane rating—pointless here because it is not legal to land in the water . . . . So Marius says you remind him of Remy? I'm not sure if that is a compliment or not."

I laughed. "He did allude to the fact that we both followed our hearts."

"Remy was a rogue." A faint smile lingered. "I do know Marius. I'll call him and check on your story."

"Do you mind if I ask what the other men said when they came here that made you ready to shoot us?"

Her smile vanished.

"The Dominicans came and I wouldn't let them in the door, so they asked if Remy left any papers behind that they could look through. I said no, and they kept whispering, then asked again to come inside. I refused and slammed the door. They tried the handle, but the lock held." She told the story calmly, but I could see her eyes blinking rapidly. "They went around to the back of the villa and tried to enter through these doors, but by then I had my gun. They said they were searching for the treasure of the *Concepcíon* and would pay me a share if I could help them. I asked what I would possibly know about such a thing, and they told the same tale about Jacques Cousteau."

"You'd never heard it before?"

She stood and moved around the room, adjusting a lampshade, moving a picture.

"I have little recollection of my grandfather," she said. "My mother spoke fondly of him and his many escapades, the movie stars at Eden Rock. . . ."

"How long did he own Eden Rock?"

"He purchased it for two hundred dollars in the early fifties and built the original inn there. People came from all over the world—in fact, Greta Garbo almost never left." She smiled.

"But no stories about treasure?"

"Not one. If there had been any treasure, he could have used it when the balance between his successes and failures tipped the wrong way."

Truck sighed.

I put my elbows on my knees and propped my chin in my hands. I had to admit it seemed like a dead end.

That left Jerry Atlas.

"Any idea why the men from the Dominican Republic would hurt Gisele? Or why they might think she'd know anything about the *Concepcion*?"

"I have no idea."

She turned toward the open doors and waved her hand for us to follow. Truck and I glanced at each other and hurried over to where she stood on the outside edge of the deck. From there, the beach and all of St. Jean looked like a postcard.

She smiled, then pointed toward the coast.

I saw she was pointing at Eden Rock. The small peninsula it was built upon jutted out into the crystal blue waters, its red-tiled roofed villas small as ladybugs from this distance.

"Their only connection was the hotel, and just after the sale it was largely destroyed in a series of hurricanes," she said. "Remy got out just in time."

And Jerry's timing couldn't have been worse.

22

NICOLE MIGHT NOT RECALL ANY MENTION OF THE *CONCEPCÍON* OR DETAILS related to the sale of the Eden Rock, but she'd made it clear that while Jerry didn't own it for long, his efforts to expand and modernize the hotel were a meaningful step toward what it was today. It was the hurricanes, his inexperience with real estate development, and his stubborn determination to do most of it himself that resulted in his giving up and selling at a loss.

Another trust-fund recipient turning millions into thousands. Sure, he could have waited for his next slug of cash, but Nicole said it was clear to everyone that he was in over his head—better to just walk away.

Yet fifteen years later, he had eight figures on deposit at BNP. How did that happen? Lou said he gave him three million a year. What a life.

"So her grandfather didn't find any treasure," Truck said.

"Not as far as she knows, provided she's telling the truth. Maybe it was just her hesitation, but I feel like she was holding something back. Still, sounds like the old man was cash poor by the end, so even if he did find some treasure, it didn't last."

"So what about Jerry Atlas?"

"People must assume that if Remy knew something, then either Jerry did too or he learned it after he bought the hotel from Remy—whoa!"

"Whoa what?" Truck said.

"Nicole. I'm thinking."

Marius had told us Remy retired to the Dominican Republic after selling the Eden Rock. Odd that Nicole hadn't mentioned it, since it was Dominicans who came by to hassle her?

"Feisty one, huh?" Truck said.

"To say the least."

"Good-looking too. Funny, she didn't warm too quickly to your usual charm, cuz."

I pulled out onto the main road and turned left.

"Isn't our hotel back the other way?" Truck said.

"Yeah, but I have an idea—I want to go see Bruno Magras.

"Who's he?"

"The president of St. Barths."

"Say what?"

I smiled and a moment later turned right into the rental car parking area at the airport. I steered the Jeep into an open spot.

"Why we stopping here?"

"Because Bruno also owns the St. Barth Commuter, an inter-island airline."

"Hmm, just like Remy."

We passed by the car rental counters—no customers now, but since planes arrived every thirty minutes this time of year, that wouldn't last long. Out in the open-air terminal, there were only a couple of check-in counters shared by the various airlines that served St. Barths from St. Martin, the Dominican Republic, Guadeloupe and others.

A deeply tanned agent with sandy blond hair was sifting through a pile of paperwork at one of the counters. I walked up.

"*Bonjour, Monsieur.*" I asked if Monsieur Magras was there.

He held up a finger and walked down the corridor that led to a few small offices and eventually outside to the airport tarmac.

A moment later, the man I'd met on my e-Antiquity yachting boondoggle came down the steps. He wore aviator sunglasses and had the air of confidence I assumed came with being the president of a jewel like St. Barths.

"Can I help you?"

"Monsieur Magras, my name's Buck Reilly. We met a few years ago—"

"Ah, *oui*, of course. I should have recognized you, but . . ." He paused. "Your hair, it is much longer now, no? And you have a plane here at the airport, a Grumman Goose?"

"That's right—"

"And there is a Widgeon, too," he said. "Small world."

"Smaller every day. I saw the Widgeon, but we're not together."

When I explained that I was here on behalf of Lou Atlas, Bruno's face turned serious. As the island's chief executive, he'd naturally be sensitive about any subject that could reflect poorly on the *gendarmes* or the government. The dead nephew of an American billionaire was potentially a nasty can of worms to open.

"I am sorry about Jerry," he said. "But rum and Jet Skis do not mix well."

"Absolutely. Lou Atlas has no concerns or questions regarding cause of death."

A small smile bent Bruno's lips. "Then what can I do for you?"

"My associate and I have crossed paths with a pair of men from the Dominican Republic. We think they may be searching for the *Concepción.*"

"So this is treasure business?"

"Not exactly." I filled him in on Gisele Atlas, Jerry's link to Eden Rock, and Remy de Haenen. I also mentioned that we'd been to see Nicole.

"I'm aware of these men," Bruno said. "We are watching them, to the extent possible."

"Could they be responsible for Gisele's beating?"

He pursed his lips. "Are you an investigator, Mr. Reilly?"

"No, but unfortunately this all seems connected."

"I've heard that the Dominicans have been researching Remy and asking about the galleon. I think they are wasting their time—I knew Remy very well, and he never mentioned anything about finding treasure. He was a man of many talents, a risk taker, sometimes even a rule breaker, but he was also a gentlemen and an idealist. One of my heroes, really."

"I wish I'd met him."

"We are watching the Dominicans. . . ." He paused. "And the Americans as well."

I swallowed.

He pointed out the window towards where my plane was tied down on the other side of the runway. I realized he was speaking about the Widgeon. I bit back a smile.

"The owner of that Widgeon, Jack Dodson, was just released from a federal penitentiary in the U.S.," I said. "I knew him years ago, and from what I can tell his incarceration hasn't made him any less ruthless."

He nodded, once. "Good to know, thank you."

A uniformed ramp agent came and spoke to Bruno. I heard him say something about "*la prochaine vol*," the next flight.

"*D'accord.*" Bruno turned back to me. "Please keep me informed of anything you learn. And be confident that we too are watching these men." He lowered his aviator sunglasses so I could see into his dark eyes. "And forgive me, but please don't cause any trouble here. If you need help, call the *gendarmes.*"

With that, Monsieur Magras walked straight out onto the tarmac, placed both hands on his hips, and looked up into the sky.

We walked away from the counter.

"Now what?" Truck said.

"Good question." I sat on one of the benches that faced back inside the open terminal. "I guess we could go back to Lou's list—"

A broad, heavily muscled man entered from the car rental area—a familiar face I'd hoped never to see again.

23

"WELL, WELL, WELL, IF IT ISN'T CHUCK REILLY." THE MAN WORE BLACK jeans, a tight black T-shirt, and the same blue mirrored sunglasses he'd had on the last time I saw him.

"Richard Rostenkowski." My stomach flip-flopped. "Or do you still go by Gunner?"

"Once a gunner, always a gunner, Reilly." He glanced at Truck, then looked him up and down.

A spark lit in my brain launched me to my feet.

"How'd you get out of Cuba?"

Gunner exposed his little square teeth.

"You mean after you double-crossed me? Left me there in the hands of the Cuban Secret Police?" He laughed. "As a matter of fact, it's a secret. The U.S. government even made me sign a confidentiality agreement, punishable by incarceration if I tell anyone." His smile grew wider. "But I been waiting for this, just to see the look on your face."

A moment dragged out. I felt sweat drip down my back.

"It was a political trade," he finally said.

"Political?"

"Me for Manny Gutierrez."

"*What?!* Why would they trade him for you? You're nothing but a mercenary—Gutierrez was a murderer and a spy!" I'd exposed the former Key

West art dealer as that, and more, and we'd nearly killed each other in the process.

"Mercenary's right. I spent a lot of years working for Uncle Sam in the Middle East. Consequently, I got a lot of secrets they didn't want the public or the Cuban government to find out about." He pointed to his head.

The pieces came together, but I couldn't believe what the puzzle revealed. I swallowed.

"How'd you get back to the States?"

His lips peeled back so far I could see his gums.

"That's the best part. You seen my plane out there next to yours? Pretty, ain't she? Looks a lot better than how you left her on that Cuban beach—"

Betty!

"Got me a partner who's a pilot too. One who's as hungry as I am."

"Jack Dodson the ex-con," I said.

"Very good, Reilly. Now here's the best part—the Cubans are backing us. Ain't that some shit?" He laughed again, then his face turned serious. "Jack was damned unhappy to see your plane here on St. Barths. Said you ignored his warning."

A hot flash washed over me.

"We heard you was here sucking Lou Atlas's tit, but do yourself a favor and stay the hell out of our way. Jack and I got bigger fish to fry. It's second chance time for me and him—got it?"

I unclenched my teeth.

"Likewise, Gunner. And stay the hell away from Jerry Atlas's family."

He laughed again. Truck took a step forward.

Gunner gave us a mock salute. "See you boys around. Not."

I watched him amble back through the terminal.

If my world had started going downhill when I saw Jack in New York, it had just fallen off a cliff.

24

I COULDN'T MAKE IT ALL THE WAY BACK TO THE HOTEL WITHOUT A PIT STOP. I pulled over in St. Jean, my hands shaking on the wheel, and parked across the street from Eden Rock. Truck pulled me out of the Jeep and practically had to carry me to the hotel's bar. After a shot of rum—Matusalem from Cuba seemed appropriate—I found my voice.

I explained how Gunner and I had clashed when he was on the hunt for the missing Atocha treasure that Truck had been accused of stealing. After I rescued Truck, I'd been shot down and crashed on a beach in western Cuba. Gunner followed me, convinced I had the treasure with me, which was why Gutierrez had shot me—Betty— down in the first place. After Ray and I gutted Betty to restore the Beast, I'd been able to capture Gutierrez and drag him back to Key West to face justice.

And the government set him free to get Gunner out of Cuba.

Who was now here.

After another Matusalem, this time on the rocks, anger finally started to overcome the shock. While Truck went out to the beach to search for sunbathing celebrities, I pulled the cell phone from my pocket and opened the contacts. I found the name I wanted and pressed Call.

"You better have something good if you're calling on my cell."

I exhaled. "Don't worry, Booth, it's good. Amazing, in fact."

"Let's hear it."

"I just found out that Manny Gutierrez was traded for Richard Rostenkowski, a.k.a. Gunner."

"*That's* Top Secret! How did you learn—"

"What the fuck were you thinking?"

"I said how did you—"

"Because Gunner *just told me*! Here on St. Barths! And he's now partnered with the Cubans, which makes sense because he's got my old Widgeon! What the fuck—"

"What do you mean 'partnered with the Cubans?'"

"He's here hunting for treasure—with Jack Dodson. Recognize that name, Booth?" Spittle shot out of my mouth.

"He's in a federal pen—"

"You're behind the times, Mr. Special Agent. Jack got out a few weeks ago and picked up right where we left off."

Booth was silent for a long minute.

"And where do you fit into that little cabal, hotshot?" he said finally,

"I fucking don't! In case you forgot, I'm here looking for Jerry Atlas, who as it turns out is at the center of not only Jack and Gunner's treasure hunt, not to mention the focus of a couple of guys from the Dominican Republic who likely beat Jerry's widow to within an inch of her life."

The bartender stared at me with his mouth opened wide. I pulled myself together and walked outside.

"Does that mean Jerry Atlas's death wasn't an accident?" Booth said.

"How the hell would I know? But there's a hell of a lot of interest in him, I can tell you that."

"Simmer down, hotshot—"

"Don't tell me to simmer down! You find out what the fuck's going on with Gunner—Rostenkowski—and call your *gendarme* friends here and check into these Dominicans—"

"What're their names—"

"I have no freaking idea, dammit. That's *your* job."

"I have no jurisdiction in—"

"How's it going to look when the press finds out you swapped Gutierrez for Gunner—and that Gunner's flying a Cuban plane with Cuban backing? You have any jurisdiction over that?"

Silence. I checked the screen to make sure he hadn't hung up, but it was still connected. So I waited.

Since I'd attracted the attention of some of the hotel guests, I took the outside stairs up through Eden Rock, past the restaurant, and up more stairs to the top.

Finally, Booth spoke.

"I'll look into all of this—"

"*And* get back to me?"

A loud exhale. "Yes, I'll call you back."

"And hurry up," I said. "This is a shit-show!"

I hit End, my mind still swirling. Gunner was just as big and scary as I remembered—the guy I'd vowed never to get into a fight with. Trickery worked once, but I doubted I'd be that lucky again. Both he and Jack had warned me to stay out of their way—my best option given the evidence Jack held over me. Second chance, my ass.

My surroundings finally came into focus. I'd sought privacy at the top of Eden Rock, which had a spacious outdoor seating area with a panoramic view back over the beach and down toward the airport. The patio itself contained small decorative cannons and sculptures of nude women bathing, in contrast to red lacquer lounge furniture and tables. The business offices for the hotel were also situated up here, as far away as possible from the guest activity down below.

Enlarged black and white photos covered the walls inside. And that gave me an idea.

25

THERE WAS NO RECEPTIONIST INSIDE, BUT AN ADMINISTRATIVE ASSISTANT SAT at one of five cubicles. I asked to see the manager. She was only gone a moment when a man in his fifties with gray hair combed stylishly back came out with a ready smile. He said his name was Monsieur Toussard and asked how he could help me.

My mind raced through all the people I'd spoken to so far and chose a name that would help me here.

"Nicole de Haenen suggested I come see you," I said.

A big smile brightened his blue eyes.

"Mademoiselle de Haenen was just here yesterday. Before that I had not seen her for a long time. And now here you are." He clasped his hands together and waited to for me to respond.

"We're doing some research on her grandfather, Remy, specifically related to when he sold the hotel to Jerry Atlas."

"*Oui*, she told me this."

Crap! What had she told him? Had she asked about the *Concepcion*?

I pointed to an old black and white photo of Eden Rock taken long before its current grandeur.

"This picture, for example. Any idea when it was taken?" I held my breath.

"Ah, *bien sur*, that is from when Remy had a small yet exclusive operation here in the 1960's. Much smaller than it is today."

"And what year did Jerry Atlas buy it from him?"

"The mid-1990's. Remy was finished with politics by then and had left for the Dominican Republic." His smile had faded. "Monsieur Atlas, well, he was looking for a project. Nicole knows all of this, of course."

Dammit. I knew she was holding out on me.

"Nicole and I haven't cross-referenced our research since before she came here," I said, "So I'm sorry if this is redundant."

He shrugged. I glanced back at the old photo. There were only a few small buildings on the piece of land that was now piled high with different suites, all tucked into rocks and ledges like a Van Gogh layer cake. It occurred to me that the peninsula wasn't all that large.

"Do you have any other photographs that show what Jerry Atlas did to expand the facilities?"

Now Monsieur Toussard's expression of genteel courtesy had faded.

"May I ask, Monsieur Reilly, what it is that you are looking for? That way I can be the most helpful."

"My interest is more related to the Jerry Atlas side of the equation." I reached into my pocket and produced the letter. "His uncle has me looking into Jerry's affairs here on St. Barths—"

"Yes, of course. So terrible—and a former owner. We are quite sad."

"So, like I told Nicole, I'm trying to get a better understanding of Jerry's history here. As far as I can tell, his effort to expand the Eden Rock may have been his most entrepreneurial project ever."

His brow lifted and his eyes widened. "Yes, I understand. Well, with Monsieur Atlas's resources, additional projects were not a necessity."

"Well said. Now, do you have any pictures from the period when Jerry owned the hotel?"

Monsieur Toussard rubbed his hands together.

"Yes, yes, of course. We have kept records of all historical images related to the hotel. I can show you the storage room—I warn you, it is a mess, but everything is in files there."

I followed him back into the small series of offices, past a large cluttered room. I noticed a cigarette smoldering in an ashtray, burned nearly down to its filter.

"So Nicole wasn't interested in these pictures?"

"No, she borrowed some old papers that belonged to Remy."

Two doors down was a room with boxes stacked high and some antiquated filing cabinets with binders, brochures, books, and other items piled on top.

"I warned you!" he said. "But let us see . . . ." He pulled open one file drawer after the next until he was at the bottom of the last cabinet. "They must be . . . ah—*voila!*"

Inside the drawer were stacks of old photos, mostly black and white. There were fewer than I'd expected, given the hotel's age—but then, anything from the past ten years was probably digital.

"Here, we shall take these out into the front room." He grabbed one bulging file and I took two smaller ones, which we carried out into the entry area. Once they were spread out on the coffee table, Monsieur Toussard organized them chronologically. The largest stack was from when Remy owned and operated the hotel, the next largest when the current owner bought it from Jerry, then there were just a few pictures from Jerry's tenure.

"Not much to show for Monsieur Atlas," Toussard said. "But he only owned it for a brief time, and of course the hotel was closed throughout his, ah, efforts to expand."

I gave him a big smile.

"No, this is great, it provides a context of what Jerry purchased, what he started, and what became of that. Do you mind if I take some time to go through these?"

"No, of course, help yourself." He paused, then glanced back at his office.

"Please, don't let me interrupt you," I said. "I'll let you know as soon as I'm finished."

I flipped through the oldest stack and quickly determined which person was Remy de Haenen. Rugged good looks, classic French shnoz, and a cocky assuredness etched into every line in his face. Several movie stars and celebrities from the era accompanied Remy in different pictures, including Dwight D. Eisenhower, president Chirac—and Jacques Cousteau, glass of wine in hand and a smile on his face.

Would that have been before or after their expedition to search for the *Concepcíon*?

The hotel itself appeared quite simple in Remy's time: a series of single-story buildings scattered around the small oasis, with large rocks, trees, and limited landscaping taking up the rest.

In Jerry's pile there were only four photos, two of which had close-up pictures of the same muscle-bound man, holding a shovel in one picture and a large pry-bar in the other. I assumed this was Jerry. Another shot was more panoramic and showed that the land had been cleared of much of the gravel and larger boulders. In the last picture, construction had commenced on additional buildings. The site was a mess, no workers or machinery visible. It looked like an abandoned property.

The most recent stack showed some early construction pictures, which compared to Jerry's time was a beehive of activity. More shots showed multiple new buildings had sprung up, and there were several pictures of the completed hotel, very similar to what it was today. There were a few pictures with people, including a much older Remy de Haenen, skinny and unsmiling, standing next to a much younger Bruno Magras. This must have been when Bruno was mayor, before they established a presidency on St. Barths.

I glanced back through the pictures. I was tempted to borrow a few, but contented myself with snapping them with my cell phone. I wanted to keep on good terms with Monsieur Toussard.

A thought struck me. Who'd taken the pictures of Jerry? He hadn't yet met Gisele.

I asked the woman in the cubicle to get Monsieur Toussard. He came back at a trot, running his fingers through his curly gray hair.

"I know Jerry did most of the work himself," I said, "but he must have had some help. Do you know if he had a contractor working with him?"

A quick shrug answered my question.

"But . . . there is a box with some receipts that I showed to Nicole, if you would like to see them."

A moment later I had a small shoebox full of yellowed papers, invoices, and lists from Jerry's brief construction effort. The receipts had a hand-stamped name on the top: Antoine Construction.

I looked up to Monsieur Toussard, who was tapping his foot.

"Have you ever heard of Antoine Construction?"

"*Oui*, they are a reputable firm. Henri Antoine is the owner."

I showed him the receipt with Antoine Construction on the top.

"That is him," Toussard said. "His offices have been down by the port, near Maya's, for the past ten years. A good man. We still use him for the occasional job here. I did not know that he had helped Jerry."

"You said Nicole took some of Remy's old papers? Any idea what they were?"

His brow wrinkled. "I'm sure she will tell you."

I handed him back the box of old papers, thanked him, and jogged down the steps outside. At the bottom I found Truck on a lounge chair holding a drink with fruit on the rim of the glass.

"Where the hell you been, man? Thought you got dragged off or something."

"I can tell you were concerned. I just dug up an idea. Come on, we've got someone else to see who isn't on Lou Atlas's list."

Truck finished the rest of his drink, grumbling. I ignored him, focused on my latest question.

What was it Nicole found here, and why hadn't she told us?

26

THE PORT OF GUSTAVIA IS SITUATED ON THE EASTERN EDGE OF TOWN. Container ships drop off shipments from France and other countries—everything from rare wines to building supplies—so it made sense for Antoine Construction to be based here. As Monsieur Toussard had said, I found their work yard on the way to Maya's, one of the better known restaurants on the island.

We pulled the Jeep into a fenced area filled with piles of rocks, rows of machinery, and multiple storage sheds, then Truck and I walked to the waterfront office. Though not much larger than a construction trailer, it had to be significant for an island the size of St. Barths. I walked up the steps and pushed open the door.

The room was open, with blueprints laid out on several tables. Hard hats hung from the walls, along with a few photographs of beautiful villas—mansions, really. Apparently Antoine focused primarily on residential construction.

A woman with a telephone cradled between her shoulder and her ear held one finger up as she spewed rapid French at the person on the other end of the line. I glanced at Truck and saw his brow raised high.

Once she finished her diatribe, she slammed the phone down and looked at us.

"*Quoi?*"

"Is Monsieur Antoine here?" I didn't want to piss her off further by butchering my question in French.

"Who are you and what do you want?"

Clearly Antoine Construction didn't get many walk-in customers.

I gave our names and said we'd been sent by Monsieur Toussard at the Eden Rock. She grimaced, then grabbed the phone as if it were a chicken whose neck she wanted to wring.

There were several doors along the back wall, some opened, some closed. The one on the end suddenly opened, and a man in his early fifties poked his head out, studied us for a few seconds, then waved us back.

The office was small, but the walls were covered with old photographs, and rolled-up drawings filled every corner. The man reached out his hand to Truck first.

"Henri Antoine."

Truck and I introduced ourselves. He glanced back and forth between us, waved us toward the chairs, pulled his out from behind the desk and brought it in front of us.

"You are new with Eden Rock?" he said.

"No, sorry, I meant to tell your, ah—"

"Jeanette is a project manager."

"Monsieur Toussard told me where to find you." I explained we were on St. Barths at the request of Lou Atlas, looking into any information about Jerry.

"I knew Jerry, but it has been many years since I've worked with him."

"You helped him with the Eden Rock, correct?"

He nodded, a scowl twisting his lips.

"I was never paid, but it was an early job for the company—one of my very first—and the exposure led to other work. So I overlooked those circumstances."

"We'd heard Jerry did much of the work there himself."

"Aside from me, there was nobody else. Jerry had used up most of his funds to buy the property—did you know two hurricanes struck just after he bought it? Of course that hurt his ability to finish the project."

I looked around. "It seems the years since have been good to you."

A toothy smile followed, with more nods and a shy, kind of boyish modesty.

"Yes, once St. Barths became the international hotspot, the demand for new and restored villas became very big. What is the American idiom—right place at the right moment?"

"Do you have any partners, or have you funded the growth yourself?"

The smile waned. "I'm sorry, Monsieur . . . Reilly, is it? What exactly are you here to discuss? Surely not my company's history."

I'd thought about this the entire ride over from St. Jean. There was no choice here but to be direct.

"It is precisely your company's history that we came to speak with you about."

Antoine crossed his arms. He wasn't a big man, but he was fit, with salt and pepper hair and a gray mono-brow above his dark brown eyes.

"How so?"

"At the Eden Rock are a few pictures of Jerry working on the property—"

"Taken by me," Antoine said. "Like any proud owner, Jerry wanted photos of himself and his new property."

"There are only a few," I said, "but they clearly document the pre- and post- hurricane condition of the property. In the latter, much of the land had been scraped—"

"All by hand. We had no heavy equipment in those days. Jerry and I worked tirelessly to clear debris, rocks, even some destroyed buildings to make room for his dreams. It was back-breaking labor."

"You seem to remember it clearly," I said.

"Very clearly. I always remember projects I am proud of—and projects where I am not paid." A fire burned in his eyes. This was a man who had built his business on hard work, starting with him as the sole laborer. "And the Eden Rock is one of the premiere hotels on St. Barths. Of course I am proud to have had a part in its history. Not just with Jerry, but the subsequent owners as well."

I paused, nodded, and smiled. Time to tack.

"Absolutely, it's an extraordinarily beautiful property. So if you don't mind thinking back to the days when you and Jerry were working to clear it, I have an important question for you."

"Yes?"

"I'm sure you know Jerry is dead?"

"Unfortunate, but not a surprise."

"And his wife Gisele was badly beaten and hospitalized."

"I have heard." He shook his head hard. "But what has this to do with me? It was many years ago that I worked for Jerry."

I leaned closer so our faces were only a couple of feet apart.

"Several treasure hunters have come to St. Barths looking for gold and silver they believe was buried on the Eden Rock property."

Henri Antoine jerked back as if I'd slapped him, eyes wide.

"Buried treasure? Ha! Had Jerry only been so lucky! He might have paid me then."

I paused. "It would have been a nice nest egg to build a construction company with."

His grabbed the arms of his chair.

"What is that supposed to mean? Are you saying I might have found something and hid it from Jerry—that's ridiculous *and* insulting!"

The fury in his eyes pushed me backwards. Truck leaned away from me.

"I think it's time for you to leave, Monsieur Reilly." Henri Antoine sprang to his feet, not deterred in the least that I was six inches taller, twenty-years younger, and had Truck with me. There is no greater insult to a man who has built a reputation of integrity than to challenge it.

I held my hands up. "I did not mean to insinuate that, Mr. Antoine, but—"

"But nothing." His hands were on his hips now, his eyes like lasers into mine. "I'd like you to leave my property."

"These men I spoke about—the treasure hunters—they are merciless. If I found you, they will too—"

"And I will tell them the same thing. The only thing Jerry Atlas found at the Eden Rock was heartbreak. And me? I learned to demand a substantial deposit up-front."

As we stepped out of his office, we passed several men standing in the room with Jeanette. They were all burly and none were smiling. Truck led the way out the door, and as we stepped out I turned back to find Henri Antoine on my heels, his eyes still ablaze.

"Thank you for seeing us," I said. "If two other Americans or two Dominicans come asking questions, please be on your guard. They're capable of worse than impugning your reputation."

He crossed his arms and the slow burn of his stare made it clear he had nothing further to say. Truck was already at the Jeep when I turned to walk across the yard.

Antoine did tell us to get off his property, so I assumed he owned all this land. With small residential parcels a fraction of this size selling for millions, this was indeed a valuable piece of property. Could business have been that good in the fifteen-plus years since he worked with Jerry, or had I struck paydirt with my questions?

"You really pissed him off, Reilly."

"Got to crack a few egos to find the truth."

Our Jeep labored up the steep hill toward the traffic circle above the airport.

"Just don't get our heads cracked in the process, okay? I got us a date with two horny British women tonight, they just dying to get back at their ex-husbands." He slapped me on the shoulder. "Let's take a break and have some fun."

Descending the hill from the traffic circle, I glanced to my left and spotted the Beast, the Widgeon still alongside her. I immediately thought of her as Betty, which twisted the knot in my already sour stomach even tighter.

So much for a relaxing research trip to my favorite island in the world.

27

TRUCK HAD A LATE NIGHT WITH HIS TWO BRITISH LADY FRIENDS, BUT TO their chagrin I begged off, needing the quiet of the evening to try and sort out the confluence of disparate details.

I was up early the next morning and itching to get a move on, so rather than waiting for Truck—or dragging him around hung over—I slipped out of the room and took the Jeep into Gustavia. The streets were quiet and the air had a chill since the sun was still low on the horizon. Rather than putting up the top, I cranked the heater and played some loud French music to take my mind off the temperature. I made my way around the harbor, through the small traffic circle, and zigzagged up the one-lane roads to the hospital.

When I got there I found Gisele had been released. Neither her less-than-friendly doctor nor the nurse we'd had to bull past was there, but the woman at the information desk was friendly and helpful.

"Monsieur Atlas paid for her medical expenses over the phone, and her parents picked her up last night."

"That's good," I said. "How did she look?"

The woman's smile turned to a grimace.

"Still bruised, I'm afraid." She shook her head slightly. I knew we were both thinking the same thing. Who would beat someone—a widow no less—so brutally, and why? I could think of candidates but not what any of them hoped to gain by that approach.

Back in the Jeep I pondered over whether to stop for coffee and breakfast, but Toiny, where Gisele's parents lived, was on the far end of the island and I didn't want the morning to be lost. I swallowed my hunger and took the high road—up through Lurin, all the way down past the road to Saline beach, and around through the quiet southeast corner of the island. With the Grand Fond beach on my right, I continued up the road until I again found the driveway leading to the Rigaud's farm.

Monsieur Rigaud was in the yard when I arrived, pitchfork in hand until he saw it was me. He walked up to the passenger side of the Jeep before I got out.

"How's Gisele?" I asked.

His lip curled. "Safe."

He studied my face. A lot had happened since the first time I'd met him, and I wanted to warn him—and his daughter.

"Can I see her?"

He shook his head. "She is not here."

"I've learned some things she should know about, and you too—"

"Two other men were here yesterday. Americans." He spoke the word as if it had a bitter taste. "Asking the same questions as the others."

I sank into my seat. "Can you describe them?"

"One was skinny and tall, the other was big, no hair, and his arms were painted. Many muscles too."

"Blue mirrored sunglasses, right?"

He nodded. "They asked if you had been here and what you wanted to know. The skinny one wanted to know if you had mentioned the *Concepcion*."

I sank into my seat. Had I?

"I told them you only asked about the Eden Rock and Jerry," he said.

"Did they threaten you—or Gisele?"

He patted the pitchfork and smiled.

"I had this. But they asked about gold and silver. Where Jerry had kept it."

Something occurred to me. "How well did you know Remy de Haenen?"

He laughed. "Everyone knew Remy, but we were not friends. I am a farmer, he was a dreamer and politician. Yet we shared some interests."

I remembered the story Marius told of Remy leading a hundred men with pitchforks to repel the tax collector sent from Paris. I figured there was a good chance Monsieur Rigaud was among them.

"Do you remember when Jerry bought the Eden Rock from Remy?"

"It was before he and Gisele were married, so all I knew was that Remy had sold the hotel at a profit to a foolish American." He shrugged. "How was I to know that the fool would soon become my son-in-law?"

To his amazement, I explained that the Americans and the Dominicans were all looking for the treasure of the *Concepcion* Remy and Jacques Cousteau might have found back in the 1970's, and that for some reason they were now focused on Jerry.

"So now you have mentioned this *Concepcion* too."

"I'm not looking for it. If the other Americans come back, please don't tell them I mentioned it. This is important, Monsieur Rigaud."

He nodded solemnly.

"I remember when Captain Cousteau was here," he said. "It was exciting, but they returned with nothing but stories. Why would this have anything to do with Gisele—or Jerry?"

"I'm not sure." I sighed. "But I *am* sure they won't give up until they've turned over every rock. And if they think Gisele's lying . . ."

He grunted. "She is protected now."

"Would you please let her know I want to speak with her about what I've learned, and about the men who're asking questions?"

His eyes caught mine and held for a long moment before he gave a short nod. He explained she was at her house in Flamands, and promised to phone her for me.

As I drove back down the gravel driveway, it seemed every goat on the Rigaud's farm had lined up along the fence to watch me pass. It sent a chill down my arms.

Did they know something I didn't?

28

AFTER A QUICK ESPRESSO AND PAIN AU CHOCOLATE AT LA PETITE COLOMBE, I turned down the road to Flamands. The descent was full of turns and twists, neither of which calmed the speed of motorists who knew the road by heart. I caught flashes of aqua blue water below, and as the road flattened and cut to the left the beauty of the water, the foliage, and the homes I passed sent a sense of warmth through me for a few moments.

Monsieur Rigaud had told me Gisele's house was the fourth driveway on the right. Once there, I turned into the gap in a stone fence taller than the Jeep and came to a closed gate. There was a call box, so I pressed the button and announced myself to the man who'd answered. The gate opened and I pulled into the beautifully landscaped compound. A pristine white villa stood between the beach and me. Jerry might have acted like a fool and a lush, but he had excellent taste in real estate.

Before I made it to the front door, a muscular man with a baseball bat came out—at least it wasn't a shotgun.

"*Qu'est-ce que tu veux?*" he said.

"I'm here to see Gisele. Her father should have called to say I was coming—"

"Book Wiley?" he said.

"Close enough. Buck Reilly."

He stepped aside and pushed the door open.

"She's resting by the pool."

The house was sparsely furnished, and what was there was disordered. Clothes were in piles, dishes were abandoned on counters, and magazines littered tables. To be fair, the family was in mourning and Gisele had just returned from the hospital. Curtains were pulled mostly closed and the sun cast odd shadows on the walls, where I saw a photo of Jerry, Gisele, and three young towheaded children seated at a picnic table. Crude modern paintings of circles and squares hung intermittently along the way toward the open double doors that led to the shimmering blue tableau out back.

I paused in the doorway. The beach was just past the low wall behind the pool, and the turquoise water seemed to thrum in a rhythmic dance throughout the bay. A warm breeze carried the scent of the sea.

Why would Jerry ever leave this beautiful spot and his beautiful wife to carouse around the island with Eurotrash?

"Monsieur Reilly?"

I stepped onto the tiled patio and followed a path between potted palms to where Giselle reclined in a lounge chair. I sat in a straight chair next to her. She stubbed out a cigarette and took a long drink from a clear plastic cup of water. Her face was still bruised, but not so bruised that you couldn't see I'd been right about her being beautiful.

"I'm glad you're home," I said. "I understand Lou Atlas—"

"Yes, he paid my expenses—I am sure he was embarrassed to learn of my predicament. Thank you for telling him."

I'd debated whether I should raise the issue of her quiet efforts to overturn what Jerry's attorney referred to as the Marital Regime. If she couldn't overturn the pre-nup, she wouldn't be able to keep this fabulous place for long—not without help.

"My father told me what you said—and about the others who've been asking about Jerry." She lit another cigarette. "Jerry was no treasure hunter, he was a spoiled trust fund brat who hoarded the money sent by his uncle every month. After the Eden Rock, he was filled with paranoia of being penniless."

That helped explain the banker's assessment of Jerry.

"These men seem fixated on Remy de Haenen as well," I said. "Aside from buying the Eden Rock from him, I haven't found any connection between your husband and Remy." No reaction. "Do you know of any?"

"With Remy de Haenen? No. He laughed all the way to the bank after Jerry bought those run-down little shacks—it is beautiful now, but back then it was nothing, neglected after Remy's years in politics. Remy was a great promoter, a visionary, some say. But he suckered Jerry into buying the hotel and then made sure everyone knew he had overpaid." A bitter laugh. "I met Jerry shortly after. He had no idea what people were saying, he was too busy trying to modernize and enlarge the hotel."

"He must have been really excited."

"Until he found out what everyone else thought—that he was a fool. And then all the stock markets dropped when the Internet companies lost value overnight. Jerry had invested a lot of his money there. It would take years of his trust fund payments to finish what he had started, so he quit. Not because he wanted to but because he had no choice. He sold out for half what he originally paid." She shook her head. "Again the laughing-stock."

There was no quiver to her voice but I sensed a depth of feeling nonetheless.

And she'd confirmed why he'd sold the hotel when he did—and why he'd stiffed Antoine Construction. Jerry's one attempt to do something with his life had failed.

I suddenly felt an unexpected solidarity with Jerry. I too had sought to build something only to have it ripped away by yet another market crash, and I too had lived beyond my means and lost everything I'd held dear. But anonymity was easier as a relocated recluse in Key West than it would have been as a very public foreigner in St. Barths.

I followed Gisele's gaze to the large island a mile or so straight out from Flamands. It reminded me of a saddle, two tall peaks with a swooping valley in the middle. White water crashed all around it, and I imagined her sitting here, staring at it, smoking cigarettes and questioning the decisions of her life. "Did Jerry spend a lot of time here?"

"Here, no. At the bar by Hotel St. Barth, yes." She pointed down to the right end of the beach. "Or at La Plage or the Yacht Club or Le Ti."

All places Lou Atlas had mentioned.

"Did he Jet Ski often?"

She smiled. "It was his favorite way to go places—no sideswiping or crashing into cars on narrow roads, nobody tailgating him. Freedom from the world is how he described it. And early in the day, before he was drinking, he would sometimes ride a Jet Ski all the way to St. Martin, or Anguilla, and sometime stay for days. He had friends there."

Women, I presumed.

She must have read my expression.

"Bankie Banx?" she said. "The reggae musician who owns the Dune Preserve on Rendezvous Bay in Anguilla? He was a good friend of Jerry's." I could tell by her tone that she was used to defending her husband. Probably for her own self-esteem, but also because she'd loved him.

If Jerry traveled that far and that often on Jet Skis, it struck me as odd that he would crash and drown so close to home.

Unless he was wasted, of course.

"Sometimes he would park on the beach right out front." She pointed toward the water. "Take the children for rides. Or pick up cash."

"Do you know Nicole de Haenen?"

"We were friends when we were girls."

I told her Nicole had also been approached by the men from the Dominican Republic. Gisele sat up straight and stared. I waited, but she said nothing.

"Tell me about Jerry after you got married."

"He ignored most of the rude talk about his failure with the hotel. He drank, but not as much." A sudden laugh caused Gisele to tilt her head back. "And he began to paint. I was so happy—I thought it would be his salvation. He didn't need to work, and after the loss of his investments he needed something to pour his soul into."

I thought of the modern paintings inside their home.

"Did he sell or show his work?"

A bitter laugh followed. "No, but friends who came to visit saw them and laughed. He dropped the interest after a few months. I tried to encourage him, but he just said he'd painted all he cared to."

"Then what?"

"We waited to have children. I was carefree and we traveled for a while, but I got restless. I wanted a family, and Jerry finally agreed."

Gisele raised a palm to her bruised eye and held it there.

"Are you okay?" I said.

"Tired. And my head is throbbing. I should go to bed."

I got up from my chair, and to my surprise she did too.

"Come, I will walk you out."

I followed her back into the house and realized she was taller than I'd thought—I'd never seen her standing.

She stopped and pointed to the wall.

"Jerry's paintings. He liked Mondrian and Rothko."

The paintings were different sizes and colors, a combination of crude circles and squares.

Once outside, the man with the baseball bat reappeared.

"Nice to speak with you, Buck," Gisele said. "And thanks for your concern, but I'll be safe."

"Do you mind if I call again, if I have any other questions?"

She held her palms up and nodded.

I decided I'd been right to not bring up the prenuptial agreement.

I drove to the end of the road in Flamands, to where the goat trail leads out to the beach at Colombier maybe a half-mile away. It reminded me of Ushuaia, the city at the tip of Argentina, at the end of the world. I would have loved to take the hike out as I'd done years ago, but a sense of urgency was festering in my gut that had me uneasy. The more I learned about Jerry, the less comfortable I felt.

Something important was missing.

Or I was missing something important.

29

I'D KEPT TRUCK WAITING LONG ENOUGH, SO I MADE MY WAY BACK UP FROM Flamands, down around the airport and St. Jean, and into Lorient. I saw Truck's lady friends lounging by the pool and one gave me a languid wave.

I opened the door to our suite, surprised to see it was still dark inside. I tripped over something, caught myself, and paused, waiting for my eyes to adjust. I ran my palm up the wall until the light switch clicked on—

The room was trashed. Furniture turned over, clothes strewn all over the place—

I heard a groan.

I jumped over debris, including our open suitcases whose contents were thrown on the floor, and took a couple of steps towards Truck's room—

Whoa! Two large men stood beside the bed—next to Truck, who was tied up, his mouth taped over. There was blood on his face and the sheets.

"We've been waiting for you, Buck Reilly," the man on the left said. He had a thick Spanish accent, dark hair, and was holding a shotgun. The other one looked the same, but had a knife in his belt, and a small club in his hand. There was blood on the club. Both men were muscular and both wore gloves.

The Dominicans.

"What the hell are you doing?" I said.

"We want information, Reilly. Your friend has not been cooperative—"

"Because he doesn't know anything!"

The one with the shotgun smiled. "Tell us what you've learned."

The other man smashed the club into Truck's shoulder—even tied to the bed and gagged, he shook wildly and howled.

"Stop! I'm telling you—there's no treasure!"

"Then why are you here? Jerry Atlas is dead—and why would his uncle send a world famous treasure hunter to investigate a drowned drunk?" White spittle caked in the corners of his mouth as he hissed at me in a low voice. "Now tell us what you've learned!"

The other man raised the club. Truck pressed his eyes shut.

"Stop! Look, I'll tell you—there's not much—but back off."

The man on the right held the club aloft.

"Jerry went broke and sold the hotel at a loss—"

"We know all about that. Why bother fixing up an old building when you found a fortune in gold?"

"He'd burned though all his trust fund money and had nothing left! He couldn't even pay the guy helping him, Henri Antoine. Talk to him, he was with Jerry during construction. We saw him yesterday—he says they found nothing. He has a big company now, Antoine Construction."

The Dominicans glanced at each other.

"What else?"

"Neither his attorney or banker know anything about treasure." I paused. "You do realize Jack Dodson is here too? He's also found nothing!"

"What did you learn at the Eden Rock? Or from Nicole de Haenen?"

"I just looked at old pictures, before and after Jerry owned the property. He left it a wreck—and there were construction receipts from Antoine. Go see him, if anyone knows something, it's him!"

They glanced at each other again.

"Sit in that chair."

I hesitated. One pointed the shotgun at me while the other one pulled the knife from his belt and pressed it against Truck's neck.

I sat down in the wood chair by the coffee table.

"Sorry, Truck," I said.

Shotgun picked some rope up off the floor and tied my hands and feet to the arms and legs of the chair, then wrapped my head indelicately in duct tape, covering my mouth. I didn't struggle, just wanted them out of here.

He pulled his arm back—I tried to dodge, but his fist hit me in the side of the jaw. My ears rang.

As my eyes fluttered, another blow caught me on the other side of my head. I slumped forward semi-conscious, their remaining movements a hurried blur. There was a flash of light as the door opened, then back to the dim glow of the room. Gray shadows drifted through my consciousness. I heard groaning—the sound made me shake my head, which hurt.

Suddenly back in the moment, I sucked in air.

Truck!

From what I could see there was no movement on the bed. I fought against my bonds, but the ropes were taut and the chair sturdy. I rubbed my cheek against the top of the chair until the tape peeled up and the corner of my mouth was clear.

"Help!" But it was a muffled plea at best.

I glanced wildly around and spotted the phone on a table ten feet away. I threw my weight from side to side until the chair fell to the ground. After several minutes of pushing my feet against the wall and tile floor, elbowing the coffee table, and digging my nails into the grout between tiles, I was close enough to head-butt the side table.

I reared back my forehead, hit it again and again until I saw stars. A clunk! The table fell over—but the damn phone fell away from me.

The sound of a dial tone lasted a long time.

When I finally heard a voice, I cried for help through the partially torn tape, my entire body convulsing with effort. Then I was silent. There was no more sound coming from the phone. Minutes dragged out.

Suddenly the room filled with light. Jean, the proprietor, his mouth agape and his face sheet white, had flipped the switch. He soon had my ankles and wrists free. I jumped to my feet—woozy—and rushed into the next room.

"Truck!"

My hand shot to my mouth. His face was swollen and bloody, his wrists and ankles tied to the bed frame. I pulled the tape off his mouth, then fumbled with the knots—one hand freed, then the other.

Truck groaned, his eyes swollen shut.

My heart raced. His face had been savaged and there were bruises on his arms, but what really worried me was his right arm bent at an awkward angle. He only groaned in response to my questions. I held a bottle of water up to his puffy lips and he struggled to drink, gagging and choking.

One eye cracked open. "My shoulder—feels busted. And my ribs . . ."

"What happened?" Jean said. "Who did this?"

"They came in the room—" Truck coughed—"I thought it was you. Next thing I know . . . they cold-cocked me." More coughing and a serious wince. "Dammit!"

Jean glanced around the room. They'd opened everything, torn every cushion, removed every drawer.

"What were they looking for?"

"Him, mostly," Truck said.

Jean stood next to me, his face pale, his hand over his mouth.

"We need an ambulance," I said.

Truck cracked his left eye open. "I look that bad?"

My face ached, but I tried to smile.

"Like you just went ten rounds with Bruiser."

Before long, the sound of a siren broke the silence. Once the ambulance arrived, Truck was quickly loaded on board and I rode with him in the back. As we drove at high speed toward the hospital, siren wailing, I clenched my fists. Jack's threat to rat me out to the FBI had been bad enough, but these guys had crossed an entirely different line.

And paybacks are hell.

My Reputation Exceeds Me

30

I WALKED OUTSIDE THE HOSPITAL, TIRED OF TALKING IN CIRCLES WITH Commander Grivet of the *gendarmes* and Truck's doctor—the same one who'd attended Gisele. Both of them made it pretty clear they thought the whole mess was our own fault— we should have kept our noses out of local affairs. The fact that the men who assaulted us were Dominican seemed not to matter to them.

Truck had a broken collarbone, and while his face looked like hamburger, his skull and cheekbones were intact. A morphine drip had him loopy, and the doctor said they'd need to hold him for observation. My face felt far worse than it looked, having only taken a few punches.

Guilt over Truck ate at my already churning stomach. The so-called missing person case had spun out of control, the shit storm that followed Jerry's death carving a wider swath each day.

I pulled the phone from my pocket and called one of the few numbers stored in its contact list. Several rings passed while I rehearsed the message I'd leave.

A voice clicked on.

"Starting to wonder about you, Treasure Hunter."

"And I'm starting to wonder about you, Lou."

"What the hell's that supposed to mean?

"My friend, Truck Lewis, was beaten viciously and hospitalized today.

Did you know there were multiple groups here on the hunt for treasure—treasure they seem to think your nephew either had or knew about?"

A brief silence was followed by a cackle.

"Treasure? How-n-the-hell would my drunken nephew have anything to do with *treasure*?"

"What do you know about Remy de Haenen?" I said.

"What? Why're you asking *me* questions? *You* work for me—"

"If you want answers, I need background."

Silence filled my ear. I waited—after all, I had nothing but time.

"I met the old bastard back when I first went to St. Barths. He was top dog back then. Arrogant, even though he was only half French, but greedy, too, so he wanted to meet me." He paused.

"And?"

"And what? I told him he was a piece of shit tinhorn dictator 'cause he tried to strong-arm me into providing money for his development plan he had. To build a resort."

From my vantage point at the front of the hospital, I watched a fishing boat putter through the harbor.

"You're talking about Eden Rock hotel?"

"Well done, Reilly. Harry was right about you. The old man wanted an investor to help him triple the hotel in size. I said no, he got pissy, I told him he was a piece of shit again and left."

I swallowed. "How long after that did he sell it to Jerry?"

"You been busy, haven't you? Few months is all. He couldn't raise the cash, so he found himself a patsy. Got Jerry ginned-up thinking he could show me he was worthy of the trust fund by developing the top resort in St. Barths. Course, Jerry'd never built so much as a tree house, and since he knew me and de Haenen had been negotiating over the property, he thought buying it was a real coup. Damned idiot didn't know he'd paid a multiple of what it was worth."

Church bells rang from the center of Gustavia.

"Then what happened?"

"Jerry came to me for money when the market went down the shitter and he lost his ass on World Com and a few other dot-bombs. I refused to advance him any funds. So, like every investor needs to do it, he learned his lesson the hard way. Dumbass should have left town with his tail between his legs, but he went and fell in love and decided to stay."

"Which is when he turned into a lush—"

"Jerry was *always* a lush, he just got serious about it after that. Don't pin his weakness on me."

"But you kept sending the money anyway?"

"My sister was sending the money, dammit. I just continued per her Last Will and Testament after she died."

This was more sordid Atlas family history than I cared for.

"Nice that you got Gisele out of the hospital," I said. "From what I can see, she's broke—at least, she has no access to her husband's money sitting in the local bank." I waited a couple of seconds, then said. "Are you going to change—or allow her to change—the pre-marital agreement she and Jerry—"

"Don't be telling me how to handle my family's affairs, Reilly."

I turned to face the inside of the hospital.

"Did Jerry have an attorney here in St. Barths? Someone I should talk to?"

"Probably one to get him out of the drunk tank, but nobody I know of. Now what have you got to tell me about Jerry's disappearance?"

"Are you asking if the treasure had anything to do with it, Lou? What are you really after?"

"Goddammit, Reilly! I'm sorry your friend got beat up, but don't turn this into some kind of conspiracy theory. You want to fly that plane of yours back to Key West, be my guest—"

"Truck's in the hospital, so I can't."

"Then go sit your ass on one of them nice beaches there and try not to piss away the whole twenty-grand I'm paying you—which, by the way, you haven't given me a hell of a lot for."

"All right, Lou. Consider this your daily check-in call. If I find out you're lying about the *Concepcion* —"

"That sounds like a threat, boy!"

I took a deep breath and bit my tongue. Lou would never tell me the truth, and getting into a pissing match with him now would get me nowhere.

"I'll continue to look around until Truck can travel, then we'll see where we are."

A loud crackling sound caused me to pull the phone away from my ear.

"Fine. Hope your pal's okay. Keep me posted, *Treasure Hunter*."

Click.

I lowered the phone. Did he not know Jerry's attorney, or did he not want me to know? Lou Atlas hadn't become a billionaire by being open and trustworthy, that's for damned sure.

31

SINCE I'D RIDDEN IN THE AMBULANCE WITH TRUCK, MY JEEP WAS BACK AT LA Banane. I walked down the hill into town and turned left at the small circle on the northwest corner of the harbor. Restaurants were packed with lunch patrons, and traffic had picked up into a midday flurry. The Yacht Club disco was locked tight, but just past that was Master Ski Pilou, the boat and Jet Ski rental business Jerry had used.

I stepped into the small office where a nicely dressed woman eyed me up and down.

"We don't need any boat hands," she said.

"Good, because I'm not here for a job."

She looked back up from her computer monitor to once again assess me. Her brow wrinkled.

"I'm not here to rent a boat, either," I said. "Lou Atlas asked me to come to St. Barths to learn more about his nephew's disappearance." I produced Lou's letter. She read it and handed it back.

"We're very sad about Jerry," she said. "He was a great . . . friend."

"Customer, yeah, I understand. Is Bernard here? I was told to ask for him."

"I'm his partner. How can I help—"

"Were Bernard and Jerry friends?"

"You could say that." She pressed a quick-dial key on her cell phone, then explained in fast French that someone was here on behalf of the

Atlas estate. I realized she was tense. If a billionaire was looking to blame someone for his nephew's death, the company who rented him the Jet Ski would be a good target.

The door sprang open and in walked a deeply tanned lean man in a white polo shirt with the Master Ski Pilou logo on his breast.

"*Allô?*"

I introduced myself to Bernard, and once he'd read the letter I followed him out to where they had a dozen Jet Skis on rubber floating docks.

"Sorry about your loss—Jerry, that is. I was told you guys were friends."

He shook his head.

"Sad, yes. Jerry ran hard and fast, usually with one eye open, but he was a friend, as you say. Things have been very different without him."

"Did he always use a Jet Ski, or did you take him out on boats, too?"

"It depended on what he was doing. He liked to dive, but hadn't done as much the past few years. He enjoyed running over to Anguilla and on calm days would use the Jet Ski. Otherwise me or one of the captains would take him in one of our speedboats."

"Why Anguilla?"

Bernard laughed. "The Dune Preserve is there, one of his favorite beach bars. Plus it allowed him to go where nobody knew his name."

"Except Bankie Banx?"

"Bankie may have been one of his best friends. They went boating together, just cruising around the deserted islands. Jerry didn't have many close friends, mostly bartenders, waitresses, people here on the dock."

I nodded. "When the Jet Ski was recovered, did you get it back?"

Bernard nodded and pointed toward a blue Jet Ski off to the side.

"That's it right there."

The sight of it gave me a chill. If only it could talk.

"What kind of shape was it in when it was recovered?"

"Fine, no scratches, nothing. Key was in it. It was out of gas, though. No automatic shut-off on this model, so it kept running until it was dry."

"Do they have GPS? So you can track them?"

"Some do, not this model. It's a little older, but Jerry liked to use the same one, so we kept it aside for him."

Bernard's voice was flat. He was handsome, had smile lines around his eyes. But the life went out of his face the more we spoke of Jerry.

"Was anything missing when it was found?"

He sighed. "Jerry."

I walked back up the street, Bernard's information rattling inside my head. Were it not for the beating of Gisele and now Truck, foul play would have seemed unlikely. And those beatings were about something Jerry had nothing to do with. User error was the natural conclusion, and with Jerry's possessions and rum still on board, his death sure looked like an accident.

Maybe it was.

32

GUSTAVIA WAS HOPPING WITH MIDDAY TRAFFIC. BOATS, CARS, DELIVERY trucks, pedestrians, a topless Russian woman shouting up the street . . . I tried to block it all out but it was impossible.

I passed by the *Banque Nationale de Paris* branch and imagined Jerry's money on deposit there. Eight figures was a substantial sum—not to mention a broad range from bottom to top. Could be anywhere between ten and ninety-nine million for all I knew.

The smell of grease drew me toward Le Select, where I snagged a table and ordered a burger at the counter. The large round sign by the gate caught my eye. Cheeseburger in Paradise, indeed. With the order placed, I went to the bar window to order a beer. As I waited for the bartender, I noticed Marius inside by the back door.

"Marius!" I spoke loudly through the bar window.

He craned around, smiled, and signaled that he'd meet me outside.

I made it back to my table with a cold bottle of Carib. Marius appeared a moment later.

"*Ça va*, Buck?"

When I told him what had happened to me and Truck—mostly Truck—his face sagged.

"Terrible news—but I'm glad you stopped by." He rubbed his hands together and lowered his voice. "A woman was here looking for you, a very interesting woman. She said she's a historian and wanted to speak with you about the *Concepcion*!"

I felt my brow wrinkle. "How would she know who I was?"

"It's a small island, Buck. With Gisele being hurt and these Dominicans getting violent—and with your background? Word gets around."

"So you told her you knew me?"

Marius smiled. "She *was* interesting, possibly even beautiful."

I'd never met a *possibly* beautiful historian.

He gave me her card: Caterina Moreau, *Societe Francaise d'Histoire Maritime*. Marius said her office wasn't far from the hospital.

Once I finished my burger I made my way back around the harbor to find Ms. Moreau. Her address turned out to be the second story above a small art gallery. I rang the bell, announced myself on the intercom when she answered. A buzz followed, and I entered the door and climbed the stairs to a bright, open room that faced the harbor.

Ms. Moreau's hair was almost black, tied into a loose bun on top of her head. Round black glasses covered much of her face, but her full lips caught my attention—that and the small upturned nose and piercing green eyes behind the glasses. I could see what Marius meant about this tall woman in a pale green top and stylish loose-fitting pants.

"I'm Buck Reilly. I understand you were asking about me?"

Her white teeth flashed in a quick smile.

"Wonderful! Come in, Buck. Do you mind if I call you that? I am thrilled to meet you after reading about all your successes with e-Antiquity!"

"You'd better keep reading," I said.

She clasped her hands in front of her.

"The work you did at e-Antiquity was ground-breaking in establishing a new understanding of Mayan culture, and the treasure troves of period jewelry and other artifacts represent some of the most popular museum exhibits in Mexico, Panama, Colombia, and Peru." She caught her breath and ushered me toward a wood chair that matched the one behind her modest desk. "The disappearance of e-Antiquity has left a gaping hole in historic discovery these past few years. And it was your role within the company to lead the research, so it's a special honor to meet you."

"Well, thank you." I felt my cheeks burning. When was the last time I met someone who actually appreciated the work we'd done at e-Antiquity? And she was right—while we rarely got credit for it, part of our pre-negotiated arrangements with host countries was to donate a significant amount of whatever we found to cultural museums. From what I'd been told, many of the exhibitions are popular tourist attractions even today.

"I would love to discuss some of your experiences, if you have time."

I'd met with a lot of historians over the years, in seaside towns and third world capitals, but none remotely like Caterina Moreau.

"Tell me, Caterina, what exactly is the *Societe Francaise d'Histoire Maritime*?"

Her eyes lit up again. "The *Societe* is a French publisher and research organization of nautical history. I am the representative here in the French West Indies."

"So, what, you write historical articles?"

"Amongst other things. I do get out in the field—or on the water, as it were."

I'd never been interested in having my targets flogged about in the press, so normally I'd have run the other way from someone like Caterina. But maybe I could use this relationship to cause problems for the Dominicans—and possibly Jack and Gunner, too.

"Are you aware of the connection between Remy de Haenen and Jacques Cousteau?" I said.

Her eyebrows lifted. "Both were notable figures in modern French history, each explorers, adventurers, and famous individuals in their own right." She paused. "And both have recently been connected to a search for the wreck of the *Concepcion* that sank off the coast of the Dominican Republic in 1641."

"You *are* well versed," I said. She glanced down for a second. "I've heard these rumors too."

"The *Concepcion* was a Spanish ship, but if these Frenchmen were successful in their efforts to locate the wreck, it would be newsworthy to our members."

If I can't search for the ship, then denying Jack the discovery would be the next best thing. How would that feel, huh, partner?

"So that is why you are here on St. Barths now?" she said. "Searching for this connection to the *Concepcion*?"

I smiled. I had several other files with more academic potential than financial upside, and if I wasn't able to get Harry to back me, I'd eventually want someone to help me pursue them. Caterina's passion, lack of greed, and focus could be exactly the combination I needed.

"While the wreck is of interest, I'm primarily here on behalf of Lou Atlas, searching for information about his nephew, Jerry."

"Do you mind if I take some notes?" She reached over and took a notepad off the corner of her desk.

I bit the side of my lip. I needed to be careful—being quoted about the *Concepcion* would really piss Jack off.

"There are men on the island searching for the *Concepcion*, including a pair from the Dominican Republic that you *might* want to avoid. And a pair of Americans—"

She pursed her lips, and full as they were the expression drew me in. Her eyes fluttered behind her glasses as she sat back and crossed her legs.

"Why—"

Her office phone rang. She glanced at her watch and jumped up.

"*Pardonnez-moi.*"

She answered the phone and I glanced around the office while she murmured into it. There were books on maritime history on shelves, maps and seafaring art on the walls—all the trappings of a maritime historian's abode. Caterina fit in too, but there was a vibrancy to her, a beauty under the glasses and hair that made me wonder what she'd look like if she let herself go a little.

Once she hung up, she turned back to me.

"I am so sorry, Buck, but I must leave for a meeting. Do you have a car or can I drop you somewhere? I truly would love to interview you about e-Antiquity and your future plans."

"I'm, ah, just walking up to the hospital to visit a friend—"

"Then how about dinner tonight? My friends who own *la Langouste* in Flamands tell me the lobster are plentiful."

My heart fluttered. "Sure—"

"And you can tell me more about the *Concepcíon.*"

We agreed on a time, and I led the way down her stairs. Once in the sun, her even tan and green eyes were even more striking. She leaned forward and we casually kissed each cheek before she started down the road. God bless the French custom—especially with a woman who actually appreciated my efforts at e-Antiquity. Now *that* was a rare find.

33

Before entering the hospital, I called Agent Booth.

"Didn't I tell you not to call me on this phone?"

"You learn anything yet? And what's an ex-con doing out of the country? Isn't that a parole violation or something?"

"This is all confidential information, Reilly."

"It won't be if the *New York Times* learns about it. And what about those Dominicans who beat up Truck—"

"Don't threaten me, hotshot!"

"I need answers! There's plenty more going on down here than meets the eye, including Lou Atlas maybe knowing more than he's sharing. There may be a payday for you here, Booth, but only if I live long enough to find the truth!"

Silence.

"Now what the hell's the deal with Gunner?"

"You sitting down?" Booth said.

"No, I'm sweating my ass off walking up a steep street to see my buddy in the hospital—"

"Dodson was remanded into Rostenkowski's supervision."

"What the hell?!"

"The Bureau had nothing to do with it! Rostenkowski's a CIA informant—he has a lot of knowledge, and it was apparently decided very high up that he could *not* be allowed to stay in Cuban custody."

I stopped halfway up the street.

"Back up, Booth. Why would *Jack* be remanded to Gunner's custody?"

"I don't have the answer—but if they're working with Gutierrez, the FBI'll arrest both their asses, that I can promise you." I knew he meant it. "If you can prove that, I'll get your slate wiped clean. You hear me?"

Giddiness hit me as the enormity of what he'd said crept into my brain. No more worries about my past—but what about the evidence Jack had on me?

I swallowed. "As in immunity?"

"Damn straight. You give me Gunner, Jack Dodson, and the Cubans in a nice neat bundle, your ass is off the list."

Wow.

That would substantially clear the playing field for the *Concepción*, except for the Dominicans. According to Booth, the fact that Jack and Gunner's plane—*my* plane—was registered in Cuba wasn't enough. But it was a start.

"Follow the trail, Reilly." He hung up.

I continued up the hill with a spring in my step.

"Broken collarbone *and* broken rib, dammit," Truck said. "Should of listened to my brother and stayed away from your ass."

I agreed we didn't have a very good track record together, but usually I'd helped Truck more than put him in harm's way. The doctor wanted to keep him overnight. I told him I was meeting a maritime historian for dinner but kept my fascination with Caterina to myself.

"Sounds boring—damn, I was supposed to see my British lady friends again tonight." He pumped his eyebrows. "You mind telling 'em I'm laid up?"

I nodded and promised to retrieve him once the doctor gave him the okay. His face was less puffy and the cuts were scabbing over, but he looked like hell and it turned my stomach to see him like this. Treasure has a way of bringing out the worst in people, whether it's gold and silver on the bottom of the ocean or the numbers on a dead man's bank account.

Truck smiled, his unswollen eye squinting.

"Have fun talking maritime history tonight."

My smile caused him to arch his brows. "You can count on that."

I MADE MY WAY THROUGH THE HOSPITAL AND FOUND A TAXI PARKED OUT BY the front entrance. At the traffic circle above the airport, I said: "Go straight, then take a quick right."

There were no planes approaching from the left, and to the right a Winair plane was taking off over the beach at St. Jean. We wound our way down to the private aviation ramp. I held my breath as we rounded the private hangar.

The Widgeon was still there.

Betty.

I paid the driver, told him not to wait, and slammed the door shut. I did a quick inspection of the Beast, checked the tie down lines (taut), the pitot tube (clean), the—

What's this? Something was taped to the portside window. I pulled it off—it was a shipping receipt for a package sent—to Special Agent Edwin Booth—Federal Bureau of Investigation, 9001 Brickell Avenue, Miami, Florida.

I held my breath and stared into the fuselage of my plane.

I was doomed. The receipt had today's date on it—and something written on the back. I recognized Jack's scrawl: "I warned you."

I put both hands against the plane and took a few deep breaths. I suddenly remembered why I'd come here just now, the importance of which had just soared way beyond the desire to rid myself of Jack and Gunner. I reached into my pocket and pulled out my keys.

My immunity was on the line. I needed to connect Jack and Gutierrez to the Cubans before that package reached Booth.

A quick glance in every direction revealed nobody, so I moved quickly to Betty and said a prayer. My keys jingled in my hand. The small black key I'd kept on the ring for sentimental reasons was squeezed between my thumb and index finger. I pushed the key toward the lock—it slid in and turned.

The lock clicked open.

"Hi, old girl," I said. "Can't tell you how sorry I am to see you like this—I mean, you look great, but with Gunner . . ."

The hatch popped open with a squeak and I stepped quickly up and in. She felt so small—the Beast was much larger. I pulled the hatch down and breathed in. The smell was different.

"Fresh leather," I said. "And look at the headliner. They did a good job with you."

The silver locker on the starboard side of the fuselage had a padlock on it. I pulled at the lock but it was solid. I'd need bolt cutters to get in there. I remembered the Gulfstream G-4 jet I'd last seen Gunner on. He had secret panels with weapons inside—machine guns, small missiles, grenades. These lockers were more obvious but were bound to contain similar hardware.

What was it he'd said at the airport? "Once a gunner, always a gunner?" I shrugged. That applied to assholes, too.

Up front I climbed into the left seat, which was constructed of fabric and frame, almost like old car seats—but the instruments in front of me, the throttle levers, the closeness of the flight deck were oh-so-familiar. All I had to do was rifle the flight log and I'd find out who owned the plane.

I looked up over the instrument panel and saw a black Jeep coming around the airplane hangar at high speed.

Shit!

How many planes were tied down here? Five? Six? Most hadn't budged since we'd arrived a couple of days ago. An electric charge shot through my extremities.

I leapt up, scraped my scalp on the low bulkhead—

What could I do?

The storage locker!

I was through the fuselage in two steps. The sound of a car door slammed outside, then another.

The storage door was locked!

My hand shook as I fumbled the keys and nearly dropped them. I jammed the black key in— it turned. I ripped the door open—my old anchor was on the deck, the compartment was crowded with ropes, the space so tight I barely fit.

There was no interior door handle!

I pulled hard at the top of the door, moving my hand at the last second. It didn't click.

I heard voices outside.

With my nails clawed into the seam where the rivets bonded two pieces of metal together, I pulled. My fingers slipped off. I pulled again—ripped a nail, but the locker door was now closed.

My heart throbbed in my ears and I was soaked in sweat.

The sound of the hatch on the fuselage squeaked open.

I'd left it unlocked!

I felt the weight of the plane shift—one man, then another.

Damn, Betty. Silence.

I reached down for the Danforth anchor and braced for the storage door to fly open—fucking Gunner was a brute.

The door didn't open. Instead, I heard a click.

I was locked in.

34

IT WASN'T THE SOUND OF THE TWIN RANGER ENGINES THAT CALMED MY breathing—it was the vibration of my old plane, refurbished and roaring down the runway.

Betty was alive.

I felt my lips stretch into a smile, albeit a short-lived one. What the hell was I thinking? I might be dumped into the Caribbean Sea at any moment.

The rattle and bounce of the tail wheel jostled me in the cramped locker. The tail lifted, the bounce stopped, and we were aloft. Betty banked to port and I fell hard into the side of the locker, my face pressed against the fuselage. We ascended to the sound of the cables that pulled the trim tabs and elevator rattling in my ears.

As the minutes passed, I considered my options. Fighting with Gunner was pointless. I'd been a moderately successful Golden Gloves boxer back in the day, but he was an animal. My only defense with him was the truth.

I could offer to help! The French maritime historian—damn—would I make it back to meet her for dinner tonight?

What was I thinking?

Would I be fish food by tonight was a more pertinent concern.

The hatch suddenly opened—the light was bright, and Gunner stood in front of me. Smiling.

"Listen, Gunner, it's not what—"

He raised a gun and extended it toward me.

"Wait!"

My eyes focused on the gun. There was a snap—my entire body convulsed.

Everything went black.

A SENSATION OF MY SKIN AFLAME TORMENTED ME UNTIL A SLIT OF LIGHT reached deep into my consciousness. My eyes cracked open.

I was alive. And not on fire.

"About time you woke up, Reilly."

My eyes slowly focused and my head fell to the side. Gunner was seated in a chair, holding a beer can. Another one was smashed flat into a disk on the side table—a bedroom table. I was lying down on a bed. Where am I?

"Had to Tase your ass four times to keep you still," he said.

I tried to lift my arms, but they were constrained. So were my legs.

My lips smacked together, dry as a desert creek bed.

"Water," I said.

Gunner smiled, guzzled the rest of his beer, put the can against his forehead, and crushed it flat against his skull. He belched.

"The hell were you doing in my plane?"

I moved my tongue around in my mouth attempting to produce some saliva.

"I don't give a shit about the *Concepcion*, Gunner." I cleared my throat. "I just wanted to see my old plane—"

"You mean you wanted to steal her."

I shook my head. We were in a well-appointed hotel suite, maybe a private villa, I couldn't tell which. The shades were drawn, but sunlight burned bright through the two large windows. Silhouettes of palm branches danced languidly on the shades.

"Where are we?"

"You're lucky to be alive." He glanced over his shoulder, lifted the blue sunglasses onto his forehead, and leaned in closer. "If I had my way—"

The door opened and Jack Dodson walked in. Gunner glared at me, then slid his shades back in place.

Jack walked over, his face hard. "Didn't I tell you to stay away from me?"

"So did I," Gunner said.

I cleared my throat again, which felt like a coffee grinder.

"I can't believe you sent that shit to the FBI—"

"How many times did we need to warn you? Now I want you out of my way, permanently."

"I can make that happen," Gunner said.

"Don't you two make a pretty pair?" I said. "You picked a winner with him, Jack. And how does Gutierrez fit in? He's not just Cuban Secret Police, he's a murderer and spy—"

"Tell us what you know about Jerry Atlas and Remy de Haenen."

He was wearing a tight fitting black T-shirt and I now saw that his arms were now covered with tattoos. Prison tats. He looked every bit as muscular as Gunner, but in a tighter package.

He watched my eyes closely. "Prison changes a man, Buck. I did five years. Hard years. And I did you a favor by sending that information to the FBI. You'll only do time. Gunner had different plans for you."

"Still do," Gunner said.

I pulled at the bonds, but Jack's eyes remained hard. I wondered when the last time was that he'd smiled. Or laughed. Had he just turned in the money when e-Antiquity filed bankruptcy, he could have avoided jail. Me? My parents died as a result of my lies. That would never change, not in five years, not in fifty. And now I'd go to prison, thanks to Jack.

"You made your choice," I said. "Neither of us got off easy. We were just dumb-asses consumed with greed, hanging onto the fantasy of wealth." The bitter taste in my mouth made me smack my lips. "And look where it got us. Here we are, at each other's throats."

"I would sit in my cell or walk the prison yard, wondering what the fuck you were doing while I rotted from the inside out. It ate at me, every day."

"You think my life's been great? Walk a mile in my flip flops—"

"What do you know about the treasure!" He stepped forward and lowered his face close to mine.

Gunner took my right hand in both of his and started to squeeze. Pain exploded up my arm.

"The treasure!" Jack said. "This isn't e-Antiquity. No King Buck, no *Wall Street Journal*." He moved his face closer with each statement. "No public company, no analysts up our asses, no 10-K's, 10-Q's, no annual reports. Nothing!" Spit hit my face.

Gunner squeezed my hand harder.

"I don't know shit! Jerry Atlas—his uncle—"

"Harry sent you, right? The day we bumped into each other in New York? Harry planned that. He's using you, Buck. Trying to use me, too—"

"What the fuck are you—"

"He's in cahoots with Lou Atlas! Sure, Jerry's dead, but my guess is they know about the treasure and they're manipulating you—and me—to find it!"

"If that's what you thought, why didn't we team up instead of you throwing me to the Feds—"

"What'd Harry tell you? That Lou wanted answers about his beloved nephew? Like he gave a rat's ass!"

"The *Concepcion*, Reilly!" Gunner said. "What have you learned?" He tightened his vise-like grip. Something popped.

"Hey—*shit!*"

"Tell us!" Jack sprayed me again with spittle. Who was this guy? Not my former partner, not by a long shot.

"Tell us!"

"Jerry bought Eden Rock from de Haenen and he fucking drowned on his Jet Ski—that's all I know!"

Another squeeze and I almost blacked out as the room spun in a circle around my nose.

I told them about Antoine Construction and Henri saying they'd found nothing. I told them about the Dominicans who'd beaten Truck and Gisele.

"I'm not on this trail," I said, "but you guys aren't the only ones who are."

Jack stood up, his expression murderous.

"How's Laurie, Jack? The kids?" I caught my breath. "They know what you're up to?"

His eyes didn't change.

"My advice is to go home and turn yourself in, Buck. They may take a year off your sentence."

"Great, thanks for the advice you son-of-a-bitch!"

Jack turned toward Gunner and nodded.

Gunner let go of my wrist and stood up.

"What are you—"

He reached into his pocket and pulled out the gun.

Snap!

Fire consumed me—convulsions—seizure—

Blackness.

35

"HELP!" I WASN'T SURE HOW LONG I'D BEEN SHOUTING BEFORE THE DOOR swung open and a woman in a maid's uniform stuck her head halfway in the door to glance around the small room.

"My hands and feet are tied to the bed, can you help me?" My throat was so dry my voice was brittle.

Clutching a broom in both hands like a club, she stepped inside.

"Where am I?" I said.

The bewilderment in her eyes turned to contempt.

"You don't know? Must of been some night!" She leaned the broom against the wall, then stood at the foot of the bed and stared at me—though the sheet covered me from the waist down, I had no shirt on. "You naked under there? I don't want to see no—"

"Please! Just untie my wrists—I was kidnapped!"

Her mouth twisted into a curl. "Umm-hmm."

"Please. I'd really like to get out of here."

After a deep breath and sigh, she stepped forward and untied my left wrist.

"I'll untie the other hand, but you can do your own feet—I want out of here myself."

"Fine, great. Thank you."

She moved tentatively around the bed, eyeing me as if I might spring up and grab her.

"Seriously," I said, "I have no idea where I am."

"Like I said, some night. You're in the Cap Juluca hotel."

Cap Juluca? There were no hotels with that name on St. Barths.

"St. Martin?" I said.

"Anguilla." Her brow furrowed and she shook her head. "West End." She hurried over and untied my right wrist, then jumped toward the foot of the bed. "I'm leaving now, then you can untie your own feet."

"Wait!"

She took three large steps toward the door.

"You see my clothes anywhere?"

Broom back in hand, she paused at the door to glance around the room, then met my eyes.

"Nope, nothing."

Crap!

I pleaded with her to check around outside. She left, grumbling under her breath, then came back and said if she found any stray clothes she'd knock and leave them by the door.

I untied my ankles and swung my legs off the side of the bed. I was completely naked and felt as if I'd been beaten with sticks and rolled over hot coals. My steps were unsteady, but I made it to the bathroom and guzzled water straight from the tap.

A knock sounded on the door.

"Find anything?" I shouted so she could hear me from the bathroom.

"They was in the trash by the beach." Her voice was muffled, but she'd emphasized *beach*, no doubt thinking I'd got drunk and into some kinky sex. I breathed a sigh of relief.

Wrapped in a towel, I took the clothing, thanked her, then checked my pockets. My wallet was there, but the Visa Black card was gone, along with all my cash. My phone was missing too.

Fucking Jack.

ONCE DRESSED, I SAT BACK ON THE BED. THE ALARM CLOCK SAID IT WAS 4:35. I rubbed my eyes and tried to recall friends or former contacts on

Anguilla, but I couldn't think of any. Understandable since I'd never been here before. But Jerry Atlas had, and one of his best friends was here.

I picked up my Top Siders and pulled out the insole on the right shoe. Thank God—my emergency hundred-dollar bill was still there.

I followed a landscaped path to the beach. Floury white sand sank beneath my feet, and crystalline water lapped the shore. I plodded toward the center of what was clearly a high-end resort and spotted the lobby. Huge Arabian-looking bulbous bronze lights hung from the domed canvas ceiling.

Inside, I approached the concierge desk with a confidence I didn't feel.

"Can I help you, sir?" The young woman with light brown eyes asked.

I glanced around the vast lobby as well-dressed vacationers moved through, their flip-flops and sandals slapping against the marble floor.

"Yes, you can." I knew how awful I looked, but the young concierge's smile never faltered. "I'm hoping to find Bankie Banx, the musician."

Bankie, she said, could be found at the Dune Preserve, where he not only performed but also owned what she described as one of the top beach bars in the Caribbean.

"It's on Rendezvous Bay," she said, "not far from here."

I thanked her and found my way to the front door, where the doorman hailed me a taxi. Once in the cab I leaned back and contemplated a future of fighting to stay out of jail. I'd have to sell the Beast to finance the court case.

Then the passing landscape grabbed my attention, partly because it was so different from St. Barths. Anguilla is largely flat, and a lot of what I saw reminded me of the Bahamas. During the short ride we saw no towns. This was a green island, not littered with resorts though I assumed there must be others like Cap Juluca tucked away.

Did they have an extradition agreement with the U.S. here? Maybe I should just stay.

When we came to a sign for the Cuisinart Golf Club and Resort, the driver turned onto a small pot-holed road that passed attractive buildings and led us to a small sign for the Dune Preserve. We pulled up to what I realized was an old beached yacht hull converted to a stage, along with a collection of open-air huts nestled on the edge of the water by a brilliant white beach. Fancy resorts with high-end restaurants had their place, but ever since e-Antiquity crashed I felt more comfortable at places like this. I wished I was coming here to while away the afternoon drinking Pain Killers and enjoying the atmosphere.

After paying the taxi, I had $82.00 left. I slipped my change back in my pocket—

Shit! My passport was on St. Barths.

How the hell would I get back there?

36

THE LATE AFTERNOON CROWD AT THE DUNE PRESERVE WAS EXACTLY AS I'D expected: bikinis, shorts, flip-flops—and laughter. I thought back to La Plage, then the Beach Bar on St. John, the Bomba Shack on Tortola, Foxy's, Soggy Dollar, and Schooner Wharf on Key West—all great waterfront bars, and the Dune Preserve fit right in. So did I as far as attire went, though my mindset was anything but chilled out.

The strong, soulful voice of a female singer rang out over the crowd. I could see her on the stage in the distance, accompanied by a tall, beautiful blonde and a guitar player.

There was a slight roll of the eyes when I asked the pretty young bartender if Bankie Banx was here. Given his celebrity, it was a question the staff must field a hundred times a day.

"I'm a friend of the Atlas family," I said. "I know Bankie and Jerry were—"

"Good friends, yeah, mon." The woman's eyes lit briefly then turned toward the floor. "Bankie's in the office. Be right back." I watched her leave the bar and turn a corner.

The singer started a familiar song—Jimmy Buffett's "Creola." My mouth dropped open as I finally recognized who was on stage: Nadirah Shakoor and Tina Gullickson, long time Coral Reeferettes, the harmony behind Buffett's band. I'd met them at a charity concert on Jost Van Dyke in the BVI last year—hell, they even sang backup on Matt Hoggatt's ballad that came out of that mess, but they wouldn't recognize me, nor did I want them to. I stood and watched—enraptured, like everybody else—as Nadirah's soulful rendition paid homage to the storyteller and made the song her own at the same time. For a moment, her voice and the melancholy lyrics helped me to forget my predicament.

The band went into a softer song, and my attention unfocused into the liquid abyss. The bar was so close to the water I couldn't even see the beach from where I stood—just aquamarine extending all the way to the horizon. It wasn't enough to soothe me.

I'd been a total shit when Jack was in prison. Why hadn't I gone to see him, sent a letter, a fucking postcard? Simple: because prisons terrified me.

The FBI had been on my ass since my parents got killed in a crash, just after they opened a numbered account at a Swiss Bank. I was scared to death that if I went anywhere near a prison they wouldn't let me out.

"Buck Reilly, is it?" A deep voice came from behind me.

I turned to find Bankie Banx. I'd seen his picture before, but he was taller than I expected. Long braided hair poked out from under his blue bandana, dark sunglasses were perched on his forehead, and a fat gold cross that looked like it doubled as a pipe rested on his bare chest.

He wasn't smiling.

"Thanks for coming out to meet me."

"Staci said you was a friend of Jerry's?"

"His uncle asked me to come to St. Barths, to check on his family and see what I can figure out about his disappearance."

Bankie's salt and pepper beard masked most of his expression.

"Was a gypsy soul, that one. Never comfortable in his own skin. But had a good heart, even if he was a little crazy."

"Jerry liked to come hang out with you, I hear."

Bankie lowered his sunglasses into place and nodded.

"Sure, man, we was tight. Jerry liked to spend money, buy people drinks. He was good to have around."

"He ever mention anything to you about treasure?" I said.

A loud laugh. "All the time. In fact, we used to go out and cruise the islands. Jerry didn't need no money, but he was obsessed with finding pirate booty."

A tingle spread through my fingers. "He ever mention the *Concepción?*"

The smile on Bankie's face vanished. "You ask a lot of questions, bro."

Nadirah Shakoor finished her song and announced they were taking a break. She and Tina walked off stage with a wave to the standing crowd.

Bankie hugged both of the ladies as he walked past the stage, which had a roof made out of an old canvas sail. He poured himself a drink at the bar, then sat on a couch built into an alcove between the bar and the stage. Big vases of sand and seashells held candles, over them was a fiery-eyed photograph of a young Fidel Castro in uniform, taken during one of his speeches.

I sat down on the couch, and handed over Lou's letter.

He read it and grunted. He wouldn't care about an American entrepreneur like Lou Atlas. I glanced back at the photo of Fidel and felt silly for showing it to him.

"Jerry hated that old man." He handed the letter back to me.

"I'm not surprised," I said. "He's an asshole. At this point I'm trying to help Jerry's wife and their kids. Gisele got nothing because of a piece of paper she signed before they got married, and she's in bad shape." Bankie looked interested. "Plus, I'm starting to think Jerry may have been a victim of foul play."

He gave me a long stare.

"We'd go around the small islands, all over, you know? Jerry liked to hike them and he carried this big metal pipe—pry bar, he called it."

"For what?" I said.

"Moving shit around. Leverage, you know? Old logs, rocks, searching for something. He'd get so excited to find old bottles or things off boats, like they was some kind of clue."

My heart double-clutched. "Did he ever find anything good?"

"Nah, man. Just trash." He shook his head again and sipped the amber liquid on the rocks. "I miss him, though. He was good people." He scowled. "And if he was killed, that'd really piss me off."

"He ever say anything about Remy de Haenen?"

"That old thief?" He laughed. "No, man—only that he got ripped off when he bought Eden Rock from him."

I took in such a long, deep breath that it broke Bankie's reverie. He lifted the sunglasses again.

"You all right, man?"

I exhaled loudly. "As a matter of fact, I'm not."

I gave him an edited run-through of all the trouble on St. Barths—Gisele and Truck beaten and hospitalized by a pair of Dominicans, the speculation about Jerry and the *Concepcion*, and finally my getting Shanghaied and left on Anguilla.

"Some serious shit there, bro."

"And my passport's still on St. Barths."

He hunched his shoulders at that.

"Any chance you could take me back across?" I said.

"No, man, got a gig here tonight." He rubbed his beard between his thumb and middle finger. "But I know some people."

I explained that the guys who'd kidnapped me had taken my cash and credit card, but Lou Atlas would replenish me and I'd happily pay someone to get me back to St. Barths under the radar. As if on cue, Bankie's song *Busted on Barbados* started to play on the Dune's sound system. Bankie gave me a handshake and a shoulder bump.

"You take care of Jerry's family, let me know what's going on. I know plenty people in these islands, the Dominican Republic too. Shit go down? I can help. I gotta go, but have some food, couple of drinks, and I'll make a call."

I sank back into the couch, grateful that Jerry had a friend in Bankie Banx. I was also grateful for some damned good barbecued chicken, a couple of ice cold Heinekens, and another inspiring set from Nadirah and Tina. But where was I going to sleep tonight? My $82.00 would cover my food and drink but not a room here. I'd already been eyeing some hidden spots in dark corners of the patio bar.

Stranded on Anguilla.

No passport and no cash.

Damn.

I watched as a beautiful forty-plus-foot speedboat cruised slowly into the bay. The setting sun cast pink, purple, and orange hues over the clouds marching slowly across the sky like costumed children in a school play. The same bartender I'd seen when I first arrived appeared at my shoulder.

"That's your ride." She pointed her chin toward the speedboat, then winked at me. "Bankie says to watch your ass."

Best advice I'd had all week.

37

TWILIGHT FADED FAST, BUT THE DULL GLOW OF ST. BARTHS WAS A MAGNETIC beacon on the horizon. Two men crewed the speedboat, neither of whom had spoken a word to me. The boat's black hull blended into the dark water, but it was the electronic signature I was most worried about. I had no idea how closely these waters were monitored.

I sat in the back on a padded bench seat and watched the bow spray spatter across the blackness of night like Jackson Pollock tossing paint on a dark canvas. Twin inboards vibrated, rattling my teeth. Based on our progress so far, the trip wouldn't take more than an hour, but the swells here were six-foot-plus rollers and had the captain, a dreadlocked man in his early thirties, throttling back. I appreciated his deft handling, preferring not to be slammed silly.

Stars began to shine above us, and the North Star and Big Dipper calmed my racing heart. Immobile and ever-present, if often hidden by clouds or city lights, they'd guided sailors for centuries. A shooting star cut a quick gash in the Milky Way that healed instantly. I turned my eyes to the horizon, scanning for running lights. I'd been reduced to human cargo, a risk to these men with no upside and no profit. Staci had comped my dinner, so I still had my $82, but that wouldn't cover a fraction of the fuel this water rocket had drunk on the crossing.

I certainly owed someone something—

Crap! I suddenly remembered my dinner tonight with Caterina Moreau.

With no way to contact her, she'd be sitting at la Langouste right now, alone, embarrassed, and angry.

Wonderful.

But standing her up was the least of my problems. Did Jack think I'd just disappear? His exposing me to the FBI left me with nothing to lose by going on full offense. If he thought he'd scare me away, he must have forgotten I didn't scare easily.

Black silhouettes of small uninhabited islands occasionally rose up out of the water. We'd passed a dozen at least. Were these the ones Bankie and Jerry had prospected?

Everything that had happened since Truck and I arrived on St. Barths played through my mind like a series of bad dreams. There was no end in sight, not until the treasure hunters either found what they were after or gave up. What worried me was the damage they'd inflict between then and now.

A spotlight suddenly panned over the water ahead of us, splashed across our bow. A loud horn sounded.

Shit!

I jumped up and nearly flew overboard as we turned hard to port and straight into a wave. I grabbed the back of the captain's chair—the horn sounded again!

"Police?" My voice was shrill over the roar of the engines.

He cut a glance back at me, his eyes sharp. I could now make out the silhouette of the ship in front of us. It was huge.

"Ferry," the captain said.

It took several deep breaths to slow my pulse. I wanted them to drop me off in Colombier, where I could hike back to Flamands and maybe see if Caterina was still at la Langouste, but wasn't about to make any suggestions. These men knew what they were doing. And Caterina wouldn't wait long.

We pulled straight into Gustavia harbor and up to the sea wall near Master Ski Pilou. The second my feet hit the concrete, the boat was in reverse and headed back out to sea.

"Thanks, fellas," I said in a whisper.

I made my way up the hill, past the dark office of the Maritime historian, and up to the hospital. I found Truck in a wheelchair, on a telephone, looking pissed off.

"Yeah, hold on, man. Reilly just posted." He held a hand over the mouthpiece of the room phone. "Hell you been, man? I'm ready to get outta here, but these Frenchies won't let me leave until they got some cash or insurance—which I ain't got."

"Me neither—"

". . . the hell you doing, Reilly?" I heard Truck's brother, Bruiser, shout through the phone.

"Hang up and let me make a call."

Ten minutes later, after a sanitized update, Lou agreed to take care of the hospital bill, send a replacement credit card, and wire-transfer funds to the BNP branch in Gustavia.

It had taken all my rusty efforts at diplomacy to keep things light with Lou. Maybe he was playing me, but without his help we'd be broke, stranded, and up to our necks in vipers. Once I had the nurse show me how to transfer Lou to the finance office, I turned my attention to Truck.

"You look like shit," he said.

"You look worse."

It was true. His right arm was in a sling, one of his eyes had a puffy half-moon bruise around the lid, and his stomach was wrapped with tape to hold the cracked rib in place. During the taxi ride back toward Lorient, I filled him in on everything he'd missed, including my little session of shock therapy with Gunner.

"Damn, cuz. All 'cause you wanted to see inside your old plane?"

I couldn't tell him about the package Jack sent to Booth. I couldn't tell anyone about that.

"These guys are focused and furious. They're ready to stomp anyone who gets in their way."

"Don't have to tell me twice."

I told the driver to make a quick stop at the airport, which was closed since it was midnight. I cajoled my way through security at the private aviation terminal while Truck waited in the cab with the meter running. The Beast was just a shape in the darkness, and I ran my palm along the fuselage until I got to the hatch.

Something felt rough—the area around the lock was scratched. The hatch was unlocked!

Once inside, I grabbed the flashlight from the storage locker and hurried onto the flight deck. On my knees, my jaw fell open. The lock on my safe was also scratched. My hand shook as I reached for the dial—the entire seat frame was bent, as if someone had tried to rip the safe out.

I entered the combination and the door swung open.

The red sheaf with all my maps and clues was still there, thank God.

I leaned my head onto the left seat and waited until my breathing returned to normal. Sons of bitches! I debated what to do, but decided to relock the safe and head back to the private terminal, where I raised hell with security and demanded the FBO give the plane a thorough mechanical inspection first thing in the morning.

Back in the taxi, I decided not to share this with Truck. If I were him, I'd already be on the brink of bailing. Whether it was the Dominicans or Jack I wasn't sure, but the stakes had again been raised.

We passed through St. Jean, looking into the darkness out the side window.

"Right now I want some tequila and decent food," Truck said.

Which is exactly what he got, as administered by the two concerned British divorcees back at La Banane. To their dismay, I opted for JoJo Burger across from the beach.

I walked down the narrow strip of sand along the water, back toward the abandoned hillside where the carcass of l'Autour du Rocher stared down on me as if to say *I warned you*.

Back at the room, I left a voice mail for Caterina, apologizing for standing her up due to being stranded and unable to communicate, and asking for a second chance. I suggested brunch tomorrow at l'Oubli, across from Le Select. During the long hot shower that ensued, I vowed to go on the offensive in the morning. Then fell asleep thinking up ways to get revenge.

38

Truck hadn't returned from his evening with his British nurses, so I left him a note and took the Jeep out on a recon mission. Too early for most and with no commercial traffic yet, there was little activity at the airport. As I drove up the hill toward the traffic circle I was able to see the private aviation lot. The Beast was there, a security guard now seated on a chair outside the building. Betty hadn't returned.

I continued all the way around the circle and headed back toward St. Jean. Caterina hadn't confirmed our brunch date, but I'd be there in case her curiosity outweighed her agitation. The road above St. Jean had a steady flow of traffic descending the hill: parents taking children to school and people headed for work. But the steep gravel drive to Nicole de Haenen's house had no traffic whatsoever.

Nicole didn't wait for a knock on the door to storm out with her shotgun. In her hiking shoes, khaki shorts, and tank top, she had the look of a woman on safari.

"Oh," she said. "It is you."

"Don't seem so glad to see me."

"Sorry," she said. "How about, 'Oh, I'm glad it's you?'"

"Better."

She lowered the gun.

"Going hunting, Mrs. Macomber?"

Her eyes narrowed. "Who is that?"

"Sorry, it was a joke. You reminded me of an Ernest Hemingway story."

"There has been a lot of unwanted traffic up here. I'm not used to visitors, especially unwelcome ones. I have work to do on the farm—it is ridiculous having to lock myself inside all the time."

I studied her face. At least she'd avoided the kind of treatment Truck and Gisele had gotten. The shotgun helped but wouldn't be enough if the serious players wanted to get to her.

"The Dominicans?" I said.

"And the other Americans. Both have been back."

"Are you familiar with the American saying, 'where there's smoke—'"

"There's fire, yes." Her chest rose with a quick breath. "Care for some coffee?"

I enjoy the smell of ground coffee as much as I do drinking the finished product, and Nicole prepared ours in her French press with the precision of an engineer.

Once she filled two steaming mugs, I followed her out to the patio down the steps by the pool. The intimacy of the moment registered in my core. Why did I always allow primal attractions to distract me?

Because I was a sucker for confident women?

Nicole turned, handed me the mug, and sat in one of the chairs overlooking the bay of St. Jean. She stared down toward the beach a mile below and ran her fingers through her sandy blond hair.

"I need someone to trust, Buck." She turned to face me, her sky-blue eyes aimed straight into mine. "Maybe it should be you."

A tingle ran through me. I took a sip of coffee and waited.

"These other men are cold-blooded—what they did to Gisele, what I see in their eyes—and I heard about what happened to your friend."

"They won't give up, Nicole."

A long breath lifted her chest.

"I went through my mother's things, including the box of mementoes she kept from my grandfather."

"And?"

"There were pictures from Remy's trip with Cousteau."

I held my breath.

"One was of a group of men poring over a chart table inside a ship, Remy amongst them. Another was of men in Scuba gear on the ship's deck."

I edged forward in the chair.

"And another photo showed all of them drinking champagne and toasting."

"Hmm." The treasure hunter in me wanted to pounce. The diplomat in me forced a nod and count to five.

"And there was a diary—totally random, mind you—but there were occasional months and years noted, along with cryptic initials and abbreviations. I found one passage from 1973 that included the initials J-YC—"

"Jacques-Yves Cousteau."

"And a reference to Bd'A and *Baie de demi lune, Hispaniola*."

"Half Moon Bay is where Burt Webber found a sizable chunk of the *Concepción* in 1978, off the coast of the Dominican Republic. The location has been referred to as Silver Shoals since the first silver was recovered there."

We leaned so close together I could smell the coffee on her breath, along with a scent of something spicy, like nutmeg, from her skin.

"Ah, *d'argent* is silver in French. Bd'A is *Banc d'Argent*—Silver Shoal!" Her voice rose and she sat up straight.

An electrical current ran between us that made the hair on my arms stand up.

"What else was in the journal? Any more detail?"

"No, nothing."

I sat back in the chair. She hadn't mentioned her visit to the Eden Rock yet. Would she?

"Well, we knew he'd gone with Cousteau to look for the wreck," I said, "but all reports were that they found nothing."

"But the champagne! Why would they be celebrating?" She spoke quickly, her eyes darting around. Impending danger? The scent of treasure? I wasn't sure what had her wound so tight.

"No mention of Jerry Atlas or Eden Rock?" I said.

"Plenty about the early days at Eden Rock—it was the first hotel on St. Barths, after all. He was very proud, and people came from all over the world—stars of the era like David Rockefeller, Montgomery Cliff, Johnny Weissmuller—he had brief notes on all of that, and their full names. Except . . ."

I sat forward again. "Except *what?*"

"Except for J-YC in 1973. Cryptic with him, but nobody else."

Now I ran my hand through my hair. Was she telling me everything?

"What about Jerry?"

She shook her head. "Only the date of sale and the price. At the time it was the equivalent of $3.7 million, U.S. That was a lot of money in the mid-1990's for a small forty-year-old hotel."

"People say Remy was cash-poor in his final years. What happened to the money?"

Nicole spread her arms wide.

"*La Villa ici.* I have the entire top of this hill—and the money spent to improve the soil for the orchards, the care—this is the largest fruit plantation on St. Barths. It was quite expensive. Remember, this was a different time—"

"Time—damn!" I checked my watch. Alone here with Nicole, time had evaporated like dew in the morning sun. "I'm supposed to meet a historian from the French Maritime Academy in ten minutes. Caterina Moreau—do you know her?"

"No, I have no interest in treasure." Her voice was a little too emphatic.

I explained that I'd no-showed the historian once already but didn't go into the whole mess in Anguilla.

"We're meeting at l'Oubli—would you like to join me?"

"Now?" She shook her head. "Impossible."

We both jumped up at the same moment. She leaned forward and kissed my right cheek, then my left. A friendly gesture, but it caused a flutter in my chest. I mumbled something about seeing her later and hurried to the Jeep.

Nicole de Haenen was a distraction, but given her access to the community, she was a worthwhile distraction. Even if she hadn't told me everything.

But I wasn't telling her everything either.

39

THE SCENE AT L'OUBLI WAS PURE FRENCH: OLDER MEN SEATED WITH YOUNGER women who were smoking cigarettes and stealing glances at younger men, along with a waitress working at her own pace as she delivered trays of espressos and café au laits to people seated nose to nose. An obese man with a Panama hat brushed past me as he cleared a path from the corner table for an anorexic bleached blonde. Since every other table was full, I waved away the smoke and sat down before the waitress cleared the plates.

With no sign of Caterina, I ordered a double espresso and a croissant. I used the pre-paid phone I'd bought at a nearby convenience store to search for information about her on the Internet. I found a couple of articles she'd written on maritime archeology—in French—and a listing of her address here in St. Barths. If Lou Atlas hadn't followed through on his promise, I'd be dead broke after paying for brunch—

"I was relieved to get your message last night."

I turned to my left—Caterina had entered from the far steps, this time in a skirt that stopped just above the knees and a translucent white blouse.

"I'm so sorry for standing you up, please accept my apologies. I really was stranded on another island with no phone and no way to get to one."

She looked interested, not angry.

"Which island?"

"Anguilla."

"*Ah, elle est tres belle.*" Her lips turned upward. "I was worried something had happened to you."

"Something did," I said. "But it's the last thing I want to talk about."

She took a moment to look around the room. Her dark hair remained in a bun and she still wore her black-framed glasses. She sat next to me, facing the crowd inside the restaurant.

"I forgive you." She shook a Marlboro Light from her leather cigarette case. "Do you mind? Terrible habit I learned at the Sorbonne and have not been able to quit."

When the waitress brought my croissant, Caterina ordered a cappuccino and we swapped biographical data. She knew all about my work at e-Antiquity, but when I mentioned Jack Dodson she didn't react. She asked several questions about some of our noteworthy archeological discoveries, but her interest felt purely academic.

"Anyway, my treasure hunting has been on hold for quite a while."

"That is not what they are saying here on St. Barths." She tapped her index finger against her full lips. "And you were so good at it!"

I swallowed.

"I came here not to find treasure but to find out what happened to Jerry Atlas. Unfortunately the two matters are becoming increasingly inseparable."

"Do you think there is any truth to the rumors about Jerry's relationship with Remy de Haenen?" she said. "There is *beaucoup de speculation* about a connection beyond the sale and purchase of Eden Rock."

"Speculation by whom?" I said.

A light laugh. "Once a rumor like that starts, it is impossible to tell where it began."

"What do you know about Remy?" I asked.

She took a quick drag on her cigarette.

"Smuggler, rascal, developer, entrepreneur, and finally the politician. The culmination of them all, *n'est pas?*"

"At least he was consistent."

"The obvious connection was Eden Rock—"

"Which Remy berated Jerry for buying at an inflated price," I said. "And I can't imagine Remy hiding treasure at Eden Rock and forgetting to take it with him when he sold the hotel."

The waitress brought Caterina's cappuccino.

"But there are rumors . . ."

"From when Remy retired to the Dominican Republic?" I said.

She leaned closer, our faces barely a foot apart.

"Exactly."

"An old man exaggerating his past?" I said.

"Remy de Haenen did not need to exaggerate. He lived the lives of ten men in his years." Her eyes narrowed. "I have heard much the same about you, Buck Reilly."

"Did I hear my family name?"

Both Caterina and I flinched, the moment broken. Nicole de Haenen stood before us. I patted the chair on the other side of me. Caterina's lips bent in a momentary frown, then her eyes lit up.

"You are Nicole de Haenen."

Nicole nodded.

Caterina introduced herself, extending her arm in front of me to shake Nicole's hand.

"We were just discussing your *grandpere*."

"Mmmm."

"Buck was asking if maybe Remy told people in the Dominican Republic that he had found the *Concepcíon* after he moved there, which would explain why two Dominican brutes came to my office last night."

Nicole and I sat forward.

"What did they look like?" I said.

"Large!" She held her hands wide as if to describe the width of their shoulders. "Short dark hair. Threatening."

"Those same men beat up my friend," I said, "and probably Gisele."

Nicole groaned. "Why did they come to you?"

"My reputation is well known in these islands. I have participated in several dives and recovered artifacts that are on display in the Academy. I imagine it was to ask if I had any information about your grandfather's voyage with Cousteau." Caterina explained that she'd moved from St. Malo, France, to St. Barths a few years before because of her expertise in European expansion into the Caribbean during the sixteenth and seventeenth centuries. As an avid Scuba diver and maritime historian, she hoped to pursue archeological opportunities and publish findings. If successful, she would return to France and make a play to become the director of the Maritime Academy in Paris. "I long to be back in the city, and there is none better than Paris."

"So the Dominicans found you in the Yellow Pages?" I said.

"What are yellow pages? Whether they found me by word of mouth or from my published work, I did not ask."

"Did you help these men?" Nicole asked.

Caterina shook her head.

"I have an idea that could help get to the bottom of this mystery." Her voice had dropped to a whisper. Maybe it was because of the smoking, or maybe the accent, but her voice was raspy, especially in that lower range. It added a sex appeal I sensed she kept bottled up.

Focus, Reilly.

"What would that idea be?" I said.

"Through my connections in France, I have access to the Cousteau family."

"Aren't they splintered these days?" I said. "Two sides that hate each other?"

She shrugged her shoulders. "Some seek to continue Jacques's legacy as an oceanographer and French icon, while others seek to capitalize on his name for profit. Both sides would be interested in helping to solve this puzzle—if, of course, there is anything to solve."

"I like it," I said.

She returned my smile. "The question is, did Remy and Jacques find anything at *la Banc d'Argent*, and if so, what became of it?"

"I have no interest in treasure," Nicole said.

Then why had she rummaged through her grandfather's remaining possessions and gone to snoop around the Eden Rock?

Caterina stood. "*Alors*, I will make contact today and call you if I learn anything." She reached out to shake my hand. "*d'Accord?*"

"Perfect, thank you," I said.

She turned to Nicole. "Your grandfather himself was a national treasure. It has been an honor to meet you. *Ciao.*"

Caterina walked quickly through the room and down the steps onto the sidewalk.

"You work fast," Nicole said.

At what?

40

"I DO NOT TRUST HER," NICOLE SAID. SHE'D TIED HER HAIR INTO A PONY-tail but loose strands fluttered in the breeze as we drove in the open Jeep above Gustavia. Green waves of vegetation spread out below and to the south, with red roofs sprinkled over the hills like berries.

Nicole's intuition didn't change my mind about Caterina, who I still saw as a potential partner to help me pursue both academic and for-profit projects. I had no intention of pursuing her romantically, although when I remembered her running her finger along her lips I—

"Did you hear what I said, Buck?"

"You've never heard of Caterina before?"

Nicole shook her head. "Seems pretty out of place in Gustavia. A historian?"

"She might be able to help figure this mess out—and if she can access the Cousteau family, maybe they can go through his memoirs to search for mention of the *Concepcion*. Do you have any idea why Remy moved to Santo Domingo after selling Eden Rock?"

"He had been in government for much of his life by then. He needed a change."

She was quiet after that and I wondered if she was thinking the same thing I was: that maybe he went back to the Dominican Republic as a result of the *Concepcion*. And maybe he told his story to the wrong people.

"What year did he die?" I asked her.

"July of 2008."

"So he lived there, what—"

"Eleven years. He was back here for his last two."

"Did he leave much behind in Santo Domingo?"

"Many of his possessions. He was ninety when he returned to St. Barths. He did not think it worthwhile to haul what he considered junk across the Caribbean. A few relatives flew to the Dominican Republic after his death, but many of his things had been picked over and the furniture was gone. Nothing of value was left to bring home, so they donated the rest to charity."

Maybe there had been clues among those items.

"Do you think Remy found treasure with Cousteau?" I said.

She shrugged. "With Remy de Haenen, anything was possible." She glanced back toward me. "So that is what you are after? Treasure?"

This was a minefield. I'd have to tiptoe.

"That's not why I'm here," I said. "But somehow Remy's past has come back to haunt us, which has been the cause for at least two people being brutally beaten." I caught her eyes for a moment. "I want to make sure nobody else is hurt, and I need to see if there's more to Jerry's disappearance than meets the eye."

Nicole crossed her arms. We pulled up to the stop sign at the small traffic circle on the coastal road at the far end of St. Jean. To the right was my hotel in Lorient, where I hoped Truck was resting comfortably. I turned left, drove through St. Jean, and turned into the parking lot at Eden Rock.

"Why are you stopping here?" she said.

"To take you down memory lane."

The valet parked the Jeep and we walked toward the beach, past the beautifully restored wood dinghy that hung from a davit. We paused at the bar to look out over the beach.

"The same view but a different world." She chuckled. "When we were young, we had the run of this beach—until my grandfather would catch us."

"What do you mean?"

"He was a very hard man. Visionary yes, adventurous yes, but also rigid. He did not like us interrupting the solitude he sought to provide here. But now—" She spread her arms wide. "There is nowhere to run anyway. Even the beach is filled with chairs."

Indeed, every inch of the rock outcropping that was the foundation for Eden Rock was covered with stone walls, restaurants, offices, foot paths, and individual suites, piled high like a red-roofed house of cards.

"Come on," I said. "I want to show you something."

We climbed halfway up the stairs, past the restaurant to the top where the patio overlooked the bay of St. Jean.

Nicole hesitated. "I do not want to go all the way up."

I wasn't surprised. But we were going to the top.

She squinted, then jabbed her finger up toward the hill above town.

"There it is—my property."

I stood behind her and sighted along her arm to where I saw the villa high atop the ridge.

"Looks lonely up there," I said.

"Can be."

"Nicole?" A voice came from behind us.

"*Bonjour, Alain, ça va?*"

"Very good, my dear! What brings you back—ah, Monsieur Reilly."

"The hotel always looks so beautiful, Alain," Nicole said. "Remy would be so proud."

Monsieur Toussard—Alain—bowed deeply at the waist.

"Just like when you were—"

"What did you want to show me, Buck?" Nicole's eyes were wide.

I turned to Alain. "The pictures we looked at the other day."

"*Bien sur*, come, please."

We followed him inside. If the secretary knew Nicole, she didn't acknowledge her.

"Please take a seat," Alain said. "I will bring them out."

Nicole sat down and wouldn't meet my eyes.

Alain returned with the stacks of pictures, still organized into the piles we'd arranged previously. As soon as he placed them on the table, Nicole said we'd let him know if we had any questions. With that, he bowed again and left.

Nicole let out a long, slow breath while looking through the pile from Remy's years. She pointed out movie stars from the '50's and '60's. While the facility was austere compared to today's magnificence, it was easy to see why it had been such an early draw for those in need of refuge. Sheer rock drop-offs provided most of the boundaries, except for where the peninsula met the land, with St. Jean beach on one side and Nikki Beach on the other.

"The small pile of rocks and refuse is after Jerry bought the property," I said.

She pointed to the picture of Jerry holding the shovel.

"That was after he'd finished clearing the debris and vegetation." She pointed to one of the pictures from Remy's pile, which showed a lot of trees, bushes, and rocks. "See what it was like before?" She studied the panoramic shot that showed the peninsula mostly cleared except for the buildings that had withstood the storms.

My attention stayed on the picture of Jerry, young, muscular, smiling, shovel in hand. He had purpose. It was the apex of his life, as far as I knew. Henri Antoine helped clear the mess and prepare the property, but Jerry was totally involved. He'd taken a gamble, sweat blood and no doubt tears to build something he could be proud of, only to have it crumble around him. And then to watch the new owners erect one of the most beautiful hotels in the world? That had to be a constant reminder of his failure.

"Do you know if Jerry had any help in doing the work here?" I said.

"He must have had, but I do not know who."

"Someone mentioned the name Antoine Construction to me."

"The big home-builder? He does large projects but I don't think Jerry could have afforded him, though perhaps he was smaller then." She frowned. "It is odd that you mention him, I heard Henri ran his truck off the road and was nearly killed—"

"What? When did that happen?"

"Early this morning. He was flown to the big hospital in St. Martin."

My stomach rolled over. The Dominicans? Jack and Gunner? I'd told them both about Henri Antoine.

"What exactly are you looking for?" Nicole said.

I tried to shake off the news but it clung to me like a poison ivy rash. I still had to answer her question.

"A connection between Remy and Jerry that would explain all this sudden interest in the *Concepcion*."

Alain Toussard had been working alongside his secretary. Now his head peered over the counter.

"Did I hear you mention the *Concepcion*?"

"Why, does that mean something to you?" Nicole said.

"It is just that two other men have come here asking if there is any documentation pertaining to that ship."

"And was there?" I said.

He held his hands up. "None that I am aware of, but these men, they were very persistent—one even demanded to review our old storage files. When I refused he made threats." He looked at the secretary. "Natalie called Security."

Nicole and I thanked him and descended the stairs toward the parking area. Something about the pictures gnawed at me, but I couldn't figure out what it was.

"How is Gisele?" Nicole said.

"Not so good. How well do you know her?"

"She is a little older than me, but we knew each other when we were younger. Once she married Jerry she became a recluse. We have not spoken in years."

"I need check in with her, would you like to come?"

Nicole smiled. "Yes, I would."

41

THE SAME GUARD WHO'D SCREENED ME LAST TIME ANSWERED THE INTERCOM. A minute later he informed me that Gisele didn't wish to be bothered.

Nicole leaned over me and pressed the button. Her hair and shoulder were in my face and again I couldn't help but smell her scent—it was from her fruit orchards, I decided.

"Tell her Nicole de Haenen is here too, and I would like to pay my respects." She paused, nearly nose-to-nose with me, and smiled. "Sorry, I didn't mean to crush you."

"Not a problem."

The gate opened slowly. I pulled the Jeep forward and parked.

"Beautiful property," Nicole said. "To be right on Flamands beach, what a joy."

Gisele met us at the door. She and Nicole held each other in a long embrace, whispering in French. Both women were choked up and teary, but they were soon laughing and bantering in a fast patois I couldn't follow. Gisele's bruises had faded considerably, and happiness gave her a whole new aura. Seated out on the back porch overlooking the beach, I enjoyed the view and gave them time to catch up.

When they stopped talking and glanced at me, I asked Giselle whether either the Dominicans or the Americans had returned. Her face hardened before I got half the sentence out.

"They are not welcome here."

Nicole told her we'd just been reviewing old photos at the Eden Rock. She said how strong and happy Jerry looked.

Gisele sighed. "That's when I met him. He was a different man."

Silence fell between the women.

"Can you think back in time for a moment, Gisele?" I said. "Did Jerry find anything important when he was clearing the property?"

Again Gisele's face hardened. "You mean gold—*mon dieu*, you are no different than the others!"

"I'm not asking for myself," I said. "I'm trying to figure out why these men are so ruthlessly chasing that belief."

Gisele began to cry. Nicole jumped over and wrapped an arm around her shoulder.

"If he found gold, why did he sell the hotel at a loss?" Gisele said between sobs. "He hated himself for taking his uncle's money, and buried treasure could have given him a way out!"

Nicole gave me a sharp glance.

"I'm sorry, Gisele—"

"No more!" she said. Nicole nodded.

I walked over to the balcony above the beach. How could I get to the bottom of this if I couldn't ask any questions? The waves splashed hard against the sharp slope of sand. A few couples strolled along the waterline or sunbathed along the broad white beach.

The twin peaks of the island straight out from Flamands took up a large chunk of the horizon, like a giant "M" rising out of the water. I thought of Bankie Banx and wondered if he and Jerry had searched that island too. Certainly Jerry would have thought about it, since it dominated his horizon—

A synapse fired in my brain.

I walked back to the women. Gisele didn't look at me.

"We should leave," I said.

The women embraced and Gisele remained in her chaise longue as we entered the house. I stopped to look at Jerry's paintings. They were different sizes and colors, but the shapes were all similar, a large imperfect oval with squares inside it and to the left side, and one of the squares was painted a different color than the others.

I stepped closer to study them.

"Buck, what are you doing?"

"One minute."

I turned from painting to painting, starting with the largest. They were all similar, just different colors and sizes.

Maps? The same map?

"Let's *go*, Buck!"

I rubbed my hands together and nearly ran from the house.

"What?" Nicole said once we were outside. "What did you see?"

"Tell you in the car."

My hands tingled on the wheel. I'd felt a momentary piece-falling-into-place high I hadn't experienced since e-Antiquity.

The front gates opened and I pulled through them slowly, wary of cars that sped along the road here. The gates closed behind us as I edged out—

Nicole screamed and I stomped on the brake.

"What—"

My question was answered when I saw a dark haired man with a shotgun pointed toward her head through the open window.

"Turn off the car." The voice came from my left. I looked out the window and found the other Dominican there, also holding a shotgun.

I thought about stomping on the gas pedal but discarded that idea when he pressed the gun to my head.

42

THE MEN CLIMBED INTO OUR BACKSEAT AND TOLD ME TO TURN RIGHT OUT OF the driveway. We passed through the small town of Flamands—two guns in the backseat didn't leave me much choice—past the beach entrance, and around the small rock in the circle at the end of the road. I knew it dead-ended at the trailhead to Colombier just ahead—

"Turn left here!" The man behind me pointed toward a driveway just past the circle. The tires spun then caught as we climbed the steep concrete drive cut into a sharp bank on the left, hidden by thick vegetation. At the top was a beautiful white villa with a pale green roof and shutters.

"Pull into the garage."

Once there, he had me turn the Jeep off and we all climbed out. He led the way while the other one prodded me in the back with the shotgun. Nicole, to her credit, was quiet, but her eyes darted between the two men and she held my hand in a Kung-Fu grip. We walked through a narrow corridor that led to a covered patio behind the house, then down a few steps to a pool.

"In there," the man behind me said. He pushed me toward a set of sliding glass doors I stepped through into a darkened master suite. Once inside, he drew the curtains and flipped on dim lights. No other houses had been visible. Nobody would have a clue where we were.

"What the hell do you want?" I said. "I already told you we don't have any information—"

A swirl of motion led to a sharp pain that doubled me over—his buddy had slammed the gun butt into my stomach. I fell to my knees, every bit of air purged from my lungs.

"No—stop!" Nicole said.

One of them pushed her onto the bed.

"Shut up, bitch! Who has the shotgun now?"

Just as I caught my breath, the other man kicked me in the chest and I sprawled onto the bed next to Nicole. When I sat up she leaned into me, quivering so much the bed was shaking. We sat on the edge facing the men.

"Guys, will you just *listen*? I'm here on behalf of—"

"Jerry's rich uncle, yes, we know," the talkative one said—his sidekick—the one who had tortured Truck, had yet to utter a word. He wore a black T-shirt stretched taut over impressive muscles. Big mouth was just as thick-set and wearing a tight blue T-shirt.

They stood side by side, sneering. Black and Blue. How appropriate.

"Dammit, we don't know anything about the *Concepción*—"

"Give it up, Reilly," Blue said. "Lou Atlas would not have sent a world renowned treasure hunter and his partner to St. Barths if he wasn't after the gold—"

"Hold on, *compadre*, Jack's here on his own. And hates my guts. He's after the same supposed treasure you are, but I'm not—"

He pointed the shotgun at Nicole. "Don't bullshit us."

Bullshit them? Hell, I needed to stall. The house was so isolated they could probably torture and kill us and nobody would hear a thing.

"Why'd you beat up Gisele?" I said. "And Henri Antoine's accident—I assume that was you?"

Blue stepped to the side, now in front of Nicole.

"And you, the great Remy de Haenen's granddaughter. You wouldn't have teamed up with Reilly for nothing. We know you're lying to us!"

I slowly lifted my hands, palms out to face them.

"Hold on, guys. I approached her once I found out someone had beat up Gisele, because of a potential connection between Jerry and Remy. She didn't come looking for me and she doesn't know shit—"

"Let her speak for herself!"

I felt Nicole shudder next to me, but all she showed was gritted teeth.

"I was a teenager when Remy sold the Eden Rock and moved to Santo Domingo," she said. "When he returned he was a broken old man and Jerry Atlas was a washed up beach bar . . . sand flea. If they had found treasure why would they live like that?"

"Sand flea is right," Blue said.

"No see-um is more like it," Black said.

So he did speak. And something about Blue's statement registered in my mind. The Jet Ski had washed ashore, but from which direction? Did B & B have something to do with Jerry's disappearance?

"Since you men first came to see me, I went back through all of Remy's things," Nicole said. "I found nothing about his adventure with Cousteau. You are wasting your time—hurting innocent people—for nothing. Nothing!"

The men stared at her. A gutter ball would force their hand—just the same as a strike would—even if we gave them specific information about what they were searching for.

"You're right," I said. Both of them turned to me. "I'm very experienced at finding missing antiquities. In fact, I even had a file on the *Concepcion*—the same one Jack Dodson has—and there wasn't a single mention of Remy de Haenen or Jacques Cousteau." I paused and looked from Black to Blue. "What makes you think otherwise? Did Remy tell someone that he and Cousteau found something?"

Blue squinted, then smiled.

"Nice try, Reilly. We're not giving you information, you're giving it to us!" He swung the gun barrel toward the side of my head. I leaned back and he missed—his momentum carried him slightly off-balance—

Black's eyes followed his partner.

"Now!" I said.

Nicole punched Black square in the crotch with every ounce of strength she had, then grabbed and twisted!

At the same time I lunged toward Blue and drove him into the curtained sliding glass door.

The crash of breaking glass shattered the quiet.

The curtain ripped off the wall and wrapped around us like a death shroud. I punched blindly, over and over.

BOOM!

An explosion froze me.

My pulse thudded in my head. Blue wasn't moving—for all I knew he hadn't been moving since we crashed through the glass door.

"Nicole?" The thick curtain muffled my voice.

I crawled backwards and pushed the fabric off me. Glass was everywhere—

"Buck!" Nicole shouted. I spun on my knees to find her holding the shotgun, pointed toward the ceiling, where sunlight shone through a fresh hole in the dark stained wood. Black was curled up in a ball—moaning, his hands in his crotch.

Blue's legs stirred. I pulled the curtain off him and he started to roll to his right—towards Black's shotgun. I kicked it into the wall—

BOOM!

Nicole fired another round into the ceiling, pumped another shell into the chamber, and swung the business end of the barrel down toward Blue.

He raised his hands. I reached down and grabbed the other gun. My heart pounded like I'd sprinted a mile and my ears rang from the last shotgun blast, but it was rage that caused me to grab the gun by the barrel and lift it over my head. Images of Gisele and Truck battered urged me to swing that gun butt down with every ounce of strength I had—

"Buck!" Nicole's voice sounded distorted to my ears. "Please, no!" I felt her wrap an arm around my waist and pull me away from Blue.

For which I was grateful. If she hadn't, I might have beaten him to death with the gun butt.

43

THE DOMINICANS SAT ON THE FLOOR OF THE BEDROOM, THEIR BACKS AGAINST the rear wall. Nicole had bound their wrists behind their backs with fabric torn from the curtains. They watched us with hard stares. The odds of our overpowering them had been virtually non-existent, but Nicole had been ready when I gave the signal. If she hadn't, Black would have had me cold.

"Now you're going to tell *us* what the hell this is all about," I said.

"You won't shoot us, Reilly—"

"But I will, *mon ami*." Nicole lowered her shotgun.

I bit back a smile as Black and Blue glanced at each other. Nicole was one bad-ass woman.

"What did my grandfather say while he was living in the Dominican Republic to make you come to St. Barths and cause so much trouble?"

Blue shrugged. Black still had his hands on his crotch and looked nauseous. If he spoke, his voice would likely be a few decibels higher.

"Tell us!" Nicole said.

"It wasn't Remy," Blue said. "It was Cousteau."

"What the hell?"

"Not Cousteau himself, but one of the crew who was briefly aboard the *Calypso* in the seventies when Remy helped them search for the *Concepcion*. He had spotted gold but did not tell anyone, then dove while everyone slept and recovered a fortune that he hid somewhere on land when they returned de Haenen here." He paused. We waited. Finally he said, "His grandson approached us for help."

In all my years pursuing treasure at e-Antiquity, I'd gotten information in many ways but never by holding somebody at gunpoint. I didn't like it, but I knew I couldn't lower the weapon.

"What did he say?" Nicole asked.

Blue looked from her to me, then back again.

"The crewman had drowned on the subsequent Cousteau voyage, and his secret was locked away until his grandson dug through his dusty sea chest after his own father died. He found a clue—"

"Why you?" Nicole said.

Blue smiled. "We're treasure hunters too. In fact, Buck Reilly's success with e-Antiquity inspired us to begin *Gamundi Hermanos Salvamento* in the DR. Our islands are littered with sunken ships. You think you're the only one entitled to profit from that?"

Nicole gave me a long glance. She wasn't smiling.

"This crewman's grandson came to you because you were in the DR?" I said.

"We have a reputation for results." His eyes were cold.

"Where is he now?" Nicole said.

Blue glanced at his brother, whose eyes remained pinched closed.

"He is no longer in the picture."

Nicole gasped.

"What was the clue?" I said.

Blue grimaced. "We could work together—"

Nicole kicked his leg. "What was the damn clue?"

"A note," he said. "It said the treasure was buried on '*la petite enfant*' and another clue was buried at Eden Rock. Together they would lead to treasure."

Blue studied Nicole, then me. He nodded.

"Maybe you really didn't know," he said. "But Lou Atlas sent you down here, so I believe there's truth to the grandson's story."

"Obviously Henri Antoine told you the same thing he told me," I said. "They found nothing when clearing the mess after the hurricanes."

Blue smiled. "Jerry said otherwise."

It took me a moment to find my voice.

"You talked to Jerry?"

Blue sneered. "He tricked us into telling him about *la petite enfant*. Said he could help us—that he'd found something that might be the clue. Then he vanished. We thought he'd double-crossed us, until they found the Jet Ski."

"That's why you beat Gisele?"

"The answer is out there, I know it!" Blue said.

I shook my head. "We need to get out of here."

"But the treasure—"

"Whatever Jerry knew, if anything, he took to his watery grave," I said. "You guys stay the hell away from us *and* Gisele Atlas. Is that clear?"

"So this is the great *King Buck*? One of the most accomplished treasure hunters ever?" Blue said. "Pathetic."

His words stung like a slap to the face, but I had words for him, too.

"If anyone else gets hurt, the *gendarmes* will be up your ass so fast you'll spend the rest of your lives shitting *foie gras* from a cell in Guadeloupe."

"Or I'll shoot you," Nicole said.

Blue smiled, but his eyes were slits.

"Don't leave here for thirty minutes." I shoved the barrel of the shotgun into Blue's nose and pressed it flat. "I'm serious, you son of a bitch, I don't want to see you again."

Nicole and I backed out of the bedroom. The sun outside was blinding after being in the dim room for so long. For a moment I thought to call the police, but I had a damned good hunch that Jerry hadn't lied to the Gamundi brothers. He'd found something.

"I am calling the *gendarmes*." Nicole made the call, spoke in rapid French, but the gist was clear. She gave the Gamundis' names and location before we were halfway down the driveway. When she hung up, she turned her gaze toward me. It wasn't friendly.

"e-Antiquity, huh?"

"That was another life—and it's nothing to do with why I'm here!"

She sighed. "I already knew. Jack Dodson told me not to trust you. I was waiting to see if you told me."

Jack?

"Everything Gamundi said was true," I said, "but that all ended five years ago. It's not what drives me but it does help me understand what we're up against." I paused. "Jack, on the other hand, is pure trouble. You'll have to choose who you want to believe."

"So you're not interested in the *Concepción*?"

"It's not why I came here, but I can't ignore the opportunity."

"What do you think happened to the *Calypso* crewman's grandson?" Her voice broke.

I shook my head, but our eyes caught and she saw the answer in mine. A shudder passed over her.

At the bottom of the long driveway, I jammed on the brakes and slid on the steep slope.

"Let's not get ourselves arrested. Throw those guns into the woods there—"

"No way, I need all the protection I can get on the top of the hill."

Neither of us spoke as we drove slowly through Flamands, up the hill, and back toward town. A sharp ache pulled at my chest, thanks to Blue's jamming the gun into my solar plexus—or was it from him calling me out?

Tears were streaming down Nicole's cheeks. I pulled over to the side of the road, got out of the Jeep, and walked over to her side to open the door. She leaned into me when I reached for her, falling into my arms as I lifted her out of the passenger seat and held her close. Her chest heaved again and again, her wet cheeks were pressed against my face. She wrapped her arms tightly around me, then pushed back to look into my eyes.

Then she pulled a strand of sandy blond hair off her face and shook her head. I fought the urge to lean down and kiss her.

"I'm scared." Her admission brought more shudders.

She pulled me back tight and I held her close. When her whuffling slowed, I put my mouth close to her ear.

"Stay with me and Truck at La Banane?"

She leaned back to gauge my statement but I held my expression at concern, even though my heart ricocheted from holding her so close. Nicole was strong, capable, smart, and attractive in an unintentional sort of way—the complete opposite of my supermodel ex-wife. Something I sensed in her touched my heart.

She nodded but let go.

"We'll see, Buck. We'll see."

44

TRUCK WAS CONVALESCING IN BED WHEN WE ENTERED THE ROOM. HE LOOKED a little more like himself and not quite so pissed off.

"Where the hell you—oh, that Nicole?"

She sat on the side of his bed and took a good look at him.

"How are you feeling?"

He ran his left palm across the top of his head, his right arm still in the sling. "I been better. Fact, let me give you some advice, stay away from this guy." He nodded in my direction. "He's cursed."

Nicole glanced back at me.

"Too late," I said. We then filled Truck in on our encounter with the Gamundi brothers, their information, the reality that they wouldn't be backing off until they ran out of options, found their prize, or the *gendarmes* captured them as a result of Nicole's call.

"Buck saved the day?" He smiled at Nicole.

"Team effort," I said.

Nicole shrugged. "You live alone long enough, people know who you are. I've learned to defend myself."

"I hope you fucked 'em up good," Truck said. "Man, just look what they did to me—in my sleep!"

"I'd guess one of 'em'll be peeing blood for a while, at least." I nodded toward Nicole.

Truck puckered his lips and whistled. Then smiled at us.

"You want me to leave y'all alone here? My British friends'll be waiting—"

"That's okay." I glanced at Nicole. "But you can have my bed tonight if—"

"That's not necessary. Jean, the proprietor, is a friend. I'll get another room." Her eyes caught mine and held for a moment.

"Truck," I said, "you feel up to joining me on some exploration?"

"Me?" Truck said. "Not really, cuz, these painkillers make me loopy. Sorry, man. I know you brought me down here to help—"

"Not your fault."

"I will go," Nicole said.

"On an antique flying boat?"

She raised an eyebrow. "I'm Remy de Haenen's granddaughter, remember? I have flown on my share of old planes."

An idea sprang to mind. "How about sailboats or Jet Skis?"

"I have done anything you can imagine under or on top of the water."

She might have underestimated my imagination—I shook that thought off.

"Jerry's Jet Ski was found near Anse de Cayes," I said. "What are the currents like in that area?"

"They can be strong—"

"I mean which direction do they flow?"

"That's a tricky area—a confluence of currents and riptides." She paused and her eyes lost focus for a moment. "But I'd say the prevailing currents come from the east."

We left Truck to convalesce and drove to the private aviation area at the airport. I was relieved Betty wasn't there, but then scowled. Booth's offer for immunity would be revoked the moment he received Jack's package. I glanced at Nicole.

God knows what Jack had told her.

The sinking feeling turned my stomach. I checked the cell phone. No messages or texts. Would Booth call to gloat? Or would he just come straight down to arrest me?

I needed a breakthrough.

WE LIT OUT OVER THE BEACH AT ST. JEAN, DRAWING POINTED FINGERS AND wide-eyed stares from onlookers.

"I love the view of Eden Rock as you first take off," Nicole said. "I often wonder what it would look like now if my grandfather never sold it." Was that a painful thought or a pensive one? It was hard to see something you'd loved dearly in the hands of others, now better off than before.

Now that we were pressed together in the Beast's flight deck, I decided it was time to get to the bottom of Nicole de Haenen.

"What's your motivation in all this?" I said.

She looked straight ahead. "What is that supposed to mean?"

"I know you went to the Eden Rock the other day to look for information."

"It is not about treasure—though I could use the money."

"Then why are you in the middle of this mess?"

She paused. I glanced over and saw her chewing the side of her mouth.

"My family's legacy," she finally said. "My grandfather's history is interwoven with almost every part of St. Barths. Most of my family is gone, so I feel like . . . how do I put it . . . like the curator of our heritage." She studied my face. "Does that make sense?"

I thought of my father's career at the State Department, his legacy of government service and diplomacy besmirched by my failure, and his death in Switzerland after getting a numbered account where he hid the maps I'd given him.

"Makes all the sense in the world," I said.

She smiled. "What are we looking for out here?"

"I'm not really sure, but I wanted to fly around near Anse de Cayes to see what it looks like from the air, try to visualize Jerry's course when he was on the Jet Ski." I thought of his paintings—I'd have my eyes open for an oval shaped island with a big rock pile. Could the Dominicans really have given him the missing link? *La petite enfant?*

We flew halfway toward St. Martin before I vectored west and entered the approach pattern into St. Barths behind a shiny new St. Barth Commuter plane. I broke off to circle around the outer edge of Gustavia. It was a clear day and Saba appeared through the mist like an ancient pyramid on the horizon, thirty-odd miles away.

Shell Beach marked the back corner of Gustavia where the shoreline turned into a steep, rocky, cactus-covered no-man's land of sharp cliffs and bluffs. I saw a couple of rock outcroppings in the water that could be loosely characterized as islands, but nothing that fit Jerry's paintings. Next came Gouverneur's Beach and a long stretch of empty open water—until we reached a decent-sized island just past Saline.

"Ever been there?" I said.

"Ile Coco? No reason to." She paused. "Anse de Cayes is on the other side of the island, why are we looking here?"

"Bernard from Master Ski Pilou—"

"I know Bernard."

"He said Jerry typically followed the coast in this direction as he circum-navigated the island. I want to follow the same course." I wiped sweat from my right palm on my shorts, my stomach in knots, wondering whether it was prudent to share my suspicions with Nicole.

We continued along the coast at an altitude of 1,500 feet above sea level, toward the rocky shore of the Grand Fond. I spotted Gisele's parents' farm as we approached Toiny, where surfers rode long waves just before the east-ernmost point on the island.

"The currents going north eddy around up to here, then press in from the east," Nicole said.

We followed the coast past Grand-cul-du-Sac, where kite and wind surfers zipped around the horseshoe-shaped harbor, and then past Le Sereno Hotel.

"That island there is called Ile Tortue." Nicole pointed. I glanced over—wrong shape.

We passed by Lorient and came to the wide bay of St. Jean, but I stayed north to avoid aircraft taking off toward us. The Eden Rock peninsula was prominent and Nicole leaned forward and tried to look past me, no doubt hoping to spot her house. I vectored the beast toward the islands to the northwest.

"And these?" I said.

"Ile Fregate out there." She pointed out the starboard side window. "And Ile Chevreau ahead."

Ile Chevreau was the big island you could see straight out from Jerry's house on the beach at Flamands.

"Anse de Cayes is right there to your left," Nicole said. "Mostly locals live there, not a lot of vacation rentals, only one major hotel. I am not sure exactly where Jerry's Jet Ski washed ashore."

There was a black sand beach below with a couple of surfers lying atop their boards awaiting a ride in. Flamands was around the next corner, and the land cut hard to the left to where the Taiwana resort and the Hotel St. Barth Isle de France marked the start of the long, wide beach. Many houses dotted the landscape, but Jerry's house, right in the middle, was one of the largest on the waterfront. Was Gisele in her chaise lounge staring up at us as we flew over?

I pressed down on the right pedal and headed straight north to Ile Chevreau, the largest of the offshore islands surrounding St. Barths. I gripped the wheel tighter. It was oval shaped with twin peaks that formed a valley. I was tempted to fly low and look for rock piles but decided against doing it with Nicole on board.

"Do people ever come out here to explore?" I said.

Nicole shook her head. "It is very rocky with strong currents and no beaches, so not really. It is a beautiful island, though. I have always wanted to come here and have a picnic on one of the high meadows, but never have."

We circled around and I saw she was right—the shore was lined with white water splashing off rocks and I saw no beaches where a boat could come ashore.

I again considered Jerry's likely course after leaving the dock in Gustavia. Any number of things could have caused him to fall off his Jet Ski, not the least of which was the bottle of rum he'd had with him. If Nicole was right and the current pressed in from the east, his accident likely happened somewhere between Marigot and the western end of the bay of St. Jean, or by Anse de Cayes itself.

We continued past Colombier and out to another large island that was also roughly egg-shaped.

"What's that one called?"

"Ile Fourchue."

I saw no other islands except for a few dots on the distant horizon toward Anguilla and St. Martin, so I turned us back into the landing pattern and flew straight toward Gustavia and the airport.

"Not much of a flight," Nicole said.

I didn't respond, focused on steering us through the narrow approach between the two peaks at stall speed, cars close enough to see their driver's faces below, the white cross on the peak now above us.

As we slowed to a stop at the end of the runway, we paused a moment to gaze down the beach to Eden Rock.

Nicole suddenly turned toward me.

"What if *la petite enfant* is Ile Chevreau?"

"Why, what does Ile Chevreau mean?"

"The closest translation I can think of is 'the kid'—the same literal meaning as *la petite enfant*."

I pictured Ile Chevreau from the air. It was a similar shape to Jerry's paintings, and there had been a number of rock piles.

"And what about the clue at Eden Rock?" she said. "The one that might have led to a location on Ile Chevreau?"

I thought of Jerry's paintings. A map. I bit my tongue.

The Gold,
The Guy
or
The Girl?

45

To my surprise, Nicole opted to go home after our flight. A quick walk around her house found the doors and windows to be secure, so we went inside and checked every room.

I walked her back to the front door.

"Your friend is right," she said. "You are dangerous company." She planted a slow kiss on my left cheek and one on my right, then shut the door without meeting my eyes.

I stood there for a long moment, wondering if I should knock and come clean, but in the end I wandered up through the apple, mango, and papaya groves toward my Jeep. I stopped with my hand on the door, glanced back again, and took a deep breath. The sweet smell swirled through my nostrils, a combination of Nicole and her orchards that—

Focus, Reilly.

Back at the hotel I found Truck by the pool, flanked by his British lady friends, both topless.

"Hello, Buck!" the one on his left said.

The one on his right smiled. "We're taking good care of Clarence."

Truck wore a shit-eating grin.

"I'm afraid *Clarence* isn't taking very good care of you," I said. "Better add some sunscreen, ladies." They glanced down and the one on the right giggled.

"Good point," she said. Then, to Truck, "You have been derelict in your duties, my dear."

I turned to walk away—

"Reilly?" Truck said.

I turned back.

"Did some checking on the tides and currents around Anse de Cayes. Pretty shifty there."

"Nicole said it comes in hard from the east across the top of the island—"

"Yeah, but after the bay of St. Jean it comes head on with water from the west. Causes a lot of chop and bigger waves."

"That explains the surfers," I said.

"Point is there's no guarantee the Jet Ski washed ashore from the east— could of just as easily come in from the other direction. You know what's over that way?"

"Flamands, and Jerry's house," I said.

And Ile Chevreau.

The woman on the left grew tired of holding the bottle of sunscreen and finally began applying it to her pink chest. The distraction caused me to miss Truck's question.

"Hey, Reilly! I said, did Gisele say anything about him stopping at home that day while he was out on the Jet Ski?"

Given the behind the scenes posturing over the pre-nup, it was a good question. Especially since, according to Jerry's attorney, his death made it easier for Gisele to accomplish the goal she'd been pursuing since long before his demise.

"She didn't say. I assumed he fell off before he reached Flamands, but that's a good question."

The woman on the left reached over Truck to hand the sunscreen to the woman on the right—his face was sandwiched between their breasts.

Truck giggled.

"Okay," I said. "Gotta go."

"Reilly?" He leaned forward, escaping the mammary assault. "Told the girls I needed to get back in the loop with you tonight!" His voice had turned to a shout as I walked away, waving without looking back.

Once inside the room, I sat to collect my thoughts. I hadn't updated Lou

Atlas today, but given my growing questions as to his motivation for sending me here, I was afraid diplomacy might be too much of a challenge. He viewed me as hired help anyway, not someone he'd share his knowledge with. But now that I felt I might have the missing pieces of the *Concepcíon* search, I needed Lou to keep the money flowing. I decided to send him a text.

That still took some effort, and I proofread it several times before pressing send.

> Lou, bit of a mess down here, a lot of people sniffing around Jerry's affairs. More violence from the Gamundi brothers from the DR. Still looking for answers. Any insights you might have would be helpful.

I hoped that would draw out some information. Had he known he was putting us in harm's way? Did he care?

Still no word from Booth—the suspense was killing me. I was on my own and the clock was ticking. With Betty gone, there was little I could do to pursue the immunity Booth had offered—

The phone buzzed. I snatched it up.

It was a text, but not from Lou Atlas.

> Meet me at Le Ti St. Barth tonight for dinner and celebration. I have news. Caterina. XO.

Was it just this morning we'd had coffee at l'Oubli? It felt like a week ago.

If she wanted to celebrate, she must have made some progress on the Cousteau angle.

The restaurant guide in the room said Le Ti St-Barth was a Caribbean tavern and mentioned BBQ. The logo caught my eye: an illustration of a gruff, scowling pirate. Le Ti was located in Pointe Milou, not far from our hotel, not close to Gustavia. Odd place for Caterina to suggest we meet, but if she had news about the *Concepcíon*, I'd be there.

And so would Truck.

46

A THROBBING BASS BEAT RATTLED MY STOMACH AS WE PARKED IN FRONT OF the valet. Torches and an arch marked the entrance to Le Ti, along with several beautiful women smoking cigarettes and chatting at a speed way beyond my ability to translate. Steps led down into a swarm of people.

"Not like no BBQ joint I been to." Truck had to shout over the music and we weren't even inside yet. He adjusted his arm sling.

A maître-d stopped us. I gave Caterina's name, and he nodded and waved us past. Dark red curtains framed the door, but lights shot out from inside, along with boisterous laughter, loud dance music, and heat.

We stopped a few steps in.

A few people along the perimeter were eating at tables with candelabras while others were dancing *on* tables next to them. On a small stage to the left, three gorgeous women dressed in captain's hats and sailor's outfits with the shortest short-shorts I'd ever seen sang and spun to the deafening yet captivating dance beat.

The triptych of Marlene Dietrichs stepped off the stage and wove through the crowd, dancing with men and women as they passed, cigarettes held high.

A waitress shoved past us with a tray of drinks and pushed us inside the bacchanal. A glance at Truck revealed a toothy smile as a woman grabbed his good shoulder, pulled him close, and started dancing.

I felt a tug on my left arm and turned to find myself face to face with—

Caterina. I'd suspected there was more to her than met the eye, but this? This was amazing.

She was dressed in a tight black midriff tank top that sparkled with rhinestones, black short-shorts, and black spiked heels. No black-framed glasses, no bun—her black hair fell down around her shoulders.

She smiled, raised her arms, and danced in a slow circle—thrusting her ass out with each bass beat. Swept into the cacophony of sound, light, and body heat, I was soon pumping my fists and grinding against her amongst the phalanx of dancers.

Celebrate, indeed.

Laser lights shot out from the back rooms, separated from us by curtains and columns. I spotted Truck being led in that direction by a tall brunette he'd been dancing with. Soon hats, long wigs, and beads began to circulate. Caterina placed a gold hat on my head, and while I suddenly felt like Elton John, the deep, pumping music was all-absorbing, and the hat only made me vamp more.

The three dancers reappeared, dropped in through a hole in the ceiling. They hung from long ribbons and spun while others danced around them—I saw a man in a pirate hat and cloak go past, followed by a woman dressed in a smidgen of a sea wench outfit. I even saw Truck go by, now wearing a pirate jacket.

Sweat had soaked through my linen shirt and pants by the time I finally took Caterina by the arm and into the back hall to catch our breath and talk. She produced tall orange drinks, sweet with fresh fruit juice but thick with rum. The pulsating crowd pressed us close together.

"So what's the news you—"

She closed the gap and pressed her lips against mine.

Startled momentarily, I put my hand behind her neck and pulled her closer. She tipped her head back, lashes thick with mascara, lips glistening.

"Is that *all* you want? Information about the *Concepcíon*?"

"Not . . ."

"Are you not surprised by what you see?"

"Totally."

"I heard you were at Gisele Atlas's today. And that you went flying with Nicole de Haenen." Her hands were on her hips now, her chin cocked forward.

That was the least of my excitement, but I didn't want to share the story of what happened with the Dominicans—not yet. She read my face.

"See, you have learned something and are not sharing with me, either!" She had to scream over the music.

"But I—"

She again pressed into me for a deep but brief kiss. Then pushed me back, swirled to the new song the DJ had started, then waved to a waitress who immediately brought us a pair of shots. We slammed them down—whatever it was tasted nasty.

Caterina smiled broadly.

Boas were now being passed around. We climbed atop a table and I caught my reflection on a mirrored wall: gold hat with a lime green boa wrapped around my neck. I laughed out loud, but the sound didn't even make it to my ears. The music became louder—more pirate outfits pressed past us—

Was that Jack Dodson standing in the shadows?

Truck, where's Truck?

I grabbed Caterina's hand and pulled her down off the table, which was a mistake. Sensory overload, too much booze and lack of food had me dizzy, and the main floor had escalated to a fever pitch. I looked around, the room whirling.

"Truck, have you seen him?"

I slipped and grabbed Caterina's shoulder for balance. She swirled in a quick pirouette and led me toward a red velvet couch. I fell into it and just kept sinking—

All the sound and colored lights spiraled into a tight tunnel of white, then synthesized into a blur.

47

LIGHT. IF I JUST OPENED MY EYES THERE WAS LIGHT OUT THERE.
I was lying flat.

It was quiet—no, there was a high-pitched *ping*, followed by a tapping sound.

My eyes fluttered. I was in bed, but not at La Banane.

A woman with long black hair lay facing away from me in the bed, black angel wings tattooed across her naked shoulder blades. I rubbed my eyes, which hurt. My head throbbed.

The woman rolled toward me.

Caterina.

"I just woke up." She stretched her arms, causing her pert breasts to rise and fall. "How long have you been awake?"

"I'm not sure I am." My voice sounded far away. "What happened?"

Her eyes narrowed for a second, then widened.

"Baby, how could you forget? You were *un animal.*" Her voice purred as she reached out and ran her hand over my chest. She pinched my nipple. I flinched.

What the hell?

I didn't recall ever having so much to drink that I couldn't remember having sex with a beautiful woman. And I'd never had a hangover like this—my mind was in a complete fog.

"Did we go to Le Ti?" I said.

Ping.

"What's that noise?" I said.

Caterina rolled back over, stood up, and scooped up her cell phone.

"I need to shower. I will be late for a meeting."

She stood for a moment, completely naked and staring at me, no shyness whatsoever. Was this really the same woman, the historian who dressed conservatively?

Ping.

She stole a quick glance at her phone as she turned toward what I assumed was the bathroom.

"I will drop you in Lorient on my way to Gustavia." She said this with her back to me as she closed the bathroom door.

"Where *are* we?"

No response.

I rolled to the side of the bed and sat up, still woozy. And naked.

With the drapes parted I recognized the scenery outside. We were still in Pointe Milou, where Le Ti was located. I had a flash memory of arriving there . . . loud music . . . Truck! Did I leave him stranded? Or did he leave me?

Why couldn't I remember anything?

My hand pressed over my eyes. Had I been drugged? By Caterina?

My head pounded as I glanced around the sparse room: modern décor, glass and black furniture. On a chair I spotted my pants. I stood—wobbling—and grabbed my shirt from the foot of the bed. The sound of the shower came through the wall. It took all my concentration to reach the chair, and I nearly fell over trying to pull on my pants.

I glanced around again. Her dress from last night was on the floor. I nudged it with my foot. Her purse was underneath it. If only my head would quiet down.

Once the black Louis Vuitton evening bag was unzipped, I pulled out her cigarettes, a wad of Euros, a piece of paper with a phone number written on it, but no name. I turned it over—my eyeballs nearly fell out of their sockets. It was a crude sketch of the painting from Jerry's house, the oval with squares inside, one of them darkened in.

Where did she get this?

Son of a bitch—did *I* draw it for her? I looked back in the purse.

A small vial, an inch in length and a half-inch in diameter, a quarter full of clear liquid. I unscrewed the cap and sniffed it. Odorless. The bathroom door opened. Caterina, now in a robe, stepped out and froze.

"You are going through my *purse?*"

"What's this?" I held up the vial.

Her face turned hard. "You have no right—"

"Did you drug me and get me to draw this?" I had the sketch in my other hand.

A slow smile came over her face.

She pulled her purse away, shook out a cigarette. She still wasn't wearing her glasses.

"You were one of the world's best treasure hunters, wealthy, the toast of Wall Street." She exhaled smoke through her nose. "Now you are a nothing. An errand boy for the rich and famous—"

Blood surged into my dulled mind and I took a step toward her. She squared her shoulders.

"You want to hit me?" Her arms were spread wide. I stopped, my breath fast and shallow, my heart rate rocketing. She snorted. "Just as I thought, a nothing!"

"All that crap about being a historian—"

"I *am* a historian!" She glared at me. "Everything I said is true—I did admire e-Antiquity! I lusted for the same success. My brains and knowledge, with your bravado—your former bravado, that is—"

"Is this how you plan to get back to Paris and be a big shot with the Academy? Or is there someone else involved? Tell me who!"

She took a small step back and again pulled on the cigarette.

"Jack? Gunner? The Dominicans?" I paused. "*Gutierrez?*"

She tsked. "It does not matter, does it?"

"Why do you say that—"

"You said it yourself! Last night you were crying—sex? Ha! No chance! So concerned about Jack Dodson, Jerry Atlas, Gunner . . ." She sneered. "And *so* concerned for *Nicole*. And you wanted me as an academic collaborator—ha!" She drew herself up and whipped her hand toward the door. "Go home, *King Buck*. Jerry is dead, you have done your job. Leave the important work to those with guts to succeed. Now get out of my apartment!"

Her words sliced through my drug-addled brain like a hot knife through ice cream. I stood breathing hard, thirty seconds, maybe longer, just staring at her.

"Go now or I'll call the *gendarmes* and say you forced yourself on me!"

I pulled on my shoes, opened the door, and walked out into the searing sunlight.

I felt like a man in a clouded bubble. Heat pressed in on me—the sun had me hiding my face. Or was it shame?

Disappointment?

Surprise?

All of the above?

Down the street I spotted a sign for the Hotel Christopher and followed it to their front entry, where I was able to call a cab. I still had the map-sketch from her purse. I took out my cell and dialed the number on the back.

"Hello?" A male voice answered—familiar, but I didn't know why.

"Jack?" I tried to disguise my voice but it just sounded like me disguising my voice.

Silence.

"Gunner? Gamundi?"

A laugh on the other end, then the call died. He'd hung up.

Damn!

A doorman walked outside to greet me. "Late night at Le Ti?"

"Why do you say that?"

He plucked a green boa feather off my collar.

During the brief ride from Pointe Milou to Lorient, I nearly ground my teeth to stubs. Errand boy? Cried like a baby?

The dizziness wasn't completely gone, but I jumped out of the taxi with a sense of purpose I hadn't felt in a long time.

Fuck 'em all. I want that treasure, dammit!

48

"CAT LET YOU LOOSE?" SAID TRUCK, WHO WAS HAVING COFFEE ON THE hotel patio when I stormed in.

"More like rat," I said.

"Caterina? You two were pretty damned cozy last night—"

"Bitch set me up—fucking drugged me!"

His brow furrowed. "Loosen up, Reilly. Women gotta rape yo ass?"

"She wanted information! About Jerry, the *Concepción*—I found this in her purse!" I threw the sketch down on the table, then realized I hadn't told him about Jerry's paintings. "And she's working with Jack and Gunner—or the Dominicans—someone!"

"They was all there at Le Ti last night," Truck said.

"Who?"

"All them motherfuckers you just mentioned. One big treasure hunters' gala in the devil's lair."

He followed me back to the suite, where I yanked off my clothes and pulled on a fresh pair of shorts and a T-shirt.

"Yeah, well, I don't remember a goddamn thing—we have to get moving, though."

Truck sipped his coffee and watched me.

"Now!"

"Damn, boy!" He sprang to his feet and winced when it hurt his shoulder. "The hell crawled up your ass?"

"I'm sick of this shit." Fucking *errand boy*? "Time to put the pieces together. I might have a lead on the treasure. You want to find it, or should we leave it to these other assholes?"

"Let me get my painkillers!"

A FIRE BURNED IN MY GUT, DIFFERENT FROM ANYTHING I'D FELT BEFORE. Ambition, sure, but mixed with anger, hurt, and humiliation, not to mention desperation. It was an inferno that could only be doused by revenge—and right now revenge meant getting the prize before anyone else.

I whipped the Jeep through the sharp turns toward St. Jean. Truck clutched the dashboard handle with his good hand.

"What did you tell her?"

"I don't know, aside from drawing that sketch—you can't remember shit on that stuff."

"What else did you *know* to tell her?"

I bit the side of my lip. "Enough to cause a race to where we're headed."

The Jeep caught air over the speed bump. Truck grimaced but didn't complain.

We blew past the airport, up the hill, around the circle, and down the road to where the Beast was tied down. A boat might have made more sense, but time was of the essence.

The Widgeon—Betty—was gone.

"Where we headed?" Truck said.

"The island shown on that sketch."

Even though adrenalin was surging through my system at a fever pitch, I forced myself to do a thorough pre-flight check. With all the hanky-panky going on around here, any one of these bastards could have sabotaged my plane. All the moving parts seemed fine, so with the twin Wasp Jr. engines fired up and the radio clear of approaching aircraft, we taxied onto the end of the runway. With only 2,100' of asphalt before it turned into sand and crystal blue waters, I held the brake, revved the RPM's to redline, and set the Beast loose. As soon as we were aloft I carved a wing to port.

"We low on fuel, huh?" Truck tapped the gauges.

"We're not going far." I leveled the Beast off at a low altitude, only 500 feet above sea level. Within a couple of minutes we reached Ile Chevreau—or *la petite enfant* as the Dominicans had called it, assuming Nicole was right.

"What're we looking for?" Truck said.

"Jerry painted pictures of what looks like a rock pile on what I think is this island."

"Maybe the dude just liked to paint?"

"Nope. It's like a map—but he didn't know which island it was. Bankie Banx told me Jerry liked to go out to different islands with a big pry bar and look under rocks."

"The hell for?"

"Long story, but the Dominicans found out something may have been buried on an island—they just didn't know it was this island." I nodded my head toward the large oval of green and brown we were aimed toward. "Plus they knew there was some kind of clue at Eden Rock, which Jerry told them he had."

"Jerry knew those motherfuckers?"

"Put the two together and maybe there's treasure buried out here."

"Great." Truck crossed his arms. "So what, we looking for a big X or something? That island's huge!"

"The painting showed rocks, so look for a pile." I pressed on the right pedal and circled back to starboard. "The rocks should be piled up to the left of some kind of marker."

I had to increase our altitude to 750 feet to get above Ile Chevreau. There was a rock-strewn valley between the peaks in the center of the land mass. I flew around the perimeter in a counter-clockwise direction, with me taking the first look—there were several rocky areas. Jerry's paintings showed detail on the left side, but there were two peaks, and was that the left side looking from St. Barths, or from the other direction? We reversed course and flew in the opposite direction so Truck could scan the island.

From what I saw, it was largely ringed in white, roiling water, although there were a couple of blank spots on the shore.

"Cut down the middle, through that valley," Truck said. "This rock's too big to see from the outside."

I banked in a circle, north of Ile Chevreau, then aimed the Beast between the peaks. We were low, almost as low as the landing into Gustavia—

"Hey!" Truck said after we passed through the center where the highest points were. "I saw something!"

"Like what?"

"I don't know man, go back toward that one!" He pointed toward the incline of land on his right side.

I circled west around the peak, maintained the loop, and cut back through the island's center again.

"Son of a bitch," Truck said.

"What?" I now vectored to the east, wanting to try and see what he'd spotted. "*What* did you see?"

"There's a dude laying under the trees down there. He wasn't moving."

49

I CIRCLED BACK AND SPOTTED WHAT APPEARED TO BE CAMOUFLAGE NETTING pulled between a few trees to create a canopy. A corner had fallen, and sure enough a man was lying under that exposed corner on the top ridge. My mind might have been playing tricks on me, but I thought he raised his arm and waved at us.

We circled the island's perimeter again, flying in a counter-clockwise rotation. No boats, kayaks, or other forms of transportation were visible. The man was stranded unless he swam—it was just a mile back to St. Barths, after all.

"What are you thinking?" Truck said.

I didn't respond.

"You told me water landings are illegal here, right? Shouldn't we be calling them *gendarmes* or whatever kind of marine patrol they got here? Tell them about that dude?"

"I don't know who's down there, but I spilled my guts to Caterina last night, and she's either working with Jack or the Dominicans, and they're probably already on their way out here. We try to alert the authorities, who knows how long that'll take—"

"You seen all that water crashing on the shore, man? Those rocks'll tear the shit out of this old tin-can!"

On my third and lowest rotation around Ile Chevreau, I confirmed that there was a small gravel beach facing due south, directly at the foot of the valley in the center of the island. Almost everything around that was a nice deep blue, but there were a few lighter circles, some crowned with whitecaps.

"Hell you doing?" Truck said.

To land from the south would mean circling back over the beach at Flamands, which would get too much attention, so instead I flew out toward the next island, Ile Fourchue, circled back around, and began my landing checklist.

"This ain't a good idea, Reilly!" Truck pulled his four-point seatbelt taut.

With flaps on full, we dropped fast. We slapped down into the waves, lifted, then slammed down again. The old plane rattled—water blasted off the props and the floats dug in and jerked us from side to side. Our forward progression came to a slow stop a hundred yards from the beach. We rocked hard in the white-capped waves, the prop wash sounding like a chain saw.

"Now what?" Truck said.

I pressed the twin throttles forward. "They don't call 'em flying boats for nothing."

We closed the gap quickly, dodging the few rocks we could see as we surged forward on each wave. The beach ahead was dark gray, which meant gravel, which meant a wheels-down beaching—a method I hated because it presented so many opportunities for mishap—but it did help to protect the fuselage. I lowered the landing gear.

"See anything up ahead?" I said. The gravel beach could also mean rocks under water.

Truck unbuckled and had his good arm on top of the instrument panel so he could get the best angle of vision ahead. He pointed forward.

"Keep going!"

Blue water led to an emerald buffer just before the shore, and a moment later the Beast rose on a wave. Her wheels hit, starboard first—the port wing dipped and the float slapped the water—then the port wheel caught and leveled us off. I added power to the port engine and the Beast shuddered, then climbed the hump until the aft fuselage scraped something. I pulled back on the power.

"Get out through the nose and set the anchor!" I said.

For a big guy with a busted collarbone and rib, Truck moved quickly into the small access below the instrument panel into the bow. Suddenly he froze—then started yelling and digging his toes against the deck, trying to move forward. His bulk had him stuck in the entry.

I placed my right foot on his ass and gave him a hard shove.

Within seconds the front hatch popped open, his head appeared, and he tossed the anchor with his good arm. He then shimmied down the side of the plane, his left arm windmilling as he dropped. After a four-count I saw the anchor line straighten, and a few moments later there was Truck's hand coming into view with his thumb raised.

I backed gently off the throttle, which slowed the props' rotation to a speed that no longer propelled us forward. The Beast slid backwards a foot, the line pulled taut—I held my breath.

We were secure.

I killed the power, shut down the magnetos and batteries, climbed through the fuselage, and pushed open the hatch, which was right on the water line.

I jumped in the water and was soaked up to my shorts.

With my heart in my throat, I stood with Truck as we stared up the steep incline of the left peak. It rose 500 feet above where we were standing. All the anticipation I used to feel when on the straightaway to finding treasure was redlined here.

"Let's go."

The valley was steep and there was a lot of loose gravel and natural debris, so we zigged and zagged our way up through the grass and cactus underbrush, then back into the trough between the hills. Heat and exertion soon had us sweating and winded. Few trees were on the slopes themselves, but there were several visible at the top. Truck had to stop once to catch his breath and mop his brow, and neither of us spoke a word until he nodded that he was ready to continue. I studied every rock pile we passed, but there were too many. How could we distinguish one from another?

"That big tree . . . there." Truck pointed. We veered to the left, away from the trough, and discovered a narrow trail leading in that direction.

"Hello?" I shouted.

We waited, but there was no reply.

We fought through the sharp underbrush where the trailhead narrowed until we reached a clearing of grass and large boulders. A man was lying under the tree. We stood still for a moment.

"What if he's dead?" Truck said.

The man held his arm up. It was shaking.

Truck and I ran the remaining distance. When we reached him my jaw dropped. The man was gaunt, almost Dachau-thin, his T-shirt shredded and filthy, his shorts barely clinging to his frame. His eyes fluttered as he tried to look up at us.

My throat was so dry I had to swallow before I could speak.

"Jerry Atlas?"

He shuddered—I realized he was crying, but with no tears.

And then he nodded.

50

JERRY COULD ONLY DRINK A THIRD OF THE WATER BOTTLE I'D BROUGHT WITH me from the Beast.

"What happened?" I said. "Did you swim here?"

"Why didn't you just swim back to St. Barths, man?" Truck glanced at a pile of garbage under rocks and underbrush. "You got food stocked out here?"

Slowly, painfully, Jerry sat up in the bed of dried leaves and grass he'd fashioned for himself.

"I used to come here to . . . hang out. I spent a lot of time on this island . . . . Away from everybody."

Truck and I waited for him to continue. It took a while.

"I was coming out one day. It was rough, windy—I'd been drinking . . . ." He rattled out a dry cough. "There's a small cut at the end of a wet weather creek on the west side of the island. That's where I beached the Jet Ski. After I'd been here a few hours—and nearly polished off the rum—I left, got hit by a rogue wave and knocked off . . . ." More coughing.

"Don't Jet Skis go in circles when you fall off?" I said.

"There was a cruise control on the throttle—" He closed his eyes a moment. "It just kept going."

Truck and I exchanged a glance. Jerry looked frail and jaundiced. We needed to get him out of here before anyone else showed up.

"Don't waste your energy, Jerry, let us carry you—"

"You're the first people I've spoken to . . . in . . . how long have I been gone?"

"Nearly a month," I said.

He stared at me. "I was stranded, just like that movie with Tom Hanks, but worse—I'm an alcoholic, chain smoker. I detoxed . . . violently." He took a few more sips of the water. "It was days before I could concentrate enough to make a funnel to catch what little rain fell into that rum bottle." He nodded toward the open meadow, where a bottle was propped up with sticks, a brown leaf rolled into the opening. There was about an inch of brown liquid inside the clear bottle, which made me cringe.

"You know what it's like to puke and dry heave with only rainwater to drink? I was so dehydrated and weak from that—must have been two weeks." His eyes shone a bright cerulean blue from deep, dark sockets.

"You lucky to be alive, man," Truck said.

"How's my family?" He shuddered again.

"They're okay, Jerry, and they'll be amazed to see you, to learn you're alive." I glanced back at St. Barths. Flamands beach was a bright white line. Jerry's house was visible from here.

He saw me looking in that direction.

"You probably know my house is right on that beach—" More spasms. "I stared at it . . . couldn't do a thing . . . about it."

Truck turned sideways so Jerry couldn't see his face. "What about the map?" he whispered.

I held a finger to my lips. Jerry's story didn't add up, but if we had him, we'd get the truth sooner or later. I bent down to grab his shoulder but felt only bones beneath the thin, filthy T-shirt.

"Let's get you out of here—"

"After all that . . . I was too weak to swim—hell, it's not even a full mile—not that I could have done it . . . when I was drinking . . . ."

"It's okay, Jerry," I said. "You're going to be fine. Let's get you back to your family."

"My family . . ." His voice was a whisper. "It's all that matters, man. I squandered so many years—" Another tremor. "And it took this . . . to get that. And the money!" His face turned sour. "Don't ever believe free money's any answer in life! Life's meant . . . to be a struggle, making ends meet working hard investing in . . . yourself . . . each other . . . . Free money . . . take it from me it's just a different kind of desperation . . . ."

"Don't try to talk any more," I said. "Let us concentrate on getting you out of here."

It took both of us to carry him—no easy task, given Truck's injuries. On steeper sections of the descent, I carried Jerry myself. His ribs cut into my back and he barely had the strength to hang on. I told him his uncle had hired us to come try to find out what had happened.

"But everybody thinks you drowned, Jerry." I was worried how he'd react to this news but he didn't seem to notice it.

"Can't believe . . . Lou . . . sent you." His voice bounced as we walked. "We aren't . . . close."

I swallowed any questions about the Eden Rock, Remy de Haenen, or the *Concepcíon.* Jerry was barely lucid. Now was not the time.

Near the bottom, he spotted the Beast.

"Thought that plane was another . . . hallucination." He laughed and one of his ribs cut into my back. "Diet of lizards can do that to you."

So would going cold turkey.

When we reached the gravel beach Jerry insisted on standing. His legs wobbled and his hands shook as he slid down the side of the fuselage toward the hatch, but his eyes were clear. I helped him inside. After he crawled toward the seat facing the aft section, he stopped and peered back outside.

"Let me take one last look."

"You won't ever come back here again?" I said.

His eyes caught mine, but he didn't answer.

51

W'E'D BEEN TO THE HOSPITAL THIS WEEK SO MANY TIMES NURSES AND orderlies greeted us like old friends when we brought Jerry in.

"Last place I wanted to be coming back to," Truck said. He had the sling pulled tight, not because he was worried about the doctor admonishing him but because he'd hurt it again while helping carry Jerry down the side of Ile Chevreau.

"At least this time nobody got beat up—"

"Beat up, my ass! Those bastards got me in my sleep! I'd of kicked their asses—"

"Buck!" Gisele ran down the open air corridor and threw her arms around me. "How did you find him?"

"We got lucky."

"I don't believe in luck—and *you*!" She placed her palm on the side of Truck's face. "You poor thing, you were attacked too—"

"Beat up." I smiled.

Truck curled an eyebrow and pinched his lips together.

"Trying to help our family." Her voice caught. "Thank you both, so much."

Her statement made me cringe. I was looking for gold when I went to Ile Chevreau—I'd long ago written Jerry off.

Inside his room, three adorable towheads sat on and around the bed. I guessed their ages to be between six and thirteen. Their faces were a collection of bewilderment, concern, and joy at the resurrection of their dad.

Jerry was beaming, and even though he'd only been here a couple of hours, he already had better color and his eyes didn't look quite so sunken.

The doctor was on the far side of the bed, along with a nurse who was replacing a spent IV bottle.

"The heroes of the day," the doctor said. It was the first time I'd seen him smile.

"How's the patient?" I said.

"Nothing short of a miracle," the doctor said. "He has a kidney infection, was seriously dehydrated, and only weighs 126 pounds—"

"I lost thirty pounds!" Jerry said.

"—but I think he'll be fine with the antibiotics and some rest." The doctor grimaced. "Assuming he takes care of himself when he's released, and starts back with a bland diet—"

"More bland than lizards, bugs, and rainwater?" Jerry laughed.

The doctor hesitated. I sensed that by "bland diet" he meant "no alcohol."

"I hate to end the party," he said. "But visiting hours are over and this patient needs rest—"

"Hell, I been lying on my ass for a month," Jerry said. "I need to get the blood moving!"

"Listen to the doctor," Gisele said. She called the children in French, each of whom hugged and kissed their father on the cheek. Jerry teared up. I hoped he'd be able to maintain the conviction he shared on the island—family first.

Gisele then kissed Jerry on the lips, hugged him gently, and promised to be back in the morning with her parents.

The doctor looked at me and Truck.

"Can we have just one second with Jerry, alone?" I said.

The doctor's smile vanished. He sighed, then crossed his arms.

"One moment only, *messieurs*."

Gisele blew her husband a final kiss and ushered the children out of the room, followed by the doctor, who maintained his sour stare all the way out the door.

"Thanks again, you guys," Jerry said. "I'll never forget what you did for me . . . for my family."

Truck and I had debated whether or not to tell Jerry everything that had been going on during his absence, but news of his return had already spread through town—and based on what the Dominicans told me, he had to know, for his safety and that of his family.

Plus I could tell he was holding out on us.

"Has Gisele told you about her encounter with the Gamundi brothers?"

"Gamundi brothers?" His smile waned.

Truck rolled his eyes.

I stepped closer to his bed. "They told me you'd met with them the day before you disappeared."

His eyes narrowed.

"They aren't the only ones who came to St. Barths looking for missing treasure from the wreck of the *Concepcíon*," I said.

"You been pretty popular since you vanished," Truck said.

"The Gamundis also told me about *la petite enfant* and the Cousteau crewman's grandson. After visiting your widow, I figured out what your paintings were." His eyes widened. "And the Gamundis just found out too."

Jerry's lips were now a thin line.

"All speculation," he said. "You know how big that island is?"

"That's exactly what I thought when we hiked up to get you." I paused. "It could take a year of hunting every day to find something—"

"Assuming there is—or was—a treasure," he said.

"Truck was attacked and hospitalized by the Gamundis." Jerry looked at Truck's sling. "So was Gisele."

He sat bolt upright.

"She hasn't said anything—"

"I'm sure the doctor cautioned her against upsetting you, but you need to know the truth. They won't give up, Jerry, especially now that you're back. They'll think you double-crossed them, and my guess is that's exactly what you did."

He bit the side of his lip. "Makes sense, *King Buck*."

"Good, I'm glad you've done your homework." I paused. "Now you know I can help you."

"I'm not saying I have a clue what you're talking about, but thanks for the concern."

The sound of footsteps stopped behind us. The doctor was probably here to throw us out—

"Isn't this a pretty scene."

I spun to find Jack Dodson filling the open doorway.

"Congratulations on surviving a month as a castaway, Jerry. Damned impressive. Man after my own heart—"

"What the hell are you doing here?" I said.

Truck stiffened. "Who's he?"

Jerry just stared at Jack, who strode right over to the bed and stuck out his hand.

"I'm Jack Dodson, CEO of Second Chance Treasure and Salvage, nice to meet you." He pumped Jerry's limp hand like a door-to-door salesman. Before I could say anything, Jack aimed a thumb back at me over his shoulder. "Buck here was my partner at e-Antiquity, but his antics and over-speculation bankrupted our company and landed me in jail—"

"That's total bullshit!" I said.

A loud knock on the open door turned us around. What now?

"Your moment's up," the doctor said. His gaze settled on Jack Dodson. The long sleeved Polo shirt covered his tattoos, but his million-watt smile actually softened the doctor's frown.

"No worries," Jack said. "I'll be back, Jerry. I just wanted to stop in and introduce myself. I have a professional operation with connections that can quadruple the value of antiquities over commodity pricing for gold or silver." He nodded toward me. "And watch out for your savior here—

there's nobody better at suckering people." With that, he gave us a two-finger salute and strode out the door.

"*Now*, Messieurs," the doctor said.

I glanced back at Jerry. Curiosity registered in his eyes.

"Like I said, Jerry—these guys are ruthless." I paused. "I'll call Lou and let him know the good news. Just remember my offer and watch your ass."

Jerry nodded once, then looked away.

52

"ALIVE?" LOU ATLAS SAID. "YOU SHITTING ME?" HE EXPRESSED HIS disbelief two or three times. Meanwhile, I had Truck in my other ear, whispering, "Ask him, dammit!"

So I reminded Lou about our deal.

"Damn right I'll send you a check. You earned it, Reilly."

His enthusiasm diminished when I shared Jerry's newfound dedication to sobriety and family. His doubt was understandable, given the years of disappointment and the side of Jerry he knew.

"I think he can do it," I said.

Lou perked up. "You never know, Treasure Hunter. After all, he *is* an Atlas."

After we'd hung up and I shared the news with Truck, he jumped up and down and I had to push him away from trying to give me a bear hug. The free trip to St. Barths and the $5,000 I'd offered for his help had been sufficient. His new British girlfriends were icing on the cake, and even though the venture had been soured by his broken rib and collarbone, the additional $20,000 as his cut for finding Jerry had him over the moon. And my $245,000 payday was the best I'd had since e-Antiquity collapsed.

WE WAITED AROUND, HOPING TO HEAR FROM JERRY, ONE DAY, THEN TWO. Truck and I had debated flying back out to Ile Chevreau, but given his condition and the size of the island, we reluctantly decided against it. Truck toured St. Barths with his lady friends and I stayed close to the hotel, waiting for Jerry Atlas to call.

I went to the hospital again, but he refused to see me. So I knew it was time to leave. Even though I knew we'd be leaving a potential fortune behind—and I'd be returning to big trouble at home.

Home? I had no home in Key West.

By now Bruce would have placed all my possessions at the La Concha into storage, Booth would be making plans to arrest me, and while I hated to admit it, Jack was probably right. Turning myself in might be the best approach.

Damn.

I hated to leave, but it was time to go.

With the Jeep returned to the car rental agency at the airport, we hailed a taxi the next morning to drive us around to the private aviation lot on the other side of the airport. Truck climbed inside while I loaded our gear.

"Sucks that we're leaving Jerry to all them vultures." Truck said.

"This is his island, we don't have—"

"Buck Reilly!" The shout came from inside the open terminal behind me.

I glanced back and was surprised to see Bruno Magras, CEO of the St. Barth Commuter airline and president of St. Barths, waving me inside.

"The hell's he want?" Truck said.

I rushed up the steps and met Bruno in front of the St. Barth Commuter check-in counter. His arms were crossed and he glanced back over his shoulder to where the sound of a plane could be heard through an open door.

"Jerry Atlas has been looking for you—some kind of emergency," Bruno said. "He called from the hospital—nice job, by the way—and pleaded with me to see if your plane was still here."

"He didn't say what the problem was?"

"Only that he needed your help—immediately."

I thanked Bruno, who gave me the number for the hospital and the news that the Widgeon had been back on St. Barths briefly but was gone again. He also reported that according to the *gendarmes,* the Dominicans had simply vanished.

On the way to a taxi, I called the hospital, asked for Jerry Atlas, and was transferred straight to his room.

"Hello—who is this?" Jerry said.

"Buck Reilly. What's up?" We climbed inside the taxi.

His voice was muffled. I thought he'd dropped the phone, then realized he was hysterical.

"You gotta . . . come get me, man! I need your help! Please, Buck, right now!"

"Whoa, Jerry, we're on our way out—"

"You can't leave—I need your help!"

"What's happened?"

Truck's head snapped toward me. The driver pulled out of the airport and was climbing the hill toward the traffic circle where we'd take a quick right back down to the private aviation area.

"Can you come to the hospital, now? I can't talk about it on the phone."

To Truck's surprise I redirected the taxi to the hospital, where we snuck back to Jerry's room. As soon as he saw us, Jerry climbed out of bed and started to pull on his IV.

"Hold on—" I grabbed his arm. "What's happening, Jerry?"

He rubbed his shaking hands over his face, snorting back tears.

"I—we've got to get back out to the Kid, ASAP—"

"Why now?"

"They've got Gisele!"

"*What?* Who?"

"They want the gold—just like you said—they have Nicole de Haenen, too—they'll kill them both if I don't give them the gold!"

My stomach twisted into a hard knot.

"Nicole?"

"Oh shit," Truck said.

"Bernie has a boat ready—"

"My plane—"

"Will take too long. The boat's at Master Ski Pilou, two-minute walk from here!" He dropped the hospital gown and grabbed a pair of jeans off the small dresser. His legs were like toothpicks, his heart visibly pounding in his chest.

"Let us go, Jerry. You're—"

"Fuck that! Took me a month to find the gold! I'm not telling anybody where it is. I'll cut you in, but we're all going."

I swallowed, my throat dusty. The stories of treasure had all been true. And Jerry found it.

"You were at death's door two days ago," I said. "You sure you can handle this?"

Jerry's jeans actually fit him—I realized they were a woman's cut. Gisele's, no doubt.

"I need you guys, Reilly, but I'm going with or without you."

"Let's help the man," Truck said.

I thought of holding Nicole after we'd escaped the Dominicans in the villa at Flamands. How she'd cracked that guy in the balls when I gave the signal. Now she was in serious danger. So was Gisele.

"Let's go," I said.

53

THE SPEEDBOAT JERRY HAD BORROWED FROM BERNARD WAS INDEED FAST, and in a couple of minutes we'd rounded the point off Colombier and were headed straight for Ile Chevreau. Jerry guided us to the hidden cut where he'd always parked his Jet Ski. Once we were tied, Truck helped Jerry out of the boat.

"You sure you're up to climbing this hill?" I said.

Jerry responded by starting to run, though after about twenty yards he slowed to a brisk walk up what I could now see as a well-worn trail. About a quarter of the way up, he stopped to catch his breath.

While Jerry wheezed, Truck glanced at me and dragged his finger across his throat. Without a word, I put Jerry's arm over my shoulders and we continued the ascent at a sustainable pace.

"So you found a map when you were clearing the land at Eden Rock?" I said.

"One of the old buildings was hit hard by the hurricanes—it was a tear-down." He coughed. "I was knocking down a wall when an old wine bottle fell out of an air vent." A few breaths. "There was nothing but an old piece of paper with a drawing on it—"

"The oval with the circles and squares, only one of which was darkened in?"

"You saw my paintings?" He shook his head. "Smart to figure that out."

"It added up with everything else going on."

We cut through a patch of sharp bushes—too sharp for talk.

"Never told anybody," he said when we were clear of them. "Always thought of it as my second chance—" He was wheezing. "But I never knew what the hell it meant. Not like it came with instructions. I spent ten years scouring islands, but the Kid was . . . so big, I never devoted . . . enough time there."

"Until the Dominicans showed up?"

He stopped and braced his hands on his knees. He was breathing so heavily I was afraid I'd need to carry him.

"They came at night, said they knew from a Cousteau crewman's relative . . . something had been stashed at Eden Rock." He huffed and puffed. "Demanded to know what I'd found." He laughed. "Said I would if they gave me a clue . . . they didn't know what it meant and didn't think I would . . . but soon as I heard *la petite enfant*, I knew it was Ile Chevreau."

Another coughing fit interrupted his story, and our climb.

"I told them I'd show them what I found in the morning . . . you needed daylight to see it. We agreed to split whatever we found fifty-fifty and planned to meet at Eden Rock. Trouble was, they pretty much told me they killed the *Calypso* crewman's grandson. I knew they'd do the same to me . . . ."

Another fit of wheezing and coughing—this one went on for several minutes. His face was bright crimson when he stopped.

"Let's take a break," I said.

"There's no time."

We walked in silence for a while, Jerry's heavy breathing the only sound. After another fifty feet, he continued.

"That afternoon, I stocked up on provisions and hauled ass out to the Kid. Parked in that same spot and unloaded everything."

"What did you do with the Jet Ski?" I said.

"Drove to the other side of the island, rigged some wet vines around the handle bars to make it go straight, locked the accelerator, aimed it toward St. Jean and jumped off."

"You ditched your *family*?" Truck said.

Jerry glared at him.

"I thought the Gamundis would give up when they found out I'd drowned—"

"They put your wife in the hospital, man," Truck said.

Jerry looked like he'd been kicked in the stomach.

"I never expected that, I was thinking the time out here would detox me . . . so I'd be a new man when I returned. I had drinking water and food to last a couple weeks."

We were almost to the top, but. Jerry's rest stops were more frequent and his color had faded to chalk.

"What about the treasure?" I said.

"I searched day and night. Any time a plane flew over or a boat ran by, I hid. I'd studied the little map so long and dug up so many islands I had a pretty good idea where it might be." He caught his breath. "Figures it was the island right outside my house."

"And?"

"I found it."

Truck's eyes lit up.

"I dreamed I'd use the treasure to get out from under my uncle. But when I finally did find it, I . . . decided I'd . . . use the gold for something good." He was panting now. "Not everyone's . . . rich here. Plenty of families . . . like Gisele's . . ." He gasped. "God . . . Gisele . . ."

"Save your breath, Jerry," I said. "It's still second chance gold—for Gisele."

After more than twice the time it had taken Truck and me to climb the island on our own, we reached the plateau where we'd found Jerry. His bed of leaves and dried grass was still intact, as was the old rum bottle. He walked straight past all that and into a thick grove of bushes.

Truck and I exchanged a glance.

Jerry crawled out backwards a moment later, dragging a long metal bar.

"Hell's that?" Truck said.

"I've had this old lever for years. I used it to slide boulders into the water on Eden Rock after the hurricane."

I took over the bar, and Jerry led us to a rocky area a few hundred feet away, about fifty feet wide and thirty feet long.

"Moved my camp over here . . . after . . . I found it. The map . . . was amazingly accurate, once I knew . . . where—"

A deep throated, belly-rumbling, all too familiar growl filled the air.

We turned around just in time to see my former Grumman Widgeon flying straight toward us at high speed from very low altitude, no more than a hundred feet above the water.

The sound shook the ground as Betty flew just over our heads. Truck dove to the ground, Jerry ducked, and I shook my fist at Jack Dodson for flying my plane like a lunatic.

He circled back around. I saw Betty's flaps drop as she glided toward the calm water halfway between St. Barths and Ile Chevreau, where she touched down smoothly and continued toward the same gravel beach where we'd landed just this morning.

Dammit, Jack, use her landing gear or you'll tear the fuselage—

"Gisele!" Jerry took off down the hill.

"They have the women?" Truck said.

"Jerry, wait!" I yelled.

He kept running, then tripped, his body moving too fast for his atrophied legs. He stumbled, rolled at least ten yards, bounced up, and continued down at a rate I didn't think his heart could maintain.

"Dammit!" I said. "Wait here, I'll go after him!"

Gravity made it hard not to fall down the hill while trying to run. As I closed the gap, I could see Gunner's mirrored shades and square-toothed smile through Betty's windshield. I didn't think about the fact that they had weapons and we didn't, or any other factors that made our odds of staying alive—much less taking them down—pathetic. I had just one thought in my head.

Time to wipe that shit-eating grin clean!

54

Jack and Gunner took their time to power Betty down. There was no sign of the women, unless they had them locked in the aft storage closet where I'd been caught.

Jerry paced until the hatch popped open and Gunner stuck his oversized head out to smile at us.

"Mind if we join the party?"

"Where's my wife, asshole!"

Gunner's smug smile faded for a moment, then returned even wider.

"And she promised not to tell you about us." He laughed.

"Funny, Gunner." I took a step toward him, my fist clenched. "Where are they?"

"We have nothing to do with any missing people!" Jack yelled from inside the plane.

"Thought you'd have learned your lesson, Reilly." He shoved me backwards and I nearly fell on my ass.

"Then what're you doing here?" Jerry said. "Where's Gisele—you told me to meet you—"

"I never told you anything," Jack said. He stepped out of the hatch and pointed at me. "We've been following him. He's always been good at finding treasure, just not too good at holding onto it."

Jerry looked from Gunner to Jack, then pushed past them to climb inside the plane.

"Gisele? You in here?"

I heard the rear hatch open, then slam shut. Not many places to hide grown women in a Grumman Widgeon. My gut said Jack wasn't lying. Gunner, on the other hand . . . .

Jerry was shaking when he stumbled out of the plane.

"They said nobody but me and Buck—you guys gotta go—they'll kill her!"

"We can help you, Jerry," Jack said. "My company—"

"You're just an ex-con!" I said.

Jack and I lunged toward each other.

BOOM!

A gunshot froze us all in our tracks.

It came from up the hill.

One of the Dominicans—I couldn't tell whether it was Black or Blue—held a shotgun. It was pointed at Truck, who held his good arm up high and the one in the sling palm out.

I caught a glimpse of black hair behind him—then Caterina Moreau stepped out.

Even at this distance, our eyes locked.

"Looks like your answer's up the hill, Jerry," Gunner said.

Jerry started up, his spindly legs wobbling. I followed after him. So did Gunner and Jack.

"We need to play this smart," I said. "Let me—"

"We can handle this, Jerry, don't worry," Gunner said.

My sharp glance only made Gunner chuckle. I held my hand up and used my thumb and index finger to imitate a gun, and held my other hand up to ask the silent question.

"No guns needed, bro," Gunner said. "We got 'em outnumbered."

The four of us climbed the scrubby hill together, totally exposed, like fools walking to a firing squad. Jerry made the entire climb without a break, but he was seriously wheezing by the time we reached Caterina and what I now saw was Blue. Truck had a fresh gash on his forehead, thanks to Blue, and blood was streaming down his neck. His eyes burned with LED intensity.

"Where's—" Jerry couldn't finish his sentence, he was breathing so hard.

"I told you to only bring Reilly!" Blue said.

"You didn't waste any time, did you?" My eyes bore into Caterina's. She was now dressed in black spandex and stood behind Blue, arms crossed.

"Just playing the odds, Buck. You know how it is—bad boys always get the girl. And the gold."

"You!" Blue waved at Gunner and Jack. "Leave now! My business is with Jerry Atlas." He glared at me. "*And* Buck Reilly."

"They're not with us." I nodded toward Truck. "I had to bring him to help me get Jerry here."

"Where's my wife!" Jerry said.

Blue's eyes narrowed and he pointed the gun toward me.

"In the boat, waiting for you to cooperate."

All eyes turned down the western side of the steep hill.

Our boat was now half-sunk, water up to the side of its gunwales. Behind it was another boat, and inside that was Black, holding a shotgun on two women.

Jerry gave a shrill wail.

"Where's the gold?" Blue said.

55

"I'M NOT TELLING YOU ANYTHING UNTIL YOU LET THE WOMEN GO," JERRY said.

Good answer.

I stood next to Jerry, with Truck now sitting on a rock to my left. Jack and Gunner were behind us. Blue was ten feet away with Caterina behind him.

"You can take the boat and the women after he leads me to the gold," Blue said. "We'll take the plane."

"I'm not taking you anywhere," I said.

"I will," Jack said.

"Not in my plane you won't—"

"News flash, Buck, it's mine and Gunner's plane."

"Finders keepers, asshole," Gunner said.

A glance back revealed Gunner watching Blue, then taking a subtle step to his left. He wouldn't care at all about Gisele or Nicole—if he could neutralize Blue, he'd have the upper hand.

"Shut up, all of you!" Blue shifted the gun toward Gunner's chest. He must have done the math on where each person's interests lay. "This is an EOD situation, my friends. Equal Opportunity Death."

Gunner scowled. "You can't kill us all with that thing."

"No? I'll kill you first and blow off Reilly's arm in the process. And my brother's instructions are to kill the de Haenen woman first if there's any trouble up here." He paused. "Think you're a hero? Make a move."

"No!" Jerry said. "Follow me, I'll take you there." He turned back over to where Truck was leaning against the rock, blood still streaming from the gash on his forehead. "I need my pry bar—"

"Wait!" Blue said. "Caterina, grab that metal bar."

She hurried over, keeping an eye on Truck, since he was closest to her, as she bent down to get it. Her eyes bulged at the weight as she lifted the six-foot steel bar off the ground.

Blue kept the gun pointed at Gunner. "How far away is it?"

"Just over here, on the edge of this field of boulders." Jerry lifted his chin toward a cluster of rocks, which I now recognized as the grouping from the painting in his home.

"You two." Blue aimed the shotgun at Gunner and Jack. "Stay back! Jerry, lead the way. Buck Reilly, you walk behind him."

Caterina carried the metal rod out in front of her with both hands like it was a curl bar. Jerry stumbled past her.

"Keep up with him!" Blue said.

I glanced back past our captor. Gunner and Jack were following slowly after us.

Hopefully they wouldn't get us killed.

Jerry leaned on the largest boulder and sucked in a deep breath.

"It's under this."

Caterina looked at Blue with her eyebrows raised.

"Step back, Reilly. Caterina, give the bar to Jerry. Move slowly, my friend, or Reilly here—hey!" He'd noticed Jack and Gunner were much closer than they should have been. "Stop right there! Get on your knees!" He took a step toward them, the shotgun raised.

Jerry took the bar from Caterina—his arms dropped down from the weight. He looked back over his shoulder, first at Blue, then me, then Gunner and Jack. Finally he turned to his left and I followed his gaze down to the boat. The women were seated, with Black glancing back and forth from us to them. He had the gun on Nicole.

My heart pounded double as I looked at each face. We were all running, all desperate in different ways, all in need of second chances.

The metal bar scraped against rock as Jerry tried to guide it down in between another boulder half the size of the big one. With the rod in place, he took a deep breath, slid his hands up to the top of the shaft, and pulled down hard, slipped and fell to the ground, the rod clanging against the rocks.

"Dammit!" Blue said. "You weak fuck!"

Jerry rolled onto his knees, sweating profusely. "It's there, I'm telling you!"

"Caterina, you try!"

She picked the bar up from the rocks, moved it around until she felt purchase, then did as Jerry had and slid her hands up to the end of the bar. Blue glanced back at Gunner and Jack, who I was certain had inched closer. The sound of the pry bar clanging against the rocks made me whip my head back.

"It's too heavy!" She let the metal rod drop to the ground.

"You two stay back!" Blue waved the shotgun at Gunner and Jack. "Reilly, pick up the rod. You make one stupid move and you know what happens!"

Blue's shirt was soaked with perspiration as he swung the gun around from man to man. Should I try to take a swing at him with the metal rod? Would Gunner jump him, or let me get shot? Knowing him, I couldn't take the chance. And either way, it wouldn't help Nicole and Gisele.

The long pole slipped into a groove and hit a definitive termination. There were several smaller boulders behind the big one, so it wouldn't roll too far when pushed off the spot. I guessed this made it possible for someone to check it without the incredible hassle of trying to manipulate a thousand pound chunk of rock each time. Had Jerry set that up, or had the Calypso crewman?

"Come on, Reilly!" Blue said.

I slid my hands up to the end and pulled straight down. The pry bar pressed against the flat boulder beneath it and the big rock moved steadily backward, first one foot, then two, before it came to a stop against the smaller rocks behind it.

All I could see was dirt and gravel underneath where it had been.

"Now what?" Blue said.

"There's about a foot of dirt on top of it," Jerry said.

"Reilly, throw the bar down and back off so Jerry can dig." He swung around—Gunner had taken a step forward. "You come any closer, you're dead!"

"I want to see the gold," Gunner said.

"Back!"

The metal rod made a loud clang when it landed in the rock field. Jerry edged past me, got on his knees, and started pulling dirt back with his palms. After several minutes there was an audible clunk.

"Keep digging!" Blue said. "How big's the trunk?"

Jerry paused, took a knee and turned toward us. He held his hands two feet apart, then three feet up and down.

Holy crap—if full, that *would* be a fortune.

Blue came to the same conclusion.

"Dig!"

I edged closer to Caterina. From my peripheral vision I spied Gunner edging closer to Blue, who was now transfixed by the metal lid that was becoming more evident with each handful of dirt brushed aside.

Jerry paused, his shirt soaked. He slipped, lost his balance, and nearly fell over.

"Don't stop, Atlas! Get that trunk out of there!"

Jerry coughed. "I need water."

"He's exhausted," I said. "Guy was almost dead a few days ago—he came here from the hospital, for God's sake"

"I said dig!"

"Let me do it," I said. "He won't be able to lift the trunk out anyway."

Blue gritted his teeth. "Fine! Get to it!"

Jerry rolled to the side and sat with his head down, panting hard.

It only took a few minutes to brush enough loose dirt away before two heavy-duty handles appeared. I took hold of the handles on each side and tried to lift the trunk. It moved slightly before dropping back with a thud.

"It's too heavy!"

Blue looked from Caterina to Jerry, then shook his head and turned back to his right.

"You! Dodson, come help him!"

Jack came. I grabbed the left handle and he took hold of the right.

"On three," I said.

He winked.

"One, two, three!"

We lifted the trunk out of the earth. I heard a grunt, and then—
BOOM!

56

WE DROPPED THE TRUNK AND I DOVE FOR COVER. GUNNER HAD BLUE ON the ground—they were wrestling for the gun.

In what seemed like a moment but was only a second, Gunner rolled over and sprang to his feet with the shotgun in his hands.

"No!" Jerry screamed.

"Sorry, Jerry," Gunner said. "Write them a check."

The rest of us stood still or lay flat on the ground, waiting for the inevitable gunshot from below. I risked a quick peek at the boat—Black stood frozen in surprise.

"Shoot them!" Blue screamed at his brother.

"Let's go, Dodson, grab the other handle," Gunner said.

My eyes caught Jack's. He glanced away.

"You can't, they'll kill Gisele!" Jerry stepped forward and Gunner swung the gun on him.

"You can buy your wife back, rich boy," Gunner said. "You can't buy your life back. Now back off!"

Jerry watched in horror as Gunner took one side of the aluminum crate in one hand, then gave Jack a sharp look.

Jack hesitated. "We'll be back for you." With that he bent down and seized the other handle of the trunk, staggering under its weight. There had to be a lot of gold in there.

"Stop!" Black's shout was barely audible. "I'll shoot one!"

Gunner laughed.

I balled my fists. *Son-of-a-bitch!*

In a flash, Blue sprinted after Jack and Gunner like a cornerback bearing down on an unsuspecting wide receiver.

"Look—" Truck started to shout, but I grabbed his arm.

I bit my tongue as Blue dove for Gunner's legs. Gunner went down and the trunk was ripped from his and Jack's hands. It tumbled forward and the gun flew from Gunner's grasp.

I dove for it.

A mid-air collision with Jack knocked us both clear of the gun and we tumbled down after the aluminum trunk. Rocks dug into my bare legs and my face pressed into gravel. We came to a stop with him on top of me. His fist reared back and aimed at my face.

"That's enough!" The voice was female.

All four of us—Jack and me in one ball, Gunner and Blue in another—froze and looked up.

Caterina scooped the gun up. She swung it back and forth between each group. I realized she could potentially mortally wound all four of us with just two shots.

Truck was creeping up behind her, but sensing the presence or hearing his foot scrape on loose gravel, she swung the gun towards him.

"On the ground! You too, Jerry!"

"Caterina!" I said. "Help us free Nicole and Gisele and we'll keep you out of this—and cut you in on—"

BOOM!

The distant shot from the boat stopped my heart.

"No!" Jerry screamed.

I couldn't bring myself to look.

57

Blue was breathing heavy and had a purple lump below his right eye. He'd weathered a wicked punch from Gunner, not something many could do. He once again cradled the gun in his hands, Caterina standing beside him. I wondered whether the shots could be heard from Flamands. Hopefully the authorities had been alerted.

The shot from the boat below had just been Black's warning. I had a fleeting hope that maybe he'd had a change of heart and wouldn't shoot the women. More likely, though, he'd seen Caterina back in control and wanted to emphasize his readiness. Either way, Jerry, Truck, and I had less brawn and firepower than either of our adversaries. As far as I was concerned, the Dominicans could take the trunk and get the hell out of here. Jerry didn't need the money and I didn't want to risk the women getting hurt.

The five of us stood in a line, shoulder to shoulder, facing Blue and Caterina.

The trunk lay open, full of brilliant gold bars that were almost luminescent as the sun hit them. There had to be a hundred pounds of gold there, easy.

Blue slammed the lid shut and licked his lips. After seeing that, there was no doubt he'd shoot anyone who got in his way.

"We *were* going to let you go," Blue said. "But I can't trust that you won't come after us, so I'll be taking the women hostage and blowing your plane."

"*Betty!*" I took a quick step toward Blue. He swung the gun on me.

Gunner chuckled. He didn't give a rat's ass about Betty—no doubt either Gutierrez or Sanchez, director of the Cuban Secret Police, had sponsored the restoration of my old Widgeon before they allowed Gunner and Jack to use it for this treasure hunt.

Jerry's knees buckled and he fell to the ground, his hands clutching his chest. I took a knee next to him.

"You okay?" I said.

"Left . . . arm . . . numb. I can't . . . can't catch . . . my breath."

Good Lord!

"This man's having a heart attack! We need to get him back to Gustavia, pronto."

Nobody responded.

"Now, guys!"

I turned my attention back to Jerry—his eyes were closed and his chest wasn't rising!

"Shit!

I began CPR, pressing on his sola plexus and started mouth-to-mouth.

"He's going to die!" I said between breaths.

"One less witness," Blue said.

Gunner laughed out loud. These two were made for each other.

"Everyone down to the plane!" Blue said.

"What about Jerry?" I said.

"Leave him!"

"We can't—"

The gun was back in my face. "Now!"

Bastard!

I smashed a fist down on Jerry's chest one more time—did he gasp?

Blue put the gun to my head and forced us all to walk side by side down the ravine between the two steep hills. A commuter plane flew out from around Anse de Cayes. I prayed the pilot would spot us and alert the *gendarmes*. Flamands beach was a white gash across the turquoise sea. My eyes followed it until I found Jerry's house. His kids could lose both their parents.

Before losing sight of one another, Blue yelled for Black to wait for them. My breathing was shallow. Jerry was dying up the hill, and they were about to blow up my Betty.

Blue had left the case of gold a quarter of the way up the hill, having had Truck use his one good arm to help him drag it down that far.

"Why don't I fly you and your brother back to the Dominican Republic with the gold?" I said. "No use shooting up a perfectly good plane."

"Nice try, Reilly. Everybody wait here!"

Blue stood about thirty feet away from Betty. She was anchored, her belly flat on the gravel—Jack hadn't deployed the landing gear—but she looked majestic.

BOOM!

Blue had fired a shot into the middle of Betty's starboard wing, and fuel began to spew from multiple holes. He glanced back at us and his eyes opened wide.

"Hey!" He lifted the gun.

Gunner had taken off.

Blue aimed the gun, but the distance was already too great for the wide spray of a shotgun. I had to draw their attention away.

"If Jerry dies, that's murder, Caterina. There's not enough treasure to go around to make it worthwhile—"

"Shut up," she said.

Blue's teeth were gritted as he watched Gunner disappear into the scrub. "Dammit."

"What about the women?" I said.

"No more foolish heroics and we set them free." He paused. "You try anything crazy, my brother shoots them both. Understood?" He narrowed his eyes. "And then we'll come back and shoot all of you, too."

He turned back toward Betty and raised the shotgun toward the other wing.

BOOM!

I took off in the same direction as Gunner, my feet sliding in the gravel.

BOOM—WHAP! Some buckshot hit my right shoulder—I stumbled

but kept going—not enough of a wound to slow me down now. My chest heaved as I ran, but no more shots were fired. I made it to the same scrubby vegetation Gunner had disappeared into, stooped down, and looked back.

Fuel was spewing out of both wing tanks. With steady streams draining from each side, I tried to guess how long it would take. Then realized I couldn't since I had no idea how much fuel there was to begin with.

Blue and Caterina ran up the hill toward the trunk. Jack and Truck were lying face down on the ground.

Damn!

58

"**F**OLLOWED MY LEAD, REILLY?" GUNNER HAD CREPT UP BEHIND ME AS I watched Blue and Caterina pick up the trunk. "We've got to get out of here before all the fuel drains out of the plane."

I looked up the hill. "Not without Jerry."

"Not without the gold," Gunner said.

He took off back toward the plane and I was right on his heels. I couldn't trust these guys not to abandon us out here, and if we didn't get Jerry to the hospital fast, he was a goner. If he wasn't already.

We got back to the plane and the smell of aviation fuel burned my nose.

"Look, Jack, we've had our differences, but I don't give a shit about the gold, I'm here to save that guy's ass. I'm going to get him now, do *not* leave us out here!" After giving him a hard stare I took off up the hill again.

"Be ready to start the engines!" Gunner said behind me. "I'm going for the gold."

My legs burned as I ran up the ravine. The damn gravel was loose, so traction was difficult. Covered with grit and soaked with sweat, I thought I might have a heart attack myself. The sound of rocks crunching made me glance back. Gunner was following me up, no doubt looking for the best angle of attack in order to surprise Blue. I couldn't let him do that—it might put Nicole and Gisele in even more danger.

As we ascended, the occasional shift in topography revealed Blue and Caterina struggling to hoist the trunk around the hill. It was damned heavy, and the footing was iffy. Not a good combination, especially for Caterina, who wasn't much heavier than the trunk.

My lungs screamed a chorus with my quads, and I had to stop to catch my breath. Gunner caught right up to me.

"They'll kill those girls, Reilly."

"Not if we don't fuck—"

"They killed the *Calypso* crewman's grandson, why would those broads be any different?" He grunted. "Use your head, boy. The fewer witnesses the better."

I recalled when they took Nicole and me to that hillside villa in Flamands. They wouldn't have let us out of there alive, I was certain of that.

Gunner was right.

"I need to get to Jerry," I said.

I quickly closed the remaining distance. The pain and lack of breath didn't register until I stopped next to Jerry's inert but still breathing form. I reached down and took his pulse while Gunner crouched next to me, watching Blue and Caterina through the low shrubs.

"Fools would have been better off having the boat meet them at the plane," he said. "Those rocks are killing their progress." Once a mercenary, ever the strategist.

I felt a sporadic pulse in Jerry's wrist. I shook him.

"Jerry, can you hear me?"

He stirred. "Gisele?" His voice was breathless. He cringed and grabbed hold of his left arm. "I'm . . . in . . . pain."

"They're getting away, Reilly," Gunner said.

Jerry's eyes popped open.

"Don't let them . . . take her, Buck. I don't care about . . . the gold—" He coughed and winced. "Forget . . . me, help her!"

My gaze shifted to Gunner.

"You ready?" he said.

Shit. How did I wind up partnered with this thug?

"Time to see what you're made of, Reilly."

"Shut up and let's go."

Blue and Caterina were struggling along, taking frequent breaks. Black held the gun on the women in the boat while walking in circles waiting for his brother. His position in the narrow, tree-shrouded cut would make it impossible to see Blue until they were nearly to the boat.

We, on the other hand, were in plain sight—if he decided to glance up the hill.

I started down its side, crouching in the underbrush that tore at my exposed arms and legs, Gunner following. My taking the lead meant I'd also take the shotgun blast if any were fired, which I was sure Gunner had considered. When we reached the halfway point we hesitated, then agreed to diverge. I looped to the right, going for Black and the women, Gunner looped to the left intending to surprise Blue and Caterina.

Just then, Jack fired up the twin Ranger engines on the Widgeon, which created a roaring distraction. Everyone in the boat looked up—I couldn't see Blue and Caterina, but Black spotted Gunner and me, and started screaming at the brother he still couldn't see. I hoped the twin engines and surf crashing along the rocks would drown him out—

BOOM!

Black had fired at Gunner! And now, back on the boat, he put the barrel of the shotgun to Gisele's head. She was seated in the bow, facing up toward me.

A shrill whistle sounded. It was Black—he pointed to where I assumed Gunner was, then to me, then back to Gisele. He held his hand up instructing us to halt, or he'd shoot.

I stopped in my tracks.

Would Gunner?

59

BLACK WHISTLED AGAIN, NOW WAVING ONLY TO GUNNER. OF COURSE HE hadn't stopped—he'd made it clear he only cared about the gold.

BOOM!

Black fired another round at Gunner, then swung the gun back toward Gisele.

"NOW!" I yelled at the top of my voice.

Nicole flung herself at Black. They fell together into the bottom of the boat, the gun on the deck.

I started running straight down the hill toward them. Gisele was screaming.

A quick glance to my left showed Gunner higher and further away than I'd expected. He was trying to circle in behind Blue and Caterina, who were perilously close to the curve of the island where they'd be able to see the melee on the speedboat.

I looked back at the boat—Gisele dove into the brawl!

My foot slipped in the gravel. I fell, rolled onto my ass, slid downward, and crashed into a cactus field.

"*Oww!*"

God knows how many cactus spikes impaled my right leg and both palms as I tried to stop my slide, but they felt like a thousand sharp needles. The deceleration sprang me back to my feet.

Gisele now held the gun on Black, who was supine on the bottom of the boat, clutching his neck. Nicole scrambled up to stand with her, Gisele handed her the shotgun.

Yes!

But Blue and Caterina were closing in fast. The women couldn't see them and I couldn't yell to warn them without alerting Blue.

Shit!

I cut hard to the left, now running at an angle down the hill toward the pair toting the treasure and a shotgun. They had to be exhausted from lugging the trunk, but this close to escape they'd also be running on adrenaline. My angle would be a surprise, but I'd be totally exposed—a thought that didn't slow me down.

Gunner spotted me and gave up his stealth for a full-on sprint from above and behind them. I was much closer: when they spotted me, they could shoot me and still be ready to defend themselves by the time Gunner reached them.

Thirty more yards and a rock cliff separated me from Blue. A loud roar sounded—Gunner!

Blue stopped in his tracks and dropped the trunk. Caterina fell to her knee. Blue struggled to find his footing as he spun towards Gunner, who was bearing down fast, still letting out a non-stop battle-cry.

Twenty yards.

Blue raised the gun.

Fifteen yards.

Caterina shrieked—she'd seen me. Blue swiveled in my direction—

I dove off the cliff.

He drew up the gun, the barrel turned toward me. I let loose a yell—

BOOM!

Blue and I smashed hard into the rocks with me on top. There was a loud crunch as I bounced off him and rolled toward the water. From the corner of my eye I saw the shotgun spinning away end over end and landing with a clatter in the rocks.

Caterina leapt on me, pounding her fists on my head and chest.

"Damn you!"

Gunner slid into the scene. Without hesitation, he seized both handles of the trunk and started an amazingly fast forty-five degree ascent to avoid the rocky shore. I held up my hands to shield myself from Caterina's punches—Blue hadn't moved but was groaning, face up.

I rolled over onto my knees and when Caterina lunged at me again, I caught her on my shoulder and flipped her over my head.

She landed with a splash in the water.

Gisele and Nicole were halfway up the hill toward Jerry. Blue's grimace indicated injury, but his eyes followed me with laser beam intensity. I grabbed the shotgun.

"Come after us and I'll shoot you. Got it?"

Gunner had already vanished through the scrub, making incredible progress. I sucked in a deep breath, looked both ways, and started back up the hill.

Blood oozed from my cuts and scrapes. Cactus needles in my face, legs, hands, and arms made pushing through the scrub excruciating, but I pressed ahead. All I could see above the bushes and rocks was concern on Nicole's face as she stood over Jerry and Gisele. When I reached them, soaked to the bone and breathless, I found Gisele seated with Jerry's head in her lap, tears streaming down her face.

"Is he . . . alive?" I said.

"Barely." Nicole's voice was a whisper.

"We've got to get him out of here!" Gisele said.

My heart skipped. Gunner!

I scanned the hillside—there! Gunner was a hundred yards from the plane! We'd never get there before him. I also spotted Blue and Caterina hurrying toward the boat—Black was tied up on its deck.

"Where's the other shotgun?" I said.

"We left it on the boat—we tied Gamundi up, so we didn't need it," Nicole said.

I handed her the one I'd taken from Blue, scooped Jerry up, and swung him on my back in a fireman's carry. Gisele followed closely behind, adjusting him as I went.

I was running on pure adrenalin. I just hoped I had enough left to reach the plane before Gunner and Jack left us here to die.

60

THE DESCENT DOWN THE HILL WAS A NIGHTMARE. JERRY HAD LOST CONSCIOUS-ness, and his dead weight made me trip and fall. We rolled a dozen yards, him flopping like a rag doll and me cracking my head on a boulder.

Once the stars cleared and the women helped me up, I stood in time to see that Gunner had arrived at Betty, which was still spewing fuel from numerous holes in the wings.

There couldn't be much left.

An outboard motor caught my attention. My heart lifted—finally, some help from St. Barths—

BOOM!

BOOM!

Shit! The Dominicans had reboarded their boat and were hauling ass around the island toward Betty. And shooting at *us*.

"Come on!"

I grabbed Jerry and carried him over my right shoulder as we sprinted toward the plane. It was excruciating to watch Gunner drag the case of gold to the plane's hatch. Jack met him there and together they hoisted it inside.

BOOM!

The boat was getting closer!

Gunner ran up to the front of the plane and untied the line from the fallen tree. He glanced our way, then hurried back to the hatch.

We were closing in fast, considering. I spotted Truck lying on the beach, using an arm to cover his face from swirling debris—a rock caught my toe and I pitched forward. I landed hard on Jerry, which produced a loud grunt from him and a series of coughs as we rolled down to the head of the gravel beach. The sound in pitch of Betty's engines, still thirty yards away, confirmed their plan. I looked up in time to see Gunner pause, one foot in the hatch, the other still on the gravel beach—

BOOM!

BOOM!

The boat rounded the corner, closing fast and shooting at Betty.

Gunner slammed the hatch shut.

I ripped the shotgun from Nicole's grasp and staggered through the deep gravel as Jack added throttle and the twin engines grew louder. The plane started backing off the beach and I saw Gunner smiling from the co-pilot's seat.

Son of a bitch!

Ten yards away, I stopped and raised the gun. Gunner was now laughing out loud. Jack worked the throttles and glanced out his side window toward the Dominicans, still a couple hundred yards away. Then he turned forward to see me.

My cheek was pressed against the dark wood stock. I stared down the barrel of the shotgun, Jack's face in the center of the sight. My hands weren't even shaking. After all we'd been through—and with Jerry close to dead, I'd shoot him if he didn't let us on board.

Our eyes locked. His widened.

Your move, Jack.

61

THE PLANE BOUNCED HEAVILY IN THE CHOP TOWARD FLAMANDS. THE ENGINES sputtered and I saw rivulets of fuel run off the back of Betty's wings.

"We've got too much weight!" Gunner said.

"She'll make it!" I said.

Jack was hunched over the instrument panel, adjusting settings, tapping the throttles, cranking the trim tab.

"The center of gravity's off!"

The women and Truck were strapped in and I was kneeling on the teak floor. Jerry, lying flat, had slid toward the storage locker. I crab-stepped back, grabbed him under the armpits and dragged him forward.

Betty broke free from the water's grasp.

"Go straight to the harbor!" I said.

"We can't land in Gustavia—we're headed to the airport in St. Jean!"

"Goddammit, Jack, he won't make it!"

"There're too many boats! We'll call for an ambulance!"

I pointed the shotgun at Gunner.

"Put her in the goddamned harbor, Jack."

He glanced back and shook his head.

"You'll get us all killed!"

He kicked the starboard pedal and shifted the wheel. Flying low in case we had to ditch when the fuel ran out, we carved a turn over Colombier, directly over Rockefeller's old house, then banked hard to port. People stared up at us as we closed in on Gustavia.

"Plane!" Nicole shouted from the starboard back seat.

A St. Barth Commuter broke its landing pattern and made a sharp turn west to avoid us.

"Damn you, Buck Reilly!" Jack shouted.

He continued west until the harbor was clear ahead, three hundred feet below us—and yes, it was packed with boat traffic. All eyes were on us as people scrambled onto their decks and swerved away from the center of the harbor. Someone even jumped off a Jet Ski when we touched down near where the ferries came to shore by the Customs office.

Jack pulled back on the throttles as we skidded, pumping the pedals to adjust course as much as possible. A huge yacht with *Lionheart* emblazoned on its hull extended way out into the harbor—Betty's port wing tip barely missed its anchor chain.

"Aim toward the Anglican church," I said.

"Where the hell—"

"Big anchor, straight ahead."

Flashing lights appeared from multiple directions in the harbor. I couldn't imagine how many laws we'd broken. A smile cracked my lips. Laws *Jack* had broken, that is.

The engines sputtered badly—the starboard one died.

"Gun the port engine," I said.

Jack slapped the throttle and the plane lurched hard to the right before that engine also coughed twice and died. The momentum of that final surge, however, carried us in a slow glide to the seawall by BAZ Bar.

Man, could I use a drink.

"I'm keeping the gold, Reilly," Gunner said. "Don't even think—"

"No way. It belongs to Jerry Atlas."

"Over my dead body!" he said.

I angled the shotgun in his direction. Gunner just laughed.

Gisele popped the hatch and started screaming for help as *gendarmes* descended on us from all directions. I felt the plane lurch when they secured it with ropes and pulled it sideways so the hatch would be by the dock. I worried that the wingtip would hit the bar—would Jack or Gunner give two shits about Betty's safety?

Jerry, who was conscious again but cringing in pain, had both hands pressed to his chest. Nicole and I lifted him through the hatch to where *gendarmes* waited, the blue lights on their silver Land Rover Defender flashing behind them. They eased Jerry into the back and with Gisele at his side took off through town toward the hospital.

The remaining *gendarmes* walked over to the hatch. I leaned back and one peered inside.

"Monsieur Jack and Monsieur Gunner? Please come with us."

"Lovely," Jack said. "My parole officer's going to love this."

Gunner laughed.

Did anything faze that guy?

Once they were out of the plane and everybody left was loaded into yet another Defender with flashing blue lights, I pulled Nicole onto my lap in one of the rear seats.

"You were amazing," I said. She placed her palm over my mouth and scanned the cuts and scratches on my face where cactus quills stuck out like acupuncture needles. She brushed some dirt off my forehead, then leaned down and kissed me delicately—on the lips.

I pulled her close, ignoring the aches and sharp pains all over my body, and was surprised to feel hot tears on my face.

When she leaned back, I saw her eyes were dry.

She gently wiped the moisture off my cheeks.

"You call yourself a treasure hunter?" she said.

I closed my eyes a moment, then looked deeply into hers.

"Just a man trying to find his way."

62

One Month Later

THE WHITE TENT WAS BLINDING IN THE BRILLIANT SUNLIGHT OF ST. BARTHS. Across the road was a beautiful cemetery, the white above-ground tombs adorned with colorful flowers both real and artificial. Names were French, some Swedish, many dated over a hundred years ago. What better place to be interred for eternity than next to the tranquil beach by Lorient, surrounded by generations of loving family members and friends who'd known each other their entire lives?

Traffic slowed and people paused to gawk as they drove by. The airport had been packed with chartered planes and the harbor filled with even more mega-yachts than usual.

With no place to go, I'd lingered on St. Barths. Nicole de Haenen held onto my arm and introduced me with a smile to friends and family members who'd arrived from places like Guadeloupe and the States especially for this day. We'd pretty much become inseparable, and I'd had the multi-faceted pleasure of staying with her high atop the hill overlooking St. Jean, surrounded by the scents of fruit trees and herbs. The only problem was that I'd known all along that it wouldn't last. Jack had seen to that by sending the package to the FBI. And Special Agent T. Edward Booth was here, seated in the same row as Harry Greenbaum. There could only be one reason for that, and while I'd still not heard a word from him, I was mentally prepared for him to arrest me.

Chairs were lined up a dozen deep, the front row mostly filled with VIP's. I saw movement by the small podium and took Nicole by the arm to edge our way through the milling assembly. Lou Atlas was holding court in front, on the other side of Harry Greenbaum. Marius Stakelborough was talking with Bankie Banx, both men nodding and using lots of hand gestures. Gisele Atlas was seated in the front row, looking apprehensive and scolding her children, who wouldn't sit still.

Someone turned on the loudspeaker, and the sudden crackle silenced the crowd. A priest stepped onto the side of the small stage, followed by Bruno Magras. On cue, everybody took their seats, Nicole and I next to Lou Atlas. I caught Booth's glance out of the corner of my eye and saw him smile—a shit-eating grin, in fact.

The priest said a short, vague prayer in French about being thankful and grateful no matter the challenges we face.

Amen to that.

The priest moved aside and Bruno Magras stepped in front of the microphone.

"Since many of you have come from America today, I will give my remarks in English." He took a deep breath. "We are here to express our love and gratitude to someone who moved to St. Barths many years ago, married into a local family, and while his path may not have always been straight, it led us here today for this solemn yet important occasion. Jerry Atlas."

Polite applause followed.

"Let his journey be a reminder to us all. Many paths can lead to destruction, but it is a narrow road that leads to new life, and a path that only a few ever find. I thank everyone for coming here today to honor this occasion, and I thank both the Atlas and de Haenen families for their generous gift to the people of St. Barths."

A louder applause followed as Monsieur Magras turned to his side and held his hand out.

Jerry stepped with a sure gait onto the stage, wearing a light beige suit and a broad smile. I hadn't seen him since the rescue and was amazed at how different he looked as he shook Monsieur Magras's hand. He'd put back on at least twenty pounds and looked not just healthy but downright handsome.

When the applause ended, he leaned into the microphone.

"I'm not a man of many words, but I welcome you all here today for the ground breaking of the Atlas de Haenen School here in Lorient." After the applause, he bent down, lifted a small case up onto the table by the podium, and opened it up. Light scattered off the gold and reflected onto the white ceiling of the tent as the crowd swooned. "It will be paid for through the sale of the gold that was buried on Ile Chevreau many years ago."

Jerry thanked a bunch of people, starting with his wife and family, and finally his Uncle Lou.

"Had Lou not sent Buck Reilly here to investigate my demise, I would have died on Ile Chevreau. But it was the month I spent there that changed my life, where I learned what really mattered—family, friends, community, and God."

He held up a gold bar in each hand.

"This gave me my second chance, but it's not the answer. Everyone lusts for wealth, but without sure feet and a steadfast heart, it's only a curse. So while we're here to break ground on this new school, I hope you will also take my experience to heart."

Jerry stepped down to a thunderous applause. I caught Lou Atlas shaking his head—whether in amazement or disagreement, I couldn't tell.

AT THE PARTY THAT FOLLOWED, JERRY APPEARED NEXT TO US AND THANKED Nicole again for donating the share of gold he'd given her, since he'd found the map in a building sold to him by her grandfather. He reiterated his promise to send me a fee for helping him, which I'd need for my imminent legal battle.

Lou Atlas pushed his way through and gave Jerry a hug.

"Your mother would be proud of you, boy," he said.

When Jerry was pulled away by others, Lou looked into my eyes.

"Can't believe that boy's transformation."

"You manipulated me into this situation, didn't you, Lou? Harry, too. Tell me straight, was it the gold or the millions at BNP that you wanted?"

His eyes lit up and he cackled.

"Nothing ever happens without manipulation, Treasure Hunter, you ought to know that."

When I turned around, Special Agent Booth was waiting for me. In the few years I'd known him, I'd never seen a bigger smile on his face. After a moment he leaned close and whispered: "Your ass is mine now, Reilly."

"Let me say goodbye to Nicole," I said.

He shook his head.

"I'm not here to arrest you—I just want to make it clear that when I call, you answer. When I say now, you jump. When I say—"

"You've said enough, Booth. I get it." I paused, all the blood rushing to my head. "And if that's all—"

"And I never found a connection between Dodson and Gutierrez. The plane was how the Cubans sent Rostenkowski home." He stared me down. "That's all, hotshot. For now." He patted my arm, walked straight out of the reception, and never once looked back.

Nicole walked over, her eyebrows lifted. She steered me by the elbow—straight into Gunner.

He was wearing a white sport coat and black jeans. The hair stood up on the back of my neck. Jack was next to him, but he was smiling, and behind his aviator sunglasses he had the look of a real jet-setter.

"A school," Gunner said. "What a waste of gold."

Jack nodded toward Booth. "Wasn't that your FBI friend?"

It was all I could do not to lunge at him. I felt Nicole's grip tighten on my bicep.

I pulled an envelope out of my pocket.

"There's a check for $245,000 in here. I'll give it to you assholes right now in exchange for Betty." It was all the money I'd been paid from Lou Atlas.

Gunner snorted a laugh. "We've got a lot more treasure to find, Reilly. We'll be putting that old bitch to work."

"Sorry, Buck," Jack said. "She's worth a lot more money than that. But I'll keep you in mind when we're ready to upgrade." He winked at me.

Jerry Atlas pressed up behind us, pushing the case of gold on a small cart.

"Here you go, Jack. Kind of poetic, having Second Chance Treasure sell the gold for me at an antiquities auction. Great that it's worth twice the bullion value because of its history."

Jack withdrew a contract from his breast pocket.

"Sign here, and we'll wire the money to your account by the end of next week."

My stomach was in my throat as I watched Jerry Atlas sign the contract and hand it back to Jack.

"What the hell?" I said after Jerry walked off.

"We get ten percent," Jack said. "Not a bad way to start our new business."

"Like I told you before, Reilly," Gunner said. "Stay away from us."

I leaned in close, my jaw clenched tight.

"No, *you* stay clear of *me*. I've got nothing left to lose, assholes."

Jack smiled and Gunner shoved his elbow into my chest as they walked past.

I was shaking when Nicole wrapped her arm around me.

"Let it go, Buck. They're leaving now."

It took a minute to find my voice.

"They'll be back, you know."

She led me down the sandy path, past the cemetery, and out onto the narrow beach of Lorient. I breathed in the salty breeze and turned my attention down past the red, yellow, and green surf shack, up to the hill atop the peninsula where the ruins of l'Autour du Rocher stood like dinosaur bones. An old construction fence had recently been fortified to keep people from entering the property. Nicole laid her head on my shoulder, then kissed my neck.

Jerry got the gold, Gunner got a cut, Jack had Betty, and Booth had my ass.

Me? Well, I still had the Beast.

A small tickle stirred in my heart. I turned to face Nicole, and leaned down to kiss her.

"Buck Reilly!"

I turned to see Harry Greenbaum shuffling down the beach toward us, mopping his brow as he approached.

"What does he want?" Nicole said.

My heart fluttered. "Looks like I get my second chance too."

The End

Acknowledgments

Writing a Buck Reilly adventure in and about one of my favorite places was a lot of fun. I've been to St. Barths many times over the years and hope I was able to produce a clear picture for those who have not had the opportunity, and those who love it like I do. And, to include real life characters, albeit in fictitious situations, with their permission, hopefully adds to the depth of the story.

To that end, I would like to thank Monsieur Bruno Magras, the president of St. Barths, and the CEO of the St. Barth Commuter Airline, for meeting with my daughter and me earlier this year, and to graciously consenting to appear in the book. You have committed much of your life to politics, first running for council in 1976, to ultimately serving as mayor and president. The people of St. Barths are fortunate to have you.

I would also like to thank the King of the Dune, recording star, Bankie Banx, known as the Anguillan Bob Dylan, who met with me just before the start of Moonsplash this year, for also agreeing to appear in the book. Bankie owns the Dune Preserve on Anguilla, which as was stated in the story, is one of the best beach bars in the Caribbean. Moonsplash is an annual Reggae festival that brings in artists from all over the world and is not to be missed. If you ever get the chance to go, do it, you won't be sorry, especially if Bankie takes the stage. And to Olaide Banks, Bankie's personal manager, thanks for making it happen.

Thank you to Marius Stakelborough, owner of Le Select in downtown Gustavia, St. Barths, for also consenting to appear. As always, it was a pleasure to see you when I was last there, and thank you for having us to your home. You are a true gentleman, ahead of your time, and you have provided an important venue for people to meet in a casual environment for 65 years. Le Select makes my favorite double cheeseburger on the planet, and in paradise, indeed. This one is for you, Marius.

Thank you to Coral Reeferettes, Nadirah Shakoor and Tina Gullickson, for also being fictionalized in Second Chance Gold, and for their lovely vocals on The Ballad of Buck Reilly, the song I co-wrote with Matt Hoggatt. At the time of this writing, Matt's CD, Workaholic in Recovery, that the BBR is included on, was #1 on the Outlaw and Progressive Country top seller list. I had the great pleasure of being with Matt when he recorded the album at Cotton Row Studios in Memphis, along with esteemed writer, musician and producer Keith Sykes and a great group of musicians. Creativity in action with the maestro at the helm, it was a total blast. Thanks, Matt.

The team at The Editorial Department for once again doing a great job in helping me develop the story, hone it, do all the interior and cover design, and doing it all well. Renni Browne, Ross Browne, Peter Gelfan, Morgana Gallaway, Jane Ryder and Liz Felix. I have worked with most of this group for 20 years.

Thank you to my publicist, Ann-Marie Nieves of Get Red PR, for her tireless efforts, creativity and friendship. Tim Harkness for his fine eye and creativity in illustration and advertising. John Wojciech for his prowess at web design and managing my ever-growing web page.

And to my increasing friends and fans who are such great support and voices of encouragement and appreciation, whether in person, on Facebook, Twitter, email or while having some rum in Key West, it's really about all of you connecting with Buck Reilly and enjoying the ride. Thank you, and I hope Second Chance Gold was as much fun for you to read as it was for me to write. #5 is already underway.

Finally, thank you to my trusty research assistant while on St. Barths, Carmen Micciche. We painstakingly fact checked drinks, food and details from La Plage to Le Ti, Eden Rock to Le Select, l'Autour du Rocher to Colombier, and many places in between. Over and over again. Research is a bitch, but we never lost focus. For long.

With love to my family, Holly, Bailey, Cortney, Jim and Mary, Jay and Beth, Ron, Linda and Cristy, and all my nieces and nephews. You guys are the best.

To read John's other books, you can go to his website and link from there:

www.jhcunningham.com

THE BUCK REILLY SERIES:

 Red Right Return

 Green to Go

 Crystal Blue

THE BALLAD OF BUCK REILLY
(Available for download, along with the album
Workaholic in Recovery from Amazon and iTunes)

CPSIA information can be obtained at www.ICGtesting.com
Printed in the USA
BVOW01s1119010315

389747BV00001B/42/P